The insufferable artist . . .

The poet slapped his chest and proclaimed in sepulchral tones, "Let us weep for civilization, which is, alas, in the final, tragic stages of decay."

"I beg your pardon?" Elena frowned.

"What could be more self-evident," he continued, "when our very bards and prophets can be victimized by malicious technocrats?"

Sarah Tolland responded with a clear-eyed smile, obviously unimpressed by the performance. Angus McGlenlevie dropped his arms and glowered at her. "You may expect to see yourself the subject of a satiric verse in my next volume, Sarah." With that threat, his fiancée in tow, McGlenlevie stalked out.

Elena turned to Dr. Tolland. "How did you happen to marry him?" she asked curiously.

"Just one of those mistakes people make when civilization is in the final, tragic stages of decay," said Sarah . . .

MORE MYSTERIES FROM THE
BERKLEY PUBLISHING GROUP . . .

JENNY McKAY MYSTERIES: This TV reporter finds out where, when, why . . . *and* whodunit. "A more streetwise version of television's Murphy Brown." —*Booklist*

by Dick Belsky
BROADCAST CLUES   LIVE FROM NEW YORK
THE MOURNING SHOW

CAT CALIBAN MYSTERIES: She was married for thirty-eight years. Raised three kids. Compared to that, tracking down killers is easy . . .

by D. B. Borton
ONE FOR THE MONEY   TWO POINTS FOR MURDER
THREE IS A CROWD

KATE JASPER MYSTERIES: Even in sunny California, there are cold-blooded killers . . . "This series is a treasure!" —CAROLYN G. HART

by Jaqueline Girdner
ADJUSTED TO DEATH   MURDER MOST MELLOW
THE LAST RESORT   FAT-FREE AND FATAL
TEA-TOTALLY DEAD

FREDDIE O'NEAL, P.I., MYSTERIES: You can bet that this appealing Reno private investigator will get her man . . . "A winner." —LINDA GRANT

by Catherine Dain
LAY IT ON THE LINE   SING A SONG OF DEATH
WALK A CROOKED MILE   LAMENT FOR A DEAD COWBOY

CALEY BURKE, P.I., MYSTERIES: This California private investigator has a brand-new license, a gun in her purse, and a knack for solving even the trickiest cases!

by Bridget McKenna
MURDER BEACH   DEAD AHEAD

CHINA BAYLES MYSTERIES: She left the big city to run an herb shop in Pecan Springs, Texas. But murder can happen anywhere . . . "A wonderful character!"
—*Mostly Murder*

by Susan Wittig Albert
THYME OF DEATH   WITCHES' BANE

LIZ WAREHAM MYSTERIES: In the world of public relations, crime can be a real career-killer . . . "Readers will enjoy feisty Liz!" —*Publishers Weekly*

by Carol Brennan
HEADHUNT   FULL COMMISSION

ACID
BATH

Nancy Herndon

BERKLEY PRIME CRIME, NEW YORK

ACID BATH

A Berkley Prime Crime Book / published by arrangement with the author

PRINTING HISTORY
Berkley Prime Crime edition / January 1995

ISBN: 0-425-14551-4

Berkley Prime Crime Books are published by
The Berkley Publishing Group,
200 Madison Avenue, New York, NY 10016.
The name BERKLEY PRIME CRIME and the BERKLEY PRIME CRIME
design are trademarks belonging to Berkley Publishing Corporation.

PRINTED IN THE UNITED STATES OF AMERICA

10 9 8 7 6 5 4 3 2 1

For the critique group

Joan Coleman
Terry Irvin
Jean Miculka

Acknowledgments

Special thanks to editor Irene Zahava and The Crossing Press of Freedom, California, who published in *Woman Sleuth* III and IV, different versions of chapters two, three, and forty-six; to Zelma Orr for access to her research on plastic explosives; to Marion Coleman for information about city government; to my husband, Bill, for advice on acids and bases; and to my son, Bill, for computer expertise.

Various members of the criminal justice system in El Paso were very generous with their time and expertise. If I got it right, it's because of their help. Any errors can be chalked up to poetic license or my failure to ask enough questions. I would like to thank Judge James Carter, jail magistrate; Sergeant Clint Porter, who gave me a tour of the El Paso County Detention Facilities; District Attorney Jaime Esparza, First Assistant District Attorney Marcos Lizarraga, and their colleagues; and from the El Paso Police Department Sergeant Bruce Manvell of Community Services, who took me on a tour of headquarters, Sergeant Pedro A. Ocegueda of Crimes Against Persons, Latent Print Examiner Robert Feverston, Toxicologist Suki Castaneda, Thelma Rivas in Photography, Captain William Adcox, and Officer Neftali Cano and his colleagues, with whom I did an eight-to-midnight patrol shift on the Westside. I can't imagine a more interesting week than the one I spent with these dedicated men and women.

1
··

Fine weather late in March had brought the Los Santos gangs out in force, armed and belligerent. Detective Elena Jarvis figured every Crimes Against Persons detective who handled homicide and aggravated assault was out in the field that night. Sergeant Holiday's entire squad had been called in to cover a teen party in the Northeast, shot up by uninvited guests.

Her own squad, under Sergeant Manuel Escobedo, was investigating four deaths and seven injuries in a gang fight at Ascarte Park when Lieutenant Beltran radioed new instructions from headquarters. Elena was reassigned to an attempted homicide at Herbert Hobart University. Campus police would serve as her backup because Crimes Against Persons was stretched so thin. Unlike the state university, whose police force investigated its own crimes, H.H.U. had an agreement with the city police to handle felonies committed on its property. The campus police assisted.

As she drove across town, Elena wondered whether she had just been subjected to a sexist division of responsibility, H.H.U. being the less dangerous situation. On the other hand, Beltran might simply have decided that a female detective with a college degree would be more acceptable to the powers that be at H.H.U.

That heavily endowed, lushly landscaped oasis of education

1

for the wealthy dominated the foothills of Los Santos to the west of the mountains. Los Santos itself was an arid, poverty-stricken city on the Texas-Mexico border. It hardly spoke the same language as Herbert Hobart, its articulate faculty, and its privileged student body. H.H.U. was to Los Santos what a magnum of Tattinger Extra Dry was to a can of Tecate. Although Elena customarily drank Tecate, with lime and salt on the side, Tattinger's was not beyond her experience. She and her ex-husband, Frank, had celebrated their sixth and last anniversary with a bottle.

Elena turned her unmarked police car off the interstate and headed up the mountain through middle-class suburbs that showcased NeoMission architecture, rock landscaping instead of grass, and cactus instead of flowers. At the ornate iron gates and stucco guardhouse of the university, she stopped for directions and was told that outsiders couldn't enter the campus after eight. "Even police?" she asked sarcastically. "Even city police called in by the university force?" The guard didn't know; nothing much ever happened here, so why would anyone have called the city police? He tried to telephone for instructions, but nobody answered.

Maybe they were at the scene of the attempted murder, she suggested. He peered at her suspiciously and asked to see her badge again. Then he decided to take a picture of it and her, which he did. They had to wait twice for the camera to whir, whine, and spit out the pictures, which the guard admired from different angles. Elena had heard that Herbert Hobart was a dingbat school. She now had supporting evidence.

"I suppose if someone dies while you're fooling around with that camera," she said, "you and the university would be legally liable."

He gaped at her, his Polaroid hanging in one hand, the other hand clutching an excellent photograph of her badge.

"If the students are as rich as people say—"

"They are," he assured her.

"Then the parents will have plenty of money to hire the best lawyers."

"Someone tried to *kill* a student?"

"Beats me," said Elena. "Here's the address. Is that a dormitory?"

"Nah," said the guard, relaxing. "That's the faculty apartment building. Still—attempted murder? You sure?" He decided to let her in; however, he provided poor directions, as if letting her in but keeping her from arriving at her destination would protect him from responsibility. In the police department they called it C.Y.A., cover your ass. Look for a ship-type building, the guard had said. What kind of sense did that make? She'd heard the architecture was funky, but she could hardly see it in the dark. The spotlights shone from the ground up so that everything above the second floor disappeared, as if a dense black cloud sat menacingly on top of the university.

What kind of attempted homicide had it been? Elena wondered. Two faculty colleagues attacking one another over some arcane scholarly point? Or a domestic squabble? Suddenly she wasn't sure about Lieutenant Beltran sending her alone. More officers died responding to domestic disputes than to gang fights. Her backup would be a campus cop, possibly as dumb as the one at the gate. He might have let the situation get out of hand. He might be dead. Or the victim might be dead. And why not? What did these campus police do on an ordinary working day—keep the rich kids from spray-painting the genitalia of the university statuary? Fine them if they defaced the tropical Florida shrubbery, which soaked up huge amounts of water from the university's private wells?

Elena scowled. The sprinklers here would have been spraying all day, while at her house, across the mountain, city water regulations forced her to water before breakfast and after dinner. But then nobody on the city council wanted to gainsay Herbert Hobart University, which brought a lot of money to town. The least she could do in the name of water conservation, Elena decided, was bust a few of the faculty, who probably took long showers and flushed their toilets excessively.

2
..

They didn't look dangerous, just mismatched, Elena thought as she inventoried the collection of people in the living room of faculty apartment #104.

One fair-haired female Caucasian, early forties, wearing a beautifully cut rose-colored suit. (Elena would have traded a week of vacation for a suit like that.)

One red-bearded Caucasian male wearing a sweat shirt that read, "Poets Do It In Iambic Pentameter."

One blond airhead in Reeboks and an expensive jogging suit. (Elena didn't jog; she got her exercise trying to delay the collapse of her house.) The poet and the airhead had greasy yellow spots on their clothes, as well as red marks and peeved expressions on their faces.

And last, one officer from the Herbert Hobart University Campus Police Force, wearing a lavender uniform that looked as if it had been inherited from the cavalry unit of a World War I middle-European army. He had put in the call and now wore a peculiar expression, almost as if he were about to laugh.

Suddenly it occurred to Elena that Frank, her ex, might have arranged this as his most elaborate practical joke to date— more attention-getting than the ad he'd placed in the newspaper, which resulted in seventeen people calling to offer homes to eleven Irish setter puppies she didn't own. She'd known Frank was behind the ad because once, when she'd wanted an

Irish setter, he told her that they were too stupid to find their way out of a small doghouse. Frank's motivation for these jokes was less easy to figure out. He might be getting even because she'd divorced him. Or he might be reminding her that he was available and always a barrel of laughs, in case she decided to take him back. Fat chance!

"What have we got, Officer Pollock?" Elena asked the campus policeman, suspicion edging her voice.

"Hard to say for sure, Detective. Attempted murder. Assault with a deadly weapon." The patrolman made an odd, snorting sound.

"What weapon?" She didn't see any weapons.

"A snail, ma'am." Pollock then succumbed to a series of undignified snickers.

Mr. Iambic Pentameter, flushed with indignation, snapped, "You think this is funny, do you? My ex-wife tried to murder me."

"How?" asked Elena. "Did she hurl the snail at you?" The call had to be a Frank-joke, but how had her ex-husband gotten these people involved, and who were they?

"I don't like your attitude," snarled the poet.

Elena didn't care much for his, either. "Let's start with your names."

The woman in the tailored suit, who had been looking amused, murmured, "As hostess, I suppose the introductions are my responsibility."

"I don't see why," said the poet combatively.

She ignored him. "I'm Dr. Sarah Tolland, Chairman of Electrical Engineering at the university. That's Miss Kowolski, my ex-husband's fiancée." She nodded toward the blonde in the jogging suit. "Miss Kowolski is, she tells me, an aerobics instructor as well as a vegetarian."

"I didn't want to come here," said Ms. Kowolski, sounding whiny and accusatory. "At least not to dinner. People like engineers and atomic scientists eat poisonous things—red meat and eggs—and they hate vegetables, and they . . ."

Did she think she'd been poisoned? Elena wondered. With a snail? Neither Ms. Kowolski nor the poet was gagging—or vomiting—or dead.

"The alleged victim is my ex-husband, Angus McGlenlevie," continued Dr. Tolland.

Elena found herself rather liking Dr. Tolland, who spoke
with wry humor.

"I'm sure you've heard of Gus." Dr. Tolland glanced at her
former husband. "He's the author of the well-known poetry
collection, *Erotica in Reeboks,* published by the Phallic Press
of Casper, Wyoming."

Phallic Press? For a moment Elena had found the professor
at least plausible. Now once again she suspected that they were
putting her on.

"Phoenix Press," snapped Angus McGlenlevie, "and you
needn't sneer, Sarah. *Erotica in Reeboks* is about to go into its
third printing."

"A tribute to the taste of the poetry-reading public," said Dr.
Tolland, and she turned back to Elena. "Be that as it may, Gus
seems to feel that I attempted to injure him with a snail."

"She did," said McGlenlevie. "She lured me over here
promising snails in garlic butter and then exploded one in my
face—and Bimmie's."

"Bimmie?" asked Elena.

"That's me," said Ms. Kowolski, "and this is a designer
jogging suit. It cost almost a whole week's salary. Now it's got
garlic butter all *over.*"

"Soak it in cold water," Elena advised. An exploding snail?
McGlenlevie had to be kidding. "How did your ex-wife cause
this explosion?" she asked. Their marital tiff had had an
authentic ring to it, but Elena seemed to remember a news
report about exploding snails.

"She turned on the blender in the kitchen."

"You think the *blender* triggered the explosion?"

"Yes," said McGlenlevie. "She probably had it wired."

"And here I thought I was making hollandaise sauce,"
murmured Dr. Tolland.

"You've never made hollandaise sauce in your life, Sarah,"
snapped McGlenlevie. "I couldn't believe it when you offered
to make snails in garlic butter."

"Everything comes prepackaged, Gus," said Sarah dryly.

"You stuff the canned snail in a shell, melt the garlic butter from the jar, pour it over the snails, and *voilà! Escargot!*"

Elena was amazed to hear that gourmet-type stuff could be prepared like that. It sounded easier than those easy taco boxes her mother found so offensive. "So it was at Dr. Tolland's suggestion that you came here, Mr. McGlenlevie, you and Ms. Kowolski?" Elena could imagine Frank howling with laughter, telling this story to every officer at Five Points; he probably had the apartment wired. On the other hand, if this was for real—and it was! she realized suddenly. It had to be, because Beltran had sent her here. He didn't like jokes, and he'd *never* team up with Frank on anything. So she had to ask questions. That's what homicide detectives did—asked questions. And what *was* that snail story she'd read?

"Well, I invited us," McGlenlevie admitted. "I wanted Sarah to meet my new fiancée."

Now *that* had to take the prize for insensitivity, thought Elena.

"But it was *Sarah* who insisted we come to dinner."

"And then she exploded the snail with the blender? While making hollandaise sauce?"

"From a mix," Sarah added.

Elena waved them all to chairs and took one herself. Five hours past the end of her shift, dead on her feet, and she was stuck with three lunatics and a giggling campus cop—for Pollock was at it again. Elena gave him a hard look. Wacky as this whole thing was, she no longer believed that Frank had set her up with an elaborate post-marital joke. Beltran aside, Frank wasn't innovative enough to think this one up. *I'm getting paranoid about Frank,* she realized uneasily.

"So your contention is that your ex-wife exploded the snail by making hollandaise sauce? Is that right?" Elena took out a notebook. Maybe she could send the story in to *Reader's Digest*.

"How the hell do I know what she was making?" said McGlenlevie peevishly.

"Hollandaise," confirmed his ex-wife. "You can check that out if you like, Detective."

"She's an electrical engineer. Can you think of anyone better qualified to make hollandaise sauce and kill me at the same time?"

"Do you have some reason to believe that your ex-wife would want to kill you, Mr. McGlenlevie?" Elena asked.

"Who can understand the nature of woman?" said the poet, and he rose, flinging both arms out dramatically. His voice dropped from a rather nasal mid-range to a powerful boom. "Women are mysterious creatures."

Oh, right, thought Elena. How had Sarah Tolland, who seemed the most normal of the three, got herself married to this jerk? "We usually hope for a more concrete motive, Mr. McGlenlevie, at least if the case goes to trial."

"Jealousy," said the poet. "She was always jealous. And she's probably still irritated about the divorce."

"You surprise me, Gus," said Sarah Tolland. "Didn't you tell me yourself that we had a friendly divorce?"

Elena noticed a certain dryness in the professor's voice and glanced at her sharply. "Is that the way *you* view the divorce, Dr. Tolland?"

"She resented my coaching the girls' intramural volleyball team," said Gus.

"How could I resent that," murmured the alleged exploding-snail perpetrator, "when the team provided the inspiration for a book of poetry that went to three printings?"

"True," Gus agreed.

Erotica in Reeboks? Had he been fooling around with the whole team while Sarah was home making hollandaise? Elena could see that it might be tempting to explode a snail in the face of a man like McGlenlevie, but would a jury buy it?

"You definitely resented all my pretty little poetesses calling the house, Sarah," said McGlenlevie angrily. "You never passed on the messages, and then you gave away the answering machine and got an unlisted number."

"Just trying to protect your writing time, Gus. I'm sure Winnie—"

"Bimmie," corrected the vegetarian fiancée.

"—Bimmie will want to do the same."

So he had been unfaithful with female students as well as female athletes, not to mention wanting to introduce his fiancée to his ex-wife. Sarah Tolland certainly had a motive, and she had created an opportunity by inviting him to dinner, which left the M.O. Could you kill a man with an exploding snail—or even injure him seriously? And how would you go about it?

Elena rose from the comfortable tobacco-brown silk chair and wandered through the dining room into the kitchen. According to the poet, Sarah Tolland had turned the blender on just before the explosion. Well, that must be the blender in question. Beside it, neatly folded, lay a no-nonsense canvas apron. Had Sarah Tolland protected her fine rose suit with that apron, then removed and folded it neatly while howls of outrage were issuing from her bespattered ex-husband? Elena grinned at the picture that brought to mind, and inspected the blender. It looked innocuous enough, didn't seem to have any suspicious attachments.

She glanced over her shoulder to make sure no one was in the dining room, drew on gloves, then threw the blender switch. It burst into whirring life. No explosion followed. She turned the machine off, lifted the lid from the container, and sampled the contents. Something lemony. Unfortunately, Elena had never tasted hollandaise. In Chimayo, New Mexico, no one served hollandaise. It probably wouldn't go well with *frijoles*. She replaced the lid and removed the container in order to examine the bottom of the base, which appeared to be innocent of any sinister tampering. Could it be rigged to explode a snail shell? If that were possible, a doctor of electrical engineering might well be the person to do it.

Should she send for an Identification and Records team to gather evidence? Would she be able to get one before tomorrow morning? Elena abandoned the blender and returned to the dining room to examine the scene of the crime—or non-crime. Nice teakwood dining set, she noted. Sarah Tolland had good taste—in clothes and furniture, if not in men. "Which shell exploded?"

"There—that one," cried McGlenlevie, jumping up to poke his finger at one of the six little compartments in the white china plate that had been his.

Elena marveled that anyone would own individual snail plates. Did Sarah Tolland have a full set of twelve? There were only three on the table. Had they been some oddball wedding present, the kind the bride would have returned if she could? Or maybe they matched Sarah's china. Amazing! Elena had six place settings of stoneware, no snail plates included. She studied the plate. Five shells intact; one in pieces. Five compartments swimming in garlic butter; one nearly empty, no doubt because its butter was now spattered on the dinner guests. She leaned forward for a closer look. Half submerged in the remaining butter lay a shred of purplish-brown stuff. She picked up a miniature fork, no doubt made specifically for dragging snails out of shells, and nudged the shred.

"Snail," said Sarah Tolland.

Elena nodded.

"She turned on that blender and ka-boom—shell fragments flying everywhere," said McGlenlevie. "It was terrifying."

Shell fragments? He made it sound like a World War II movie on late-night TV. Frank had been addicted to that bloodthirsty garbage. Evidently no one had ever told him that war was hell. He'd liked the army, and he *loved* the war on drugs.

"Look here." Gus pointed to a small cut on his cheek. "I'm lucky I didn't lose an eye, and we were both scalded by hot garlic butter."

Scalded by hot butter—that rang a bell.

"I offered you antiseptic burn cream," Sarah reminded him. Then she smiled at Elena, a tolerant adult dealing with hysterical children.

"What good will burn cream do me?" Bimmie whimpered. "I probably need plastic surgery."

Elena examined the three red splotches on the girl's face. "First degree," she judged. The injuries, if you could call them that, were definitely minor.

"Is that bad?" asked Bimmie anxiously. "Will I be scarred?"

"You'll be as good as new in a week," Elena assured her.

"She will not. Whose side are you on, anyway?" Gus ruffled his red beard, scowling. "An attempt has been made on my life. I'm a respected poet. My following . . ."

Elena stopped listening because she had finally remembered about exploding snails. "Mr. McGlenlevie, snails have been known to blow up on their own," she pointed out. "I read in the newspaper a year or so ago about some fellow at a restaurant who got burned when an exploding snail spewed hot garlic butter in his face."

Had Sarah got the idea from the news report and manufactured her own exploding snail, Elena wondered, or was she just lucky? Either way, Elena didn't think the D.A. would want to prosecute. Howl with laughter, yes. Prosecute, no. Especially with a victim like Angus McGlenlevie in his Poets-Do-It-In-Iambic-Pentameter sweat shirt. Thank God she hadn't sent for I.D. & R. She'd never have lived that down.

Elena tucked her notebook into her heavy leather shoulder bag. "I don't have enough evidence to make an arrest, Mr. McGlenlevie. Officer Pollock, maybe you could see Mr. McGlenlevie and Ms. Kowolski to their car."

"Gus lives upstairs," said Bimmie.

"That's it?" McGlenlevie's face went redder than his beard. "She tries to murder me, and all you do is see me to my car?"

"Well, no, Mr. McGlenlevie, not if you don't have one."

The poet slapped his chest and proclaimed in sepulchral tones, "Let us weep for civilization, which is, alas, in the final, tragic stages of decay."

"I beg your pardon?" Elena frowned at him, having been taken by surprise a second time when his voice suddenly changed timbre and tone.

"What could be more self-evident," he continued, "when our very bards and prophets can be victimized by malicious technocrats?"

Sarah Tolland responded with a clear-eyed smile, obviously unimpressed by the performance. Angus McGlenlevie dropped his arms and glowered at her. "You may expect to see yourself the subject of a satiric verse in my next volume, Sarah." With that threat, his fiancée in tow, and Officer Pollock snickering along behind, McGlenlevie stalked out.

Elena turned to Dr. Tolland. "How did you happen to marry him?" she asked curiously.

"Just one of those mistakes people make when civilization is in the final, tragic stages of decay," said Sarah.

"Uh-huh." Elena grinned. "And how did you manage to

explode that snail shell?" Although she knew she couldn't make a case against Sarah Tolland—unless, of course, Sarah confessed—Elena had just the tiniest niggling suspicion that she might have been investigating an assault—or something. She'd like to know what. Dr. Tolland just laughed and relaxed into a chair, her long legs crossed comfortably at the ankle.

If the woman had actually tried to blow up her ex-husband, then Elena felt an obligation to head off any further attempts. "Look, Dr. Tolland, maybe you ought to consider therapy. Divorce can be traumatic. No one knows that better than I."

"Oh? Are you divorced, Detective?"

"Recently divorced, and I belong to a very good support group." If she could get Sarah Tolland into the group, she could keep an eye on her, keep her from exploding any more snail shells in her husband's vicinity, if that's what she had done. And get to know her, as well. Aside from having married an irritating man, something that could happen to any woman, Professor Tolland seemed an interesting person. "I'd be glad to take you along to the next session." Elena debated the second part of her invitation, expecting a turndown. Still, why not ask? "We could have a bite before the meeting if you're interested."

"I'd like that." Sarah Tolland smiled.

Pleased, Elena smiled back. "I'll give you a call."

3
..

Friday, March 27, 9:45 P.M.

Once she saw through her little round ocean-liner windows that Detective Jarvis had driven away, Sarah strolled over to the dining room table and stared thoughtfully at the purple-brown shred nestled among the shell fragments and congealed butter. How unusually astute of Gus to realize that his exploding snail had not been a natural phenomenon. It hadn't even been a snail—not that one. Fortunately, snails were much the same color as plastique, a fact of which Detective Jarvis seemed unaware, although the lady had obviously guessed that something was amiss.

Of course, it hadn't been an attempted murder, just a little electronic hint to Gus, but it hadn't gone exactly according to plan. Sarah certainly hadn't *planned* to be visited by the police. On the other hand, a partial success was good enough. She had judged the amount of the plastic explosive nicely—no one had been hurt—and she'd accomplished her purpose. Gus was unlikely to suggest any more cozy evenings involving her and his fiancée, his cow-eyed poetesses, or his nubile volleyball players. Sarah had endured quite enough of that kind of thing during their marriage.

Then she smiled. Detective Jarvis might well turn out to be an interesting acquaintance. Sarah hadn't met any police persons socially, or even professionally, until tonight. Gathering up the three snail plates, she went into the kitchen to see if her hollandaise was salvageable. Maybe she should have invited the detective to share the rest of the dinner. No, she'd see Elena Jarvis at the therapy group, not that Sarah felt she needed therapy, but she did relish the idea of meeting non-university people for a change. In the meantime, there was the pseudo-snail to dispose of—carefully, very, very carefully.

4
..

Lili Bonaventura knocked softly on the door of faculty apartment #407. She was wearing designer jeans, a mesh T-shirt from Rafaela's of Miami, and her Mafia undies, which Coach Gus had admired on her last visit to his apartment. Her father would have a fit if he ever saw the panties with the embroidered gun pointing at her crotch. Actually her father would have a fit if he knew about Coach Gus.

Papa was old-fashioned when it came to the Bonaventura women; he believed in virtuous daughters who stayed home with their parents until an acceptable husband, preferably a friend of the family, came along. Her father had considered Lili's going away to college a revolutionary idea and, with a contingent of bodyguards, had flown to Los Santos to inspect the territory himself. Fortunately for Lili, Giuseppe Bonaventura had been impressed. The Herbert Hobart University campus looked like the historic district of Miami Beach, only better, and the students were filthy rich. The place had class; that's what Mr. Bonaventura had said to his attorney, Arturo Spengler.

Lili knocked again. No answer. She grinned and took out her key, anticipating that Coach Gus had thought up some new game. Like the time he hid in the closet wearing only a glow-in-the-dark condom and then fucked her among the coat hangers. Or the time she found him in the bathroom dressed

15

like King Neptune—or so he said. How was she supposed to know that a naked, bearded guy with a pitchfork was dressed up like the king of the sea? Anyway, they'd had a lot of fun playing King Neptune and the Mermaid in his bathtub. Intellectual sex was what she figured she was getting. Gus was a poet—besides being coach of the girl's volleyball team. She and Gus had been getting it on every two weeks since she made captain.

Lili closed the door quietly behind her and tiptoed to the coat closet. No one there. Then she glided toward the kitchen. Nothing there but a half bottle of beer on the table. She had saved the bedroom and bath for last, but he wasn't in the bedroom either. She tiptoed across the carpet, which was green with a black streak of lightning that ended at the bed. The bathroom door stood ajar, so Gus had to be in there, but not playing King Neptune. Coach Gus prided himself on the "fecundity of his imagination." Lili had had to look up *fecundity*, figuring it meant something dirty and not wanting to look dumb by not knowing. Gingerly, smiling what Gus called her little-girls-like-to-play smile, she pushed the door open wider and peeked in.

Then Lili Bonaventura, who knew a thing or two about death, having eavesdropped on her father's business associates whenever she got the chance, began to scream.

5
..

Detectives Elena Jarvis and Leo Weizell were working overtime when they took the call, Elena gladly. They had been going door-to-door on a drive-by shooting and getting nowhere. No one knew anything. No one had seen anything. And they treated Elena like an Anglo cop, although she spoke to them in Spanish—all those women in the public housing project, women working as maids, or sewing at the pants factories for employers who didn't always pay their wages, or not working at all and living hungry from welfare check to welfare check.

They acted like she was the enemy, *La Migra*, although they ought to be able to tell the difference between a plainclothes cop and the Border Patrol. Maybe it was her accent—northern New Mexico as opposed to border Spanish. Or her skin—she had the white skin of her mother, Harmony Waite Portillo, flower child of the Sangre de Cristos. The white skin made Elena an outsider in the *barrio*, even though she also had her father's Indian cheekbones and black hair.

She smiled to herself in the darkness of the unmarked car, thinking of the tale so often told in their family. Thirty years ago Ruben Portillo, then a deputy sheriff in northern New Mexico, had found true love while raiding a hippie commune, true love with long hair, a poorly tuned guitar, and a half-finished degree from Berkeley. A year later their fair-skinned, dark-haired daughter Elena was born. Her ex-husband Frank used to say Elena's hair absorbed light. The black hole of hair, he called it. *Up yours, Frank,* she thought.

It took Leo about fifteen minutes to drive from the *barrio* to the parking lot of the faculty apartments on the Herbert Hobart University campus. Fifteen minutes, and you wouldn't know you were in the same world, she thought. She'd visited the building more than once since meeting Sarah Tolland six weeks ago, but late enough in the evening to miss its finer points—the curved walls, the porthole windows. It looked like an ocean liner being launched off the mountain. She mentally apologized to the guard at the gate for questioning his description.

As she skirted the statue of the ubiquitous naked Charleston dancer, Elena glanced at the lobby decor—art deco, according to Sarah. Leo was quite taken with the statue and had to be urged to the elevator. Elena wondered what kind of university put up naked Charleston dancers everywhere.

Well, obviously a university that had very flaky administrators. For instance, Sarah had told her that the president was an ex-TV evangelist who wanted to break into prayer at every opportunity. The faculty, on the other hand, refused to be prayed over. They said H.H.U. was a nonsectarian institution and threatened to bring suit in defense of their constitutional rights. According to Sarah, who had been on the faculty negotiating committee, the administration and faculty had compromised. The president got to pray, but only every two weeks and then only if drinks were being served. Thus a new university tradition was born: the Wednesday afternoon prayer meeting and cocktail party. Elena loved it. Nothing that bizarre ever happened in the police department. One of the joys of having dinner with Sarah was hearing her stories about the university.

The elevator they'd been waiting for arrived. Elena followed Leo in and punched Four. Even the elevator was bizarre—five-sided, red carpet on every surface including the ceiling, mirrors on each wall etched with long-limbed women. A little more breast and bottom on the women, and you'd have a perfect whorehouse elevator. If whorehouses had elevators. She'd have to ask Frank next time she saw him, if he ever came out from under cover again. Having worked both Vice and Narcotics, he'd know about whorehouses.

Before the elevator door opened on Four, she could hear the screaming. It led her straight to 407, where a curly haired girl in jeans and a mesh T-shirt sat on a sofa, fists covering her eyes, screaming steadily. Three members of the university police force surrounded her, obviously appalled that she was making a scene in the faculty apartment building. The one with his tie askew, probably called away from his dinner, introduced himself to Elena as Chief Clabb. He all but embraced her, evidently thinking that she'd perform some miracle, get the hysterical girl to shut up.

"Where's the body?" Leo asked.

"In there," said an officer who looked familiar to Elena. He waved toward the bedroom, and the university cops returned to remonstrating with the screamer. Elena followed Leo and glanced around the bedroom, found no evidence of a body, crossed the black arrow that pointed to the bed, and halted at the open bathroom door, peering over her partner's shoulder.

As a Crimes Against Persons officer she'd seen bodies before. Strictly speaking, this wasn't a body. And it made her flinch. Submerged in a modern-looking bathtub, which was full to within an inch of the lip with a moderately cloudy liquid, lay a skeleton. The round tub was six feet across and three feet deep with a comfortable curved edge—big enough to hold your ideal American family—mother, father, two point something kids—if there were any families like that anymore. This tub held bones—lying flat on the tub floor, hands crossed piously on the rib cage, empty eye sockets staring up through the cloudy liquid at Elena and Leo.

"Is it a fake?" asked Elena hopefully.

"Looks like the real thing to me," said Leo. He peered down at the bones and said, "Take a note, Miss Jarvis. One skeleton wearing a ring on the right ring finger. No other identifying—"

"Oh, take a note yourself," said Elena, grinning. "Let's see—Detective Elena Jarvis wishes to make a charge of sexual harassment against Detective Leo Weizell for treating her like his secretary."

"Jeez, you broads are so touchy," said Leo.

"Broads. That's another one. Didn't they warn you against sexist words in that sensitivity class?"

"Mostly I learned a bunch of new ones," said Leo. "I'm a real quick study, don't you think?"

"The chief is gonna be real happy you got so much out of that class," said Elena, "since it was his brainstorm."

"You want me to let the water out now that you've seen the deceased?" asked one of the campus cops, sending a puzzled glance from one detective to the other.

Elena turned and stared at him. Of course. He was the snickerer who had answered the call at Sarah Tolland's place. Then she turned back and studied the tub. "You'd have to reach in to flip the drain lever."

"Right."

"With your hand," said Leo.

"Yeah."

"Which is covered with the same kind of skin that dissolved off him—or her," Elena pointed out.

"Jesus," said Officer Pollock.

"Besides which you'd be draining away whatever that stuff is—and it may have killed him." Again she studied the crime scene. "Actually, I think someone crushed his skull before they dissolved him."

Leo stayed in the bathroom, taking his own notes. Elena returned to the living room, called for I.D. & R., then called the medical examiner, and finally waved off the university police. She always got stuck with the women in hysterics. "Your mascara's running," she said loudly into the ear of the screamer, taking a seat beside her on the sofa. Rooting through her handbag, Elena found a Kleenex under her police revolver. "Here, wipe your face off." The girl had stopped screaming and reached for her fanny pack as soon as Elena mentioned her mascara.

"I'm Detective Elena Jarvis." Elena shifted the gun again and located a blue and white foil-lined package, which she handed to the girl.

"Is that a condom?" the girl asked tearfully.

"No, it's not a condom." Elena pointed to printing on the

package, which said "MOIST TOWELETTE the instant cleanser and refresher." "For the mascara. You're a mess."

The girl nodded and began to scrub black tear tracks from her cheeks.

"What's your name?"

"Lili. Lili Bonaventura."

Bonaventura? Wasn't that the name of a Miami crime lord? Hot damn! A mob hit right here at off-the-wall Herbert Hobart University. Suppressing a grin, Elena said casually, "Pretty scary in there, huh?" The girl nodded and sniffed. "I don't suppose you could give us any idea who the deceased is?"

"It's Gus," she replied, dabbing at fresh tears with the Kleenex, then removing the new smudges with the towelette.

Elena handed her the whole Kleenex pack, plus a second towelette. "Of course, there's no way to be sure," she mused.

"Yes, there is. He's wearing our championship ring. I'm the team captain." The girl's voice rose into a keening wail on the last revelation. "And he's the coach."

"What sport would that be?" asked Elena uneasily.

"Volleyball," said Lili.

"And the name of the deceased?"

"Coach Gus—McGlenlevie."

Oh shit, thought Elena. And Sarah had been doing so well, attending the support group, acting like a normal person. Well, actually Sarah had missed the last meeting, but still Elena had been almost sure that the Chairwoman of Electrical Engineering hadn't really tried to blow her ex-husband up with an exploding snail. Now this. Dissolving him in his own bathtub. "How did you happen to discover the—ah—remains, Ms. Bonaventura?"

"What do you mean?"

"Well, you had to get into the apartment to find him. Did someone let you in?" The girl stared at her from under a mop of curly hair. "Maybe you had a key."

"There's a key here on the table beside the door," said one of the campus cops, starting to pick it up.

"Don't touch it," Elena snapped. He jumped as if bitten. Great, thought Elena. No telling how much evidence these university cops had destroyed. If an LSPD patrolman had responded, that wouldn't have been a problem. They knew enough to secure the scene.

"You think I killed Gussie?" Lili Bonaventura's full lower lip trembled.

"I didn't say that. Maybe the door was ajar. Maybe the key won't have your prints on it." Maybe the girl, not Sarah, had killed him.

"I want a lawyer."

"Right." I.D. & R. arrived, and Elena gestured toward the bedroom. "Look, but don't touch," she called after them.

"Very funny," Charlie Solis called back. Not two seconds later she heard him mutter, *"Madre de Dios."*

"You were telling me how you happened to be in Mr. McGlenlevie's apartment, Ms. Bonaventura."

"No, I wasn't."

"Having discovered the body does not automatically make you a suspect."

"I want a lawyer."

Elena sighed and thought, *Smart girl*. Did Lili Bonaventura sense how much Elena hoped that she was the murderer? She—or anyone but Sarah Tolland.

Good lord! Elena had been having dinner with the woman once a week since the snail incident. Sarah was the smartest, most interesting friend Elena had ever made. Intelligent people didn't commit murders! Well-controlled people didn't, and Sarah was the epitome of self-control. Look at how calm she'd been during the snail investigation. Elena shivered. What if that *had* been an attempted murder? And she'd ignored it and let the murderer go. Not just let her go, made a friend of her.

No. That wasn't what had happened. Onofre Calderon, the medical examiner arrived, and Elena waved him through to the bathtub.

A noisy sniffle called her attention back to Lili. "You need another Kleenex?" Elena asked. Around them, surfaces were being dusted for prints; photographs were being taken, evidence bagged.

Calderon stuck his head out of the bedroom and said, "I think he's dead."

6
··

Elena sat in a Mexican ladder-back chair at her gaily painted table, sipping coffee and reading the newspaper. In one corner of her kitchen was a rounded adobe fireplace, which she never used, and certainly not in May with the morning temperature pushing seventy-five. Several of her rooms had those fireplaces, which gave a Hispanic ambiance to the house and provided a nesting place for birds in the chimneys. She could hear them twittering if she happened to be home when they were settling down for the night. Other nods to her mixed heritage included the drapes, upholstery, and bed covers made by her mother, a secret weaver in Chimayo, New Mexico.

Since her mother was Anglo and not associated with any of the traditional weaving families, Aunt Josefina sold the material as if she'd produced it herself, which made the tourists happy because Aunt Josefina looked like a weaver—very Indian, more Indian than Elena's father, Sheriff Portillo. Unused fireplaces and bright, clandestine, nonwashable fabrics. Mixed genes made her an anomaly in a world of central heating, microwave ovens, and machine-washable polyester. Elena grinned and poured herself another cup of coffee, reached out to pluck a piece of toast from the toaster, spread it with ambrosial apricot jam made by Leo's stubbornly old-fashioned wife, Concepcion, and began to read the lead story.

POET DIES IN ACID BATH

23

Well maybe, thought Elena, but it hadn't looked like acid to her. On the theory that it might be, the crime-scene team and the medical examiner had taken forever to fish the bones out with tongs. Elena had snagged a vial of the stuff herself.

The remains of poet Angus McGlenlevie were discovered last night by Miss Lili Bonaventura, captain of the Herbert Hobart University intramural girls' volleyball team, of which McGlenlevie was coach. The body lay in his bathtub, little left but the bones, thus generating the police conclusion that McGlenlevie had been immersed in an acid bath.

That was Leo's conclusion. Elena thought the liquid looked like diluted whitewash, but that wouldn't make good copy. Who wanted to read a headline that said "Poet Dead in Whitewash"?

McGlenlevie's skull had been crushed by a powerful blow to the back upper left quadrant, raising the possibility that he may have been dead before being put into acid.

She scanned the rest of the article, which identified McGlenlevie as the famous author of *Erotica in Reeboks* and other popular and critically acclaimed books of verse. Did books of verse actually achieve popularity? Maybe books of dirty limericks. *Erotica in Reeboks* sounded as if it belonged to the dirty-limerick genre.

Abandoning her newspaper, she snapped on her nine-inch, black and white kitchen TV, which she'd bought cheap at a garage sale. The local news anchors were interviewing the Chairman of the Chemistry Department at Herbert Hobart University.

"It couldn't have been acid," said Professor Abelard Moncrief. "Acid would have eaten up the tub. You'd have it all over the floor and burning its way into the apartment below. You could have dangerous fumes, and believe me, the neighbors would have noticed. If you flushed it down the drain, it would have eaten up the pipes. They didn't do that, did they?" He sounded alarmed. "I could have told you what the compound was," continued Professor Moncrief reprovingly, "but no one bothered to call me or bring me a sample."

Elena wished they had. In deference to the pipes and sewer system, the stuff was still sitting in the tub. She supposed no matter what it turned out to be, the newspapers would continue to call it an acid bath.

Although it was Elena's turn to take the late shift, from noon to eight, which wasn't for four hours, the case goaded her like a burr inside a hiker's boot. She wanted to move on it. Find proof that Sarah hadn't killed McGlenlevie. Do it before the day's case load swamped her. With the temperatures rising into the mid-nineties, the people of Los Santos, those without air conditioning, would be turning mean and killing each other. Crimes Against Persons would be run ragged—as usual.

7
..

"Hey, Carmen. Great hair," Elena said to the police receptionist, who was a good deal more interested in hairstyles than
she was in Crimes Against Persons.

"You're on twelve-to-eight," said Carmen, jabbing a bobby
pin into a complicated, odd-looking roll at the side of her head.

"Right," said Elena. "Being a dedicated officer is a real
pain."

Carmen grinned. "If I could get the overtime you do, I'd be
a real pain too," she said, then turned her attention to a small
boy nearby. "Hey, kid, did you just blow your nose into that
potted plant? If you did, this lady, who's a detective, is going
to arrest you for aggravated assault on a plant." The little boy
dived for his mother, who was occupying one of the five chairs
in the small reception area.

Elena waved to the kid and started down the aisle toward her
cubicle on Homicide Row in the back, just where she'd wanted
to be.

Between the academy and C.A.P., Elena had done two years
on patrol, as all officers did, the first year on the Westside,
tracking runaway teenagers and soothing their distraught
parents, arresting under-eighteens for public possession of
alcohol, chasing suspicious persons around neighborhoods,
being the first on the scene for burglaries, breaking up bar and
family fights, patrolling the projects and picking up tips from

the guards there, lots of aggravated assaults but not too many homicides. Twice she'd caught homicide calls and made some friends in C.A.P. by being diligent in securing crime scenes and keeping witnesses around and busybodies away.

The second year, they'd moved her to Central, where her Spanish and her ability to think on her feet stood her in good stead in an area that was always jumping. A slow night in Central was the exception rather than the rule. Six months there and they moved her to the East Valley, which was bigger and just as violent. She'd won some commendations in East Valley. The Gang Task Force had asked for her when she passed her detective exam at the top of the list, but so had Lieutenant Beltran of C.A.P.

He admitted up front they needed a woman because it looked bad that they didn't have one, but that was O.K. It got her in, even if it meant four months in the front with the Sex Crimes and Robbery squad. How she'd hated that! Not the robberies. The sex crimes. The traumatized rape victims, all those kids she had to sit with on the blue polka-dot sofa, getting them to tell her the awful things that had been done to them by parents, stepparents, brothers, and sisters; you name it, somebody did it to a kid.

After four months and quick solutions to a couple of rape-murders, she'd asked for transfer to Sergeant Manny Escobedo's Homicide and Aggravated Assault squad, and Beltran hadn't blocked it, probably because they had another woman, not as high on the list as Elena, but still very good. She'd had commendations even as a patrol officer on child abuse and rape cases. Nadine Collins. Elena had been glad to see another woman make C.A.P. even if she didn't interact much with Nadine.

Sergeant Manny Escobedo, whose small windowed office she was passing, swung his chair around, knocked on the window, and yelled, "Hey, Jarvis."

She stuck her head in. "You're my man on the twelve-to-eight shift," he chided her. Each of the three squads contributed one detective to late and weekend shifts. "I hope you haven't forgotten that."

"I'll be there," said Elena. "I just didn't want to let the acid bath case get cold. Given the news coverage it's generating, we're gonna start getting heat from Lieutenant Beltran, maybe even Captain Stollinger." Beltran was the head of Crimes Against Persons, Stollinger of Criminal Investigations.

"You're right about that, and Leo won't be in till noon. Community Services O.K.'d him to talk to a bunch of kids in some damn kindergarten."

"Uh-huh. He's this morning's Show and Tell for one of Concepcion's fourteen nieces and nephews."

"Shit," said Escobedo. "What a great way to fight crime. They see a police detective, they'll all want to carry guns." Elena turned to go, and Escobedo called to her again, saying, "Jarvis, your stomach go all to hell after you got divorced?"

She turned back. "Why, has yours, Sergeant?" The sergeant was more recently divorced than she.

"Oh, yeah."

"Well, mine didn't," said Elena, "but then I was eating the same food I ate while Frank and I were still sharing a house. What are you eating?"

"Whatever I can pick up," Escobedo admitted.

"And then you got two kids visiting you once a week, right?"

"Yeah. I never have 'em but I get a call in the middle of the visit and have to take 'em back home to Marcella, which, of course, pisses her off, and she has to go over for about the millionth time all the reasons she divorced me. Or maybe she's not there, and I'm even unluckier because her mother's there. That old woman always did hate me."

"Try Maalox," said Elena. "That or the gym. They tell me all those exercise machines really reduce stress."

"Just what I need," Manny Escobedo muttered. "A whole bunch of pulled muscles to go with my stomach trouble."

Elena nodded. "Try Maalox," she advised again and went on down the aisle, past the two small interview rooms, past the C.A.P. computer, which would do anything including put out a wanted poster, but not a thing to speed up the processing of physical evidence, almost all of which had to be sent to the Department of Public Safety Labs.

In her own cubicle she settled into her rolling chair with its gray tweed upholstery. Partitions were covered with the same fabric. Someone must have got a good price on gray tweed. Still, Elena had read enough police procedurals to know that Los Santos C.A.P. looked pretty good. Almost restful. Detectives didn't have their own offices, but most of the time they weren't here; they were out in the field. When they were in, it was fairly quiet. Computer terminals, which they all had, weren't noisy, and if you didn't have a door, you did have the partitions around you. Of course, when other detectives were in, they were usually smoking, and she could have done without that, but you couldn't have everything. From the descriptions she'd read of facilities in other cities, it was better here.

Elena began her investigation on the telephone. The night before, after leaving Gus McGlenlevie's apartment, she and Leo made two stops, the first at Sarah's apartment downstairs; she wasn't home. Why not? Elena had wondered uneasily. The support group didn't meet until next Thursday, and finals week should have eliminated night classes and academic meetings. Sarah didn't date. So why wasn't she home?

Bimmie Kowolski, the aerobics fiancée, was. They located her address in Gus's address book and visited her to ask when she had last seen him. "When I told him that he either set the date for the wedding or the engagement was off," said Bimmie, her face hot with resentment. "He's never even given me a ring, and I don't need that kind of treatment from my boyfriend. I'm asked for dates all the time."

"I'm sure that's true," said Leo, who had been examining her as if she were an important piece of evidence. "When was that, Miss Kowolski?"

"When was I asked for a date? Well, this cute masseur—"

"When did you last see your fiancé?"

"The night he gave his final in English four-ten—that's the dirty poetry class," she replied sullenly, and told them that she remembered very well because it was the night she caught Gus feeling up one of the poetesses. "He claimed he couldn't help himself; he was turned on by the sonnet she wrote for the final. I tore it up," said Bimmie with satisfaction, "but Gus said it didn't matter because he was going to give her an A anyway.

So that's when I said the thing about setting the date. Gus ignored me—like he always does. He just sat there making out the final grade sheet." Pouting, Bimmie had brooded over Gus's intransigence while Elena and Leo waited—none too patiently.

"He didn't average the grades," Bimmie then added. "Does that seem right to you? My teachers always averaged grades. Gus just goes, 'An A for you, sweetheart, and a B for you.' He gave A's to the girls and B's to the boys. I told him, 'That doesn't seem right to me, Gus,' and he goes, 'What do you know about it, Bimmie? You're not exactly a brain surgeon.' And that's the last I saw of him. I walked out, and he hasn't called me. So why do *you* want to know?" she had asked Elena. "You finally decided to do something about the snail?"

A disquieting question, thought Elena.

"Well, it's too late," said Bimmie. "I sent the jogging suit to the cleaners. All the spots are—"

"He's dead, Miss Kowolski," said Leo. They left Bimmie in tears, remorseful that she had spoken ill of her beloved Gussie when he was dead, convinced that the dangerous exploding snail had got him in the end—although they'd assured her that such was not the case.

They couldn't ask where she had been when he died because they didn't know when it happened, nor were they likely to. All the guidelines a coroner uses to fix the time of death had disappeared with Gus's flesh, which might explain why the murderer had dissolved him. Bimmie had a motive, Elena supposed, although her gut reaction was that Bimmie hadn't done it. She'd have been afraid of burning acid holes in her designer jogging suit. Then Elena remembered Sarah, and told herself not to be so quick to eliminate perfectly viable suspects like Bimmie.

With Bimmie's information in mind, Elena made her first call of the morning to the English Department at the university and was told by the departmental secretary, who had read the morning paper, that the final for the late Professor McGlenlevie's The Conception and Writing of Erotic Poetry had been held on Tuesday, May 5, at 7 P.M., which was against the rules. "Holding a final in the evening isn't allowed, but no one ever yet convinced *him* to follow any rules," said the secretary in a petulant voice.

It was obvious to Elena that Mr. Lance Potemkin, secretary to the English Department, disliked or disapproved of the late Gus.

"At least, I *suppose* he gave a final," said Mr. Potemkin. "I guess I should check to see if he turned in any grades."

"Where would you check that?" asked Elena and, being given the information, called the registrar's office and found another, later day on which Gus McGlenlevie had been alive, Wednesday, May 6, when he turned in grades at the registrar's office late in the morning. "He looked like he was going on safari," said the registrar's clerk. "And he patted my behind when I got up to give his grade sheet to the girl at the computer." Elena was entering information into her own computer as she got it, phone held between shoulder and ear as she typed. She'd always meant to get herself one of those doohickeys that held the phone to your ear, but she always forgot. Result—a stiff neck from telephone interviews.

Neither piece of information from the registrar's clerk surprised Elena. As she told Leo, when he arrived at 10:30 and accused her of bucking for promotion by coming in so early, Gus McGlenlevie was a known lecher and given to idiosyn-cratic clothing, the Poets-Do-It-In-Iambic-Pentameter sweat shirt being a case in point. "And how come you're not at Show and Tell?" she added. "You afraid I'd solve the case before you could get here?"

"Oh hell, they only wanted to see my gun—bloodthirsty little boogers. I don't know why anyone has kids these days. Television turns them into juvenile delinquents before they're three."

"Uh-huh." Elena didn't comment further. She knew how much Leo and Concepcion wanted a child of their own.

"Then I offered to show them a really good soft-shoe routine, and they asked about my handcuffs."

Elena laughed. "No one appreciates the fact that you're the Fred Astaire of the LSPD."

"You laugh," he retorted. "Just wait till the talent show. I ought to make sergeant just on the basis of the routine I'm working up." He did a few steps, then asked, "So how come you happen to know McGlenlevie was a lecher? You date the guy or what?"

Elena told him about the snail case.

"If his wife killed him," said Leo, "you're going to be in deep shit, babe, for not arresting her first time around."

Elena knew that; the prospect gave her cold chills, and not just because of the teasing she'd take in the station house. Her sergeant might ignore it—he considered Elena and Leo his best homicide team—but Beltran wouldn't. She wasn't sure what interpretation he'd put on her failure to arrest Sarah, but it wouldn't do Elena's career an ounce of good if Sarah had actually killed her ex-husband.

Her second series of calls did nothing to solve her problems. First, she rang Sarah's apartment and got the answering machine, as she had when she tried the night before. Then she called the Electrical Engineering Department and was told by the secretary, Mrs. Virginia Pargetter, that Dr. Tolland was out of town. She would not tell Elena where, and agreed to do so only after she'd telephoned Police Headquarters to be sure that Elena was, in fact, a police officer pursuing a legitimate investigation.

The secretary evidently hadn't read of Gus's death, or if she had, she wasn't letting on. Elena's last call was to the Chicago hotel where Sarah Tolland was said to be attending a national conference for electrical engineers. Had Sarah mentioned a conference at any of those dinners they'd shared? Elena didn't remember any such information. Maybe her friend had meant to mention it and hadn't been able to because— The front desk at the hotel took her off hold and informed Elena that Dr. Tolland had checked out early that morning. Was Sarah coming home? Elena fervently hoped so.

She then called the close-mouthed Mrs. Pargetter back and elicited the information that, no, Dr. Tolland was not coming home; she was going on vacation. Although the secretary initially assured Elena that Dr. Tolland had left a vacation address—"Dr. Tolland always leaves word where she can be reached," said Virginia—no such information was in the computer when she tried to retrieve it. Elena could tell that the woman was very upset to discover the void in her computer files. Had Sarah deleted her destination, killed her ex-husband, and then disappeared? Elena asked herself.

Unfortunately, with that crazy report about an exploding snail on the blotter and her inexplicable disappearance, Sarah was looking more and more like the prime suspect. Even the fact that she hadn't told Elena she was leaving seemed suspicious. Gloomily Elena reminded herself that Sarah had seemed to be a nice person. At the woman's support group, at the dinners they'd shared, she hadn't given the impression of being angry about the divorce, more like amused.

Elena was the angry one, and she hadn't killed Frank, so why assume cool, calm Sarah had killed Gus? But Sarah was gone. According to the secretary, she'd left Los Santos on Friday, May 8, early in the morning, 5:30, although according to the desk clerk at the hotel, the conference sessions hadn't started until Monday. Had Sarah killed McGlenlevie sometime between Wednesday, which was, so far, the last time he had been seen alive, and Friday when Sarah herself left? Otherwise, why leave Los Santos early? Otherwise, why leave that message on Elena's answering machine that she was too jammed up with last-minute chores to attend the support group or go out to dinner? Last minute before what? Killing her ex-husband? Skipping town?

And then she'd left the conference early. Meetings were scheduled for today, but Sarah had skipped them, checked out, and disappeared—on the morning when news of Gus's murder appeared in the papers. Had someone called her, sending her into panicked flight? It didn't look good to Elena. It looked even worse to Leo when she told him.

"Sounds like she's our murderer," he said. "Could she have killed him? I mean physically. Is she strong enough, tall enough?"

"Maybe," Elena hedged, feeling too depressed to offer an opinion. "We don't have the coroner's report—angle and force of the blow, that sort of thing."

"Coroner's report won't be in till Monday, so we better hit the streets. You want to interview the residents of the apartment building? See if anyone saw or heard anything. Did you notice that all the suspects are female? Just goes to show that women are making their mark. Women detectives, women murderers."

"Yeah, yeah. You don't think there are any men who hated him? Like the men connected to the women. The secretary at the English Department is a man; he sure seems to dislike Gus. Funny name," she mused. "I wonder if he's related to my neighbors."

"McGlenlevie?"

"No, Potemkin." *I'm whistling in the dark,* thought Elena, *hoping for any murderer except Sarah.* "Let's try interviewing colleagues, his and hers. No one's going to be home at the apartment house on Friday morning."

"O.K., and if all else fails, there's always that drive-by shooting. We haven't cleared that yet."

"That and forty other cases."

"Manny shifted some of our load to other guys. The brass wants this one solved."

Elena rose, settled her shoulder holster more comfortably and pulled on a lightweight jacket. "Then let's do it."

8
..

"It looks like one of those temples in Mexico where the Indians cut out people's hearts," said Leo, scowling at the Humanities building with its turquoise and salmon tile trim.

Elena, having read the "Architecture of Herbert Hobart University" pamphlet, knew that they were looking at Mayan Revival, an American offshoot of art deco. Since Sarah had given her the pamphlet, Elena didn't pass the information on to Leo. No use reminding him that she had failed to arrest a woman who might be guilty of dissolving her ex-husband after an unsuccessful attempt to kill him with an exploding snail.

Since the university was in the interim between spring finals and summer school, the detectives found few faculty members in their offices. The English Department secretary was at his desk, but the chairman was gone. As they went down a hall to visit Professors Donald Mallory and Anne-Marie LaPortierre, Leo said, "He's gay, right?"

"Who?"

"The secretary. He's gay."

"Lance is? Son of a gun!" said Elena. "I thought he was cute."

"Cute? You thought he was cute? Come on."

"Well, he's got nice blond hair like yours and a better than average build."

"The hell," muttered Leo, who was over six feet and very

35

thin. "He's short. Lemme ask you this. Would you go out with a secretary?"

"Why not? Concepcion was a secretary when you met her."

"Well, yeah, but Concepcion's female. I mean secretaries are supposed to be—"

"That's a sexist remark, Leo," said Elena. "You owe me a quarter." Since the sensitivity training class, they had a bet on that he couldn't go a whole week without making a sexist remark. Leo had maintained that he never made sexist remarks. Elena claimed a quarter every time he did. In the month since the class, she'd collected $2.75 and had to argue for every penny of it.

"I don't see anything sexist about expecting a secretary to be female," said Leo. "That's just—"

"Sh-sh." She knocked at the door of Professor Donald Mallory, who told them, among other things, "Angus McGlenlevie was a fraud—poetry-wise. Our departmental secretary is ten times the poet McGlenlevie was. Angus wrote pornographic doggerel. It doesn't scan, has no rhyme scheme, has no metaphors of note. How a man of his meager talents could put himself into the same literary category as William Shakespeare and John Donne . . ."

Dr. Mallory, it turned out, was a Renaissance scholar who disliked not just Angus McGlenlevie but any poet who postdated the Jacobeans—except Lance Potemkin. Leo didn't know who the Jacobeans were. Elena remembered that they had flourished during the reign of James I. She thought Ben Jonson, whose plays she had detested, was one. Dr. Mallory, she noted, was neither surprised nor dismayed to have read that Angus McGlenlevie had been murdered. Could Professor Mallory be the murderer? Motive—professional jealousy? Critical disgust?

Professor Anne-Marie LaPortierre wasn't surprised either, although she hadn't read the morning paper. "The man tries to seduce anything female from the veriest freshman to me, and I'm fifty-five and uninterested."

"She may be fifty-five," Elena remarked as they headed for the College of Engineering through a corridor of tall palm trees, "but she looks in good enough shape to have delivered the fatal blow, walked to the bathroom with the corpse under her arm, and with the other hand carried in enough acid or whatever to dissolve him."

"Nah," said Leo. "She's old enough to be someone's grandmother. Grandmothers don't do stuff like that."

"What about the grandmother who beat her son-in-law to death with a tamale steamer?"

"Well, there was her," Leo conceded. "How do you figure they got palm trees this size in here? They sure as hell didn't grow in Los Santos on their own, and the university's only been around three years. You figure they dug 'em up in California and sent 'em in by train or what?"

"Florida," said Elena, and they entered the Engineering building, on whose first floor were the offices of the Department of Electrical Engineering and the super-efficient Virginia Pargetter, Executive Assistant to the Chairwoman. Virginia was a stern, gray-haired lady, slat-thin with a square-jawed face, who informed them that she did *not* inadvertently delete things from her computer files, that if Dr. Tolland's vacation telephone number was gone, which it was, then it had been feloniously deleted, and she thought the felony should be investigated. Leo promised her that they would look into it.

"I hope you didn't mean we personally are going to look into it," Elena muttered as they began knocking on doors in the Electrical Engineering Department. "The only computer I know anything about is the terminal at my desk, and you're not much better."

"Hey, I was just putting her off. But if this chairlady was going to kill her husband and disappear, she wouldn't want anyone to know where," he pointed out. "And she's a computer whiz, right? I mean the sign in the hall says Electrical Engineering and Computer Science. So she'd know how to get rid of the information. Right?"

That supposition had already occurred to Elena, although she wasn't sure *what* Sarah did. Research—Sarah had mentioned research, but not on what. Being chairwoman, teaching— but again Sarah had never been specific about *what* she taught. Maybe she was a specialist in—Elena tried to imagine what electrical engineers did—power plants, perhaps. Or lighting—

like lamps, football fields, those weird green street lights they had across the river in Mexico.

"We can get a computer expert over here from I.D. & R. if we need to," said Leo.

"Wouldn't we have to get a search warrant for that?" Elena asked.

"Damned if I know."

Three electrical engineering professors, one an Indian woman who seemed to be suffering some kind of nervous collapse, all looked blank when asked if they could shed any light on who might have killed Angus McGlenlevie, the ex-husband of their chairwoman. None of them had met Angus McGlenlevie.

One said brusquely, "Well, it wasn't Sarah," and swung around to his computer, a clear signal that he didn't care to talk to them anymore.

Another said, "Are you sure Sarah was married to this person?" He was puttering around in a lab full of mysterious equipment.

The Indian lady burst into tears and said she was returning to India the next day and had no thoughts on the death of Mr. McGlenlevie, whose name she mispronounced badly.

"Don't you think it's strange that she never introduced him to any of her colleagues?" Leo asked.

"You wouldn't ask that if you'd met him," Elena replied. "I wouldn't have introduced him to anyone."

"Why not? If I remember right, you introduced Frank to people."

Elena scowled at him and returned to the departmental office to ask Mrs. Pargetter if she happened to remember where Sarah had said she was going after the Chicago meeting.

"Boston," said the secretary curtly.

"Do you remember where in Boston?"

"No."

"Why didn't she just tell you that in the first place?" asked Leo as they went out into the intense dry heat of the afternoon.

"She's a New Englander," said Elena. "Didn't you notice the accent? If you don't ask the right question, they don't volunteer any information. I read that in a book."

"Bad habit—reading. The lieutenant wouldn't like it. He

thinks women should stay in the kitchen, illiterate and pregnant." His face lit with delight at Elena's angry reaction. "Let's hit the apartment house like I said in the first place. Since no one's in the offices, they're all home. Right?"

Among the neighbors of Angus McGlenlevie there was a consensus of opinion. The only unusual sound they'd heard from his apartment recently was silence. No one agreed on how long this blessed silence had lasted. One week, two. The silence had been broken by screaming. Last night. That had been closer to normal than silence, so only one neighbor had called the campus police. "I'm glad I didn't go up there," said a redheaded lady. "Imagine having a grisly murder right above one's head." That witness lived on Three.

"Most of the time we heard noisy sex, loud music, and people shouting lines of poetry," her husband explained. He was a cello professor who liked to play his instrument in the second bedroom when McGlenlevie wasn't drowning him out. "I just thought the screams meant he was back home again. I put my cello away and got out the earphones, which usually works. You can't use Bach or Vivaldi, but even McGlenlevie can't overpower Wagner. By the time the first act of *Das Rheingold* was over, the screaming had stopped." The professor ruffled his thinning hair and added with an ingenuous smile, "He was a satyr, you know."

None of them seemed unduly grieved by Gus's demise. None had seen Sarah entering or leaving his apartment—ever. Several recognized pictures of Bimmie Kowolski and Lili Bonaventura, although they couldn't say for sure when they'd last seen these ladies in the lobby, elevators, or hall. Several said other women visited his apartment, but they didn't know who and couldn't describe them very well. "After all," a portly economics professor remarked, "women streamed in and out. There must have been something attractive about him, although what it could have been—well, that's always puzzled me."

"Female masochism," said his wife, a chunky psychologist with a squint in her left eye. "The man attracted women who thrive on psychic pain. Many a time I thought of putting hidden cameras in McGlenlevie's apartment. Three or four days out of his life would destroy feminist psychology. Now it's too late. Damned shame too."

That was as close as anyone came to mourning Angus McGlenlevie. Certainly no one was surprised that someone had killed him.

"I could have done it myself," said the birdlike wife of a professor of Balkan language and culture. "He kept borrowing things—sugar, coffee, my mother's crystal dessert dishes, the *New York Times*, tampons. And he never returned anything. I don't see why he couldn't buy his own *New York Times*—and tampons? He asked my husband if I could spare him a tampon. My husband slammed the door in his face.

"And do you think that discouraged him? Oh, no. He was back the next day wanting to borrow my car. He smashed up Professor Tolland's car. Did you know that? You think she killed him? She wouldn't even speak to him. When you remove that crime tape from his apartment, I'd like to go in and get my mother's crystal back. Of course, he may have sold the whole set. I wouldn't put it past him. Do you think I could sue his estate . . . ?"

She was still talking as Leo and Elena, smiling apologetically, backed down the hall.

9
..

Monday, May 18, 9:15 A.M.

Strictly speaking Elena was off today, but anxiety impelled her to visit the basement at headquarters in search of information about the acid bath case, as the papers were still calling it. Then, if she wasn't facing the end of her career—because, for instance, they'd found evidence of Sarah's presence at the crime scene—Elena had some home-repair errands to run. She armed the security system and locked the heavy carved door of the house she still thought of as the place that Frank bought.

They hadn't been married two months before he purchased at auction a crumbling adobe in one of the pretty, older sections of town. It was a foreclosure sale and, as he pointed out, dirt cheap with his V.A. loan. They'd fix it up together; that was Frank's idea until he'd actually taken part in some of the fixing up.

Elena paused for a moment to study her house, white walls, mellow red roof tiles drowsing in the May sun among the slender spearhead cedars. With forested mountain around it, she might have been back home in New Mexico, but here all the green that surrounded the house had been planted by her or by previous owners, certainly not by Frank. Two weeks on the home improvement detail had killed his enthusiasm.

Work done on the house thereafter—the adobe patching, the painting, the rotten wood replacement, the floor sanding, the nailing up and yanking down, the plumbing and electrical

41

work, the gardening—she'd done it all in the years when she was finishing up her degree at the state university and then in her spare time after she joined the force. World-class home handyperson—that was her. Fellow officers asked her advice on rusting evaporative coolers and clogged drains. There were crooks in town who stopped stealing cars and burglarizing houses long enough to give her a call because their fruitless mulberries had bag worms.

Turning away from the house, she cut over to her Ford pickup truck parked beside a satin-green Palo Verde tree. She thumbed the security disarmer, without which the truck would have said, when she first laid her hand on the door handle, "Back off," in a loud, threatening voice. Then if she persisted, the alarm would have gone off, bringing to their front doors all the old folks who lived in the neighborhood. Frank liked to break into her truck and move it over a few parking places or a few blocks just for the hell of it, to remind her that he hadn't disappeared since the divorce, but she thought that she and Coronado Perez down at Safe Auto Supply had finally thwarted him.

She climbed in and headed for Five Points, deciding that besides the cement to patch up the stone walls that edged her property, she'd buy a little straw, mix up some adobe, and slap it onto the bad places on the east side of the house where the August rainy season had made inroads. And of course, she'd need whitewash.

Once on Montana, she began to think about work. She'd made an arrest in the drive-by shooting just yesterday, in the case where nobody saw a thing. It came together because Leo got Crime Stoppers to put up a thousand dollars for information leading to arrest and indictment. Lo and behold, within twelve hours they had a make on a 1974 rusted red Pontiac with, as the female informant had said, "big pipes sticking out the back."

So they—she and a detective from Sergeant Holiday's squad, both on weekend duty—arrested four boys, three of them juveniles, who probably thought they'd put in a few years down at Gatesville and come on home. Elena doubted it. People were getting sick of the drive-by shootings where grandmothers died in front of their TV's and little girls took a slug in the shoulder while doing their geography homework at the kitchen table. The judges were certifying the shooters to stand trial as adults, and the juries were sending them off to Huntsville for long stretches, which was fine with Elena.

Then there was the acid bath case, which was taking up part of her day off and in no way an easy arrest. The coroner's report was in. Probable cause of death, a blow to the back of the head, crushing the skull, delivered with a blunt instrument, not found. However, they couldn't be sure the blow had killed him, or when, because they had only bones left and a few strands of hair on the edge of the tub, which looked like the hair found in a brush from the bedroom dresser. D.P.S. would tell them for sure, but not in time to help the investigation. The height and build of the bones matched what she remembered of McGlenlevie. And there were teeth. Teeth with enough fillings so that dental records should have given them a positive I.D.

She had called, first, every dentist on the list provided by the university health insurance company, and then every damn dentist in town, and finally about fifty dentists across the border in Mexico. If Angus McGlenlevie had ever been to a dentist around here, nobody would admit it, so he couldn't be identified by dental records, which meant they didn't really have a positive I.D. on the remains—beyond the early statement of Lili Bonaventura that the ring on the skeletal finger was the Girls' Intramural Volleyball Championship ring that Coach Gus and all the players had got at the end of the volleyball season. And of course, the corpse had been found in McGlenlevie's bathtub, so why wouldn't it be him? As Leo said, "Who the hell else would it be?"

Three days after she discovered the body, Lili Bonaventura still refused to talk to them. However, interviews with other members of the volleyball team had yielded information about Lili and Coach Gus. Some of the girls had said she was the team captain and let it go at that. Some of them had taken their last finals and flown home or to the French Riviera or wherever rich girls migrated in the summer, but two, who had stayed for summer school, said Lili had been getting it on with Coach Gus every other Thursday since she made team captain. One of them said Lili claimed that sex with Coach Gus was very creative, him being a poet and all. Elena believed that. A man who ran around in a sweat shirt that said "Poets Do It In Iambic Pentameter" and had a beard like a small tumbleweed, except that it was red—well, the wonder was, not his sexual proclivities, but that Sarah had ever married him.

So even if she wouldn't say, they knew why Lili Bonaventura had been at the apartment. She probably had her own key. Fingerprints would tell them about that, but Elena didn't think the volleyball captain had killed him—not that Elena said so. Leo, on the other hand, was more forthcoming. "Once she dissolved him," he asked, "why have a screaming fit? She'd be smarter to leave and wait for someone else to discover him."

Elena said, "You think she's smart?" Leo had been off over the weekend, but she'd talked to him a couple of times by phone.

The interesting thing was that Lili Bonaventura actually turned out to be the daughter of Giuseppe "Fat Joe" Bonaventura, the Miami mob boss, so maybe McGlenlevie's death had been a Mafia hit. Leo had said, "Oh, come on." But Elena knew a little about how fathers in Hispanic families felt about their daughters. Her father, Sheriff Ruben Portillo, had asked her as soon as she announced her impending marriage to Frank, "Did that Anglo weasel dishonor you on the backpacking trip? I knew I shouldn't have let you join the Sierra Club."

So Elena wouldn't have been surprised to hear that Italian-American fathers took the same attitude toward their daughters and guys who might have been fooling around with their daughters. Maybe Fat Joe Bonaventura had gotten wind of Lili's biweekly adventures with Gus McGlenlevie and decided to take Gus out, as a matter of family honor. Elena hoped so because the best alternative suspect wasn't Bimmie, the aerobics instructor, fiancée of the deceased, whom they had left in remorseful tears because she'd spoken ill of the dead, but probably not because she'd killed him.

Elena parked her truck and entered headquarters by the side door. She was downstairs, heading for the fingerprint room in I.D. & R. when she saw Fernie Duran, better known as Fernie the Flirt. They had been in the same class at the Police Academy; Fernie made detective six months after Elena and was down the hall in Special Investigations, assigned to Organized Crime.

"So you're finally coming to the gym to work out and give us another look at the famous Jarvis body," said Fernie, grinning. He had on shorts, gym shoes, and a T-shirt with the sleeves cut off—ready to work out in the headquarters gym, Elena surmised.

"You wish," she retorted.

"It's a great stress reliever," said Fernie, giving her an exaggerated leer. "Almost as good as the number one stress reliever, which I'd be glad to demonstrate."

"What'd you have in mind? A *ménage à trois*?" asked Elena dryly.

"Sounds good to me. What is it?"

"You, me, and Angie." Fernie was married to Angie Duran, one of two toxicologists in I.D. & R.

"Shucks," said Fernie, looking disappointed. "I don't think Angie'd go for it."

"Me either." Elena had been a bridesmaid at their wedding, along with Angie's three sisters and one of Fernie's. He had two more, but they had been too pregnant to be in the wedding party.

Elena had two stops to make in I.D. & R. before she could go after her unslaked lime. The first was with Steve Curry in Fingerprints, who turned from the AFIS computer, delighted to see her. He had pale red, receding hair, freckles, and more girlfriends than any man Elena knew.

"You've decided to marry me, right?" said Steve.

"How's your new girlfriend going to feel about that?"

"How'd you know about her?"

"Stands to reason. Who is she?"

"A librarian at Main Library. Actually reads books. You don't find too many of those anymore."

"Sounds like the girl of your dreams," Elena agreed. "I've got a favor to ask you, Steve."

"Anything for you, sweetheart."

"Did you get any makes on the fingerprints from the acid bath case?"

"Only the three guys from the university police force. No known criminals in that apartment."

Elena opened her shoulder bag and handed Steve a lavender metallic gift box in which a birthday present from Sarah had come. It was carefully but loosely wrapped in tissue paper. "Could you lift prints from here, eliminate mine, and see if what's left matches anything they got from the apartment?"

He rose and went to a bench where he dusted the box, then examined it under a magnifying glass. "Two good latents, three, one partial," he muttered. He passed the glass to Elena.

"The one with the left slant loop would be mine," she said.

"I'll treasure it forever," said Steve.

"Sweet, but I'm already in the system."

"No feeling for romance." He lifted two prints and a partial, prepared them, and fed them into AFIS, a computer that would match them to the 150,000 prints in the Los Santos system. "Here we go," he said and put two prints on the screen. The computer threw up tiny circles at points of similarity. Using a mouse, Steve put up more. "I'd need to do a manual, but I'm pretty sure we've got a match here."

Elena sighed. "Where was that print found at the crime scene?"

Steve pulled up the information. "Only one place. On a photo frame and glass."

Elena hoped it wasn't Bimmie or any other girlfriend whose picture Sarah had picked up while she was in Gus's apartment. And what was she doing there when she avoided her ex-husband? Or so she'd always said.

"You don't look too happy," said Steve. "You want to give me information on the print. I can't put a name on it."

"Sarah Tolland," said Elena grimly.

She went on to the lab to find Angie looking beautiful, hovering over the intoxilyzer. "Catching lots of DWI's?" Elena asked.

"You bet." Angie looked up and took in Elena's outfit. "All dressed up for work, I see."

"It's my day off," said Elena, who was wearing old jeans and a T-shirt that read SANTA FE'S NICE, BUT I CAN'T AFFORD IT. "I'm going down to get myself a couple of barrels of lime to whitewash my house, but before I—"

"Didn't I hear my husband down the hall propositioning you?"

"I didn't accept, did I?"

"*Ménage à trois* isn't accepting? You've fueled the man's vanity for months."

Elena grinned. "Listen, I'm here about the acid bath case. You heard about it?"

"Uh-huh."

"I wondered if you could find out what was in that bathtub."

"Hasn't D.P.S. got—"

"Yeah, but I don't want to wait three months. If I knew what it was, it might help me with the investigation."

"I'll sure be glad when the new labs open," muttered Angie. "At least I can tell you whether it was acid."

Elena handed her a vial of the cloudy liquid. Angie rooted around in a drawer while Elena stared at the hunks of bloody gauze drying in a glass case. That would be blood sopped up at some murder scene. Angie dried it out and sent it to D.P.S. for typing.

"It's not acid," said Angie. "It's a base." She held a strip of litmus paper that had turned blue where it touched the liquid. "Beyond that—" She shrugged, studied Elena, and said, "You're really worried about this one, aren't you?"

"Yeah. If it turns out a friend of mine did him, I could be in big trouble, not to say that she wouldn't be in bigger trouble."

"A friend? Naughty, naughty." Angie turned back to her DWI's. "Maybe you could get one of the university labs to do an analysis for you," she said over her shoulder.

Elena thought back to the original television broadcast about the case. A chemistry professor from H.H.U. had said if they'd brought the liquid to him, he could have told them what it was. "Can I use your phone?"

Elena called Abelard Moncrief, who said he had a postdoctoral fellow who could run the test for her—free. That was important. The police department wasn't going to pay for private testing when eventually D.P.S. would tell them what it was—maybe even in time for the trial if anyone was indicted.

Within an hour a skinny young man with beige hair that stuck out from his head in untidy tufts told her that she was dealing with simple unslaked lime in a dilute solution with water. He admitted, when asked, that a body could be dissolved with it. "No question it'll heat up and boil if you put water in it, and it will eat flesh, but to get the job done, you'd have to stay there a couple of days. Dissolve, drain, dissolve, drain. A couple of days—a lot of lime. That's kind of a weird idea if you ask me."

Elena shrugged. "Someone did it. Right in your neighborhood more or less."

"Wow! The acid bath case?"

"Right, but we'll have a better chance of catching the murderer if you don't mention this to anyone."

"I won't say a word. And if you need any other analyses, just give me a call."

Support from the public, thought Elena. That was new. "The big question is why lime?" she murmured.

The student thought about the question. "It's cheap. It's easy to get hold of. It's easier to handle than acid. Maybe you've got a very neat murderer. With the lime, you'd get no messy decaying corpse, no offensive odors to tip off the neighbors."

"And by leaving only bones, the murderer ensures that there's no way we can tell when the deceased bought it," said Elena thoughtfully, and wondered if anyone at the faculty apartment house had seen the lime being hauled in. They'd need to go back with a whole new set of questions. She sighed, asked to use the chemist's phone, and called headquarters to suggest that someone from the eight-to-four shift go door-to-door trying a new line of questioning.

"Sorry, sweetheart," said Beto Sanchez. "No one to do it. We're going out on what looks like a murder-suicide. You and Leo will have to pick it up yourselves tomorrow. Oh, and say, babe, got a message for you from Frank."

Elena gritted her teeth.

"Frank says that the narcs have had their eye on McGlenlevie; he's into drugs—funny-farm mushrooms—so maybe you should look for a drug connection in the acid bath case."

"We don't even know for sure that McGlenlevie's the corpse," said Elena.

"Well, anyway, Frank says you ought to look into the drug connection, and he'd be glad to help."

"Tell him to butt out," said Elena. The corpse had to be McGlenlevie, she assured herself. Who else would those bones belong to? And she guessed she'd have to look into a drug connection, but she'd get her information from some other narc. Mushrooms? Who had McGlenlevie thought he was— Carlos Castaneda?

She picked her shoulder bag up off the floor by the lab bench and set off to make her second-to-last stop—back to the Eastside, to the morgue near Thomason General, where the coroner mentioned odd markings—scrapes and scratches—on the bones. "Could we have done it getting the bones out of the tub?" Elena asked.

"Nope," said Wilkerson. "Not as many as I found."

Finally she returned to headquarters to do a detective's supplement, then put in for her overtime.

Fifteen minutes later she was taking the West Yandell overpass to the acetylene factory. Five minutes after that she was shoveling up bright white sludge, a by-product that sat around in thick puddles waiting for the public to haul it away free of charge. She'd brought along two garbage cans to hold it. Put a little salt in, water it down to painting consistency, and it made great, cheap whitewash.

And evidently it also made a poor but feasible dissolver of corpses. Elena tried to picture Sarah bashing Gus's skull in, then watching the lime boil up around the corpse. Sarah, who read the *New Yorker* and went to see art films but had never been to a slasher movie. Sarah, who believed rapists should go to prison for life but disapproved of capital punishment. Sarah who, unless she was the world's greatest actress, couldn't have killed Gus.

Am I kidding myself about her? Elena wondered.

10
..

Elena and Leo, now both on the eight-to-four shift, divided the telephone chores. He took the hardware stores and building supply outlets, looking for someone who had bought a lot of unslaked lime, particularly someone who looked like Sarah Tolland.

"She wouldn't be buying unslaked lime," Elena pointed out. "She lives in an apartment.

"Right," said Leo. "If she bought any, we've got her."

"Not necessarily," Elena muttered.

"Well, you don't see it because you botched the case when she tried to blow him up with a snail."

Elena began calling doctors, trying to find out whether Gus McGlenlevie had had some kind of bone disease that would explain the scratches. Neither she nor Leo had any luck. The only doctor Elena could find who had ever seen Gus McGlenlevie was the one at the university clinic, a woman, who had given him an employment physical. Elena made an appointment to interview her.

Then she and Leo went off to a little hole-in-the-wall cafe for *enchiladas verde con dos huevos* with refried beans, after which they planned to head for the university and another door-to-door in the apartment building, looking for someone who might have seen a couple of barrels or boxes of unslaked lime hauled in. "His place wasn't broken into," Leo pointed

50

out, putting hot sauce on a cluster of tacos. "So who would he let in? His ex-wife. Right?"

"With a big barrel of something and a weapon in her hand?" Elena asked sarcastically.

"Maybe you ought to get off this case. Did you two get to be friends or something?"

Elena looked out the grimy window and didn't answer. She and Sarah had become friendly, she admitted silently, but that didn't mean she'd ignore a murder; she just didn't believe that Sarah had killed him. If she were to make a guess, she'd pick Lili Bonaventura's relatives or "friends," or maybe someone else among the large crowd of Gus's past and present lovers and their husbands and boyfriends. She'd called Fernie and asked him to look into an organized crime connection, since that was his department. She'd asked a detective in Narcotics, not Frank, to follow up on the mushroom tip, even though it seemed like a long shot to her. People killed over cocaine, over crack, over heroin, and even marijuana—but mushrooms?

Leo zipped into the parking lot behind the faculty apartment complex, and they split up to do the interviews. As she trudged from door to door, Elena wished she'd worn comfortable tennis shoes, but she didn't suppose that degree of informality would impress a bunch of Ph.D. professors, not that some of them didn't look pretty scruffy in their off hours. By 3:30 she and Leo had talked to everyone who was in.

"You find anything?" asked Leo.

"No one saw Sarah with him or on any floors but her own and the lobby," said Elena, "with or without unslaked lime, and they all knew her. What about you?"

He flipped through his notebook. "One woman thinks she saw Sarah on Four, doesn't remember when. Another woman two doors away from McGlenlevie was taking her washing downstairs to the laundry room and saw a delivery man. She thinks it was the Sunday night during finals week. That would be the tenth. And no one saw McGlenlevie after—let's see." He flipped back in the notebook. "After Wednesday, the sixth. Anyway, this woman saw a delivery man with one of those dollies, and it had two big boxes, gift-wrapped. She said he could have been heading for Gus's apartment, but she didn't know because she was getting on the elevator while he was getting off."

"Gift-wrapped? The murderer gift-wrapped the lime?"

Leo shrugged. "A couple of presents would get him—or her—in the apartment."

"I thought you said it was a delivery *man*."

"She said it was a man wearing a uniform, ill-fitting, complete with hat. A woman could disguise herself that way."

"How big?" asked Elena.

"Slender. About five nine or ten."

"Sarah's only five five, maybe six."

"The witness was a very short woman. You know how short people tend to overestimate height."

"Except that Sarah left town Friday."

"Maybe she came back Saturday or Sunday—to give him one or two all-night doses of lime. The actual conference sessions didn't start until Monday. She didn't have to be in Chicago Friday, and no one would have noticed if she wasn't there. Maybe she killed him on—oh—Wednesday after he turned his grades in. Thursday she slipped back into his apartment to change the lime. She was still in town then."

Elena remembered Sarah's absence from the support group on Thursday night.

"Friday she leaves. Maybe she's afraid she's been seen. Maybe she just wants to establish herself as being somewhere else. Sunday she registers for the conference. Then she flies back here, dissolves the last of the ex-husband, and gets back to Chicago in time for the first meeting on Monday morning. We know she kept the hotel room in Chicago, so that gives her an alibi of sorts."

"It's too complicated, Leo. Murders are usually a lot simpler than that."

"You're looking for a simple solution? A murderer who'd dissolve the victim in unslaked lime isn't going to offer any simple solutions, and your friend, Professor Tolland, was acting peculiar. Leaving town two, three days early, leaving the conference early for parts unknown, trying to blow him up with a—"

"So we'll check the flights," snapped Elena. "But if she came back, she'd be crazy not to use cash and an assumed name."

"So we'll check for cash fliers. Check to see if she could have got back here Sunday and still make the Monday morning meetings in Chicago."

There were cash fliers, but Elena and Leo had no way to tell whether Sarah had been one. They'd have to interview flight attendants, most of whom were always somewhere else. There was a middle-of-the-night flight from Los Santos to DFW. From there Sarah could have made a connecting flight to Chicago, but would she? Elena knew that Sarah Tolland expected to get a full night's sleep each and every night. Still, if you wanted to cover up a murder, you might be willing to break even the most cherished routines.

"It's too complicated," Elena protested.

"So she's a complicated woman."

She was, thought Elena with a heavy heart. The very complexity of the scheme might appeal to Sarah. And there were the fingerprints.

11

Wednesday, May 20, 8:30 A.M.

"Hey, Elena, you wanna take an acid bath call?"

"Lime bath," she muttered and picked up. "Detective Elena Jarvis."

Silence. Then the caller stammered, "You're a cop?"

"Right. Detective Elena Jarvis." He'd been caught off guard by the idea of a woman police officer, she thought. "What's your name, sir?"

"I'm Hector Montes, head of Buildings and Grounds out here at the university."

"Which university?"

"Well, Herbert Hobart."

"And you have information on the case?" she prodded.

"Yeah. Well, I don't know, but I read in the paper the other day how they found unslaked lime in that bathtub. First, you know, they said it was acid, but then they said—"

"That's right, Mr. Montes," Elena interrupted, swiveling her chair around and staring at her gray tweed partition. The post-doc who had promised silence told the first reporter nosing around the university that he'd discovered the bath was lime, not acid. "It was unslaked lime and water, Mr. Montes," said Elena.

"Yeah, well, I got to thinking. I ordered some of that. In fact,

I ordered it twice. We got these rock walls that we stuccoed over. Then we whitewash 'em."

Elena nodded, letting her silence nudge him on.

"Well, anyway, you mix this unslaked lime with salt and water, so I ordered a bunch of it. You know—for whitewash. And it never showed up. Company swore they sent it, but it never got to us, so I had to reorder. I got the second batch, all right."

"How much did you order, sir?" Elena swung back and logged onto the computer.

"Just three barrels—each time. I don't like to keep a whole lot around because it's a bitch—ah—I mean it's bad stuff if it gets exposed to water by someone who don't know what they're doin'."

"Would you know if there's any way to trace what happened to the missing order?" She typed in "three barrels" beneath Montes' name.

"Ask the company, I guess—fat lotta good that did me. Maybe ask Central Receiving here at the university. All the orderin' an' routin's done by computer. Maybe the Computer Center. I just couldn't tell you for sure."

Elena sighed. "Thanks for your information, Mr. Montes. Could you describe the barrels for me?" She typed the description—weight, dimensions, appearance. "Damn people," she muttered after she'd hung up. The papers had made that correction two days ago, and it took Montes forty-eight hours to decide his missing unslaked lime might be important. Three barrels. That ought to be enough to dissolve Gus McGlenlevie and a few other people. To be sure, however, she called the university and talked to Abelard Moncrief himself. He said two barrels would be sufficient in his opinion.

After hanging up, Elena thought about the information she'd just received. Somebody had appropriated Mr. Montes' lime. Who? Was it the lime used in Gus's bathtub? Probably no way to tell. But if they could find the third barrel—the barrel the murderer wouldn't have needed—oh hell, unslaked lime was unslaked lime—generic. If they found the third barrel, it might confirm their suspicions—hers and Leo's—but it wouldn't prove anything in court. A good defense attorney could suggest all kinds of innocent reasons for his client to be in possession of unslaked lime. He could point out that Detective Elena Jarvis used unslaked lime, and ask if the jury considered her a suspect.

12
..

Like the Humanities and the Engineering buildings, the administration building was another Mayan Revival temple, except that it had a salmon and turquoise marble presidential reception hall, which President Sunnydale's secretary, a beaming little white-haired, rosy-cheeked Mrs. Santa Claus type, had insisted on showing Leo and Elena while they waited for their appointment with the university president.

"Start at the top," Elena had decided as they ran over the list of university officials they wanted to visit that day. She was dying to meet President Sunnydale, the wacko ex-California evangelist Sarah had told her about. Leo agreed, and they had called first for the appointment with President Sunnydale. Mrs. Santa Claus informed them that Dr. Harley Stanley, Vice-President for Academic Affairs, would attend the meeting also.

Bingo! thought Elena. Another oddball to add to her collection. When he wasn't busy with academic affairs, Harley Stanley sponsored the Herbert Hobart Desert Adventure Club, a gang of student motorcyclists who were, according to environmentalists, ruining the delicate desert ecology. Sarah said he rode his motorcycle in a suit and tie—and, of course, a helmet.

Leo, who wasn't paying much attention to the president's secretary, tried out a little tap dance on the marble floor of the reception hall. Elena elbowed him when Mrs. Santa Claus's back was turned. "She'll think you're weird," Elena hissed.

"I think she's weird," Leo whispered back after executing a lively shuffle-off-to-Buffalo and looking very pleased with himself. "Those kindergarten kids should have let me dance. I'm a better dancer than anyone in town."

"There's my beeper," cried the presidential secretary. "Don't you just love all this modern gadgetry?" She ushered them back to the president's office. "Someday soon I expect I'll even get around to trying the computer President Sunnydale bought me. Here we are. President Sunnydale, I've brought you these two fine young policemen—persons—goodness, what do people call you, dear?"

Before Elena could answer, the secretary added, "They're going to solve our murder, and no doubt they need your spiritual guidance, President Sunnydale." She beamed maternally at the president, who was at least her age but had more white hair and a startling tan for someone with a rather ethereal look—or was *vague* the word Elena wanted?

"I've been with President Sunnydale through his church career as well as his academic career." The last was addressed to Elena, who was now mulling over the idea that she might be expected to accept spiritual guidance when she had been hoping for carte blanche to snoop in the university computers and question the university administrators. Having made all the necessary introductions, Mrs. Santa Claus tottered away with a promise of coffee and cookies, neither of which materialized.

Vice-President Stanley eyed them solemnly. "Detective Jarvis, Detective Weizell, we know why you're here and want to assure you of the university's cooperation in this most unfortunate matter."

"Most unfortunate," echoed President Sunnydale. "It must have been some maniac, don't you think, Dr. Stanley? Well, perhaps not a maniac. One hardly likes to think of a maniac roving the groves of academe, but who would want to kill a poet?" He considered the matter, hands folded as if in prayer, and added, "An eminent poet. We were very proud here at Herbert Hobart to have a literary figure of the stature of Mr.—er—" The president looked at a loss.

"McGlenlevie," prompted Harley Stanley.

Elena could think of quite a few people who might have wanted to kill Angus McGlenlevie. She and Leo discovered more every day. But with Sunnydale having been such a famous TV evangelist—if the rumors were true, his ministry ran afoul of the IRS and lost its tax exemption—perhaps the more scandalous aspects of Angus McGlenlevie's personality and character had been kept from the president.

"So if there's anything at all we can do," said Dr. Stanley, "to help resolve this unfortunate business, please do call upon us."

"Unfortunate. Most unfortunate," murmured President Sunnydale.

"We don't want to cause our parents undue anxiety over the safety of their offspring," said Dr. Stanley.

I'll bet, thought Elena. Every parent connected with the university was probably worth a million dollars. They'd cut off the contributions, stop paying the outrageous tuition rates, withdraw their kids, and enroll them in some other university.

"We're planning a memorial service for our poet, Angus— ah—"

"McGlenlevie," prompted Dr. Stanley once again.

"Yes, McGlenlevie. We do hope you'll attend." President Sunnydale nodded at them with ecclesiastical benevolence.

"Do either of you know of anyone who might have had it in for him?" asked Leo.

The president and vice-president looked astounded that they might be expected to have such information, and both shook their heads vigorously. "He was very eminent," said Dr. Stanley.

"And well loved—no doubt," said President Sunnydale. "Do come to the services. This afternoon at two. In the chapel."

Elena wondered what an art deco chapel would look like. Maybe they had the Virgin Mary doing the Charleston, *au naturel*. Then Elena recalled President Sunnydale's agreement with the faculty—no drinks, no prayer. Would cocktails be served at the memorial service? To placate the faculty?

In her head she heard her mother's voice saying, *Shame on you, Elena. One must always show tolerance and respect for the religious beliefs of others.* Mother wasn't much of a

Catholic, although she certainly showed tolerance for her
husband's beliefs, and Sheriff Portillo, although he thought of
himself as a Catholic, didn't attend mass all that often. They'd
been a very nominal family, religion-wise. Her mother, if
anything, was a pantheist. She could see God in a flowering
chamisa bush but was always more interested in the ancient,
home-carved *santos* in the church than anything the priest had
to say.

"The memorial service will be followed by our biweekly
prayer meeting and cocktail party. We'd be delighted to have
you attend. The gathering after finals week is always quite
festive." Elena tried to imagine cocktails being served at the
Sanctuario de Chimayo and had got as far as Aunt Josefina in
her black church shawl with a Bloody Mary in her hand. The
fantasy was interrupted when she noticed Leo on the verge of
unseemly laughter as he accepted the invitation and then told
the two university administrators that although the department
wasn't ready to make an arrest, he and Elena felt they were
making progress.

Some progress, thought Elena. *We don't know when Angus
died. He thinks Sarah did it. I don't. That's our progress.*

They secured a promise of access to the university's records
and computer files, left the president's office, and split up for
separate interviews: Leo to corral additional members of the
English department, with whom he now had appointments,
Elena to visit Dr. Greta Marx at the Herbert Hobart University
Health and Reproductive Services Center. *What services are
those?* she wondered as she entered the waiting room, which
had no patients that day, so many students having gone home.

"Detective Elena Jarvis," she told the nurse receptionist. "I
have an appointment with Dr. Marx."

"Jarvis." The nurse looked at her bare appointment book.
"Right this way, please. Here's your next appointment, Doctor.
Ms. Jarvis."

Without looking up from her paperwork, Dr. Marx said,
"Take a seat. What kind of birth control are you using?"

Elena blinked.

The doctor looked up impatiently when she received no
answer. "Well, you are using birth control, aren't you? And

don't tell me you're not sexually active. All you young people are. And let me say this: I'd rather prescribe the pill for you now than have to provide an abortion later. I do not consider abortion the birth control method of choice, although, of course, I do them. Better an abortion than an unwanted child." The doctor laid down her pen and glared accusingly at Elena. "You might keep in mind that we're bound to be hit sooner or later by those pro-lifers, and you won't much like having to force your way through a crowd of screaming fanatics to keep yourself from becoming an unwed mother. And then there's AIDS."

"Look," said Elena, "I'm from the police department. Detective Elena Jarvis. I'd like to ask you some questions about the late Angus McGlenlevie."

The doctor squinted at her suspiciously as if she might be a student trying to evade the subject of responsible sex. "Doctor-patient relationships are privileged," she said. "No matter how many girls have showed up at my door before or after being with that man, I can't give you their names. God knows what they saw in that obnoxious twerp. What are we dealing with here? A charge of statutory rape? Just tell the parents he's dead. That ought to—"

"That's right. He's dead, and you're evidently the only doctor in town that ever saw him. All we've got to work with are teeth and bones, strange bones at that."

At the mention of strange bones, Dr. Marx's eyes lit with interest, and she managed to overcome her fixation on safe sex. "Strange bones?" She wheeled her chair and worked rapidly at her computer keyboard, staring at the records that came up on the screen.

"The county coroner said they had—well—scratches on them," Elena explained.

Dr. Marx turned away from her screen and cast Elena a skeptical glance.

"He's never seen anything like it, and we wondered whether McGlenlevie might have had some sort of bone disease?"

Dr. Marx scrolled through the file. "Nothing that he mentioned, and certainly no such thing would have been detectable in a routine physical examination. How long had he been dead?

Perhaps the scratches were the result of wild animals attacking the corpse."

"We don't know how long he'd been dead, probably less than a month, and it's unlikely that any wild animals got into the faculty apartment building."

"He didn't have a dog?"

"Not that we know of, and if he did, the dog would have had to dive into an unslaked lime and water mixture to get at the bones. No dog would have persisted, believe me."

"Peculiar," said the doctor. "I'm afraid I can't help you."

"Well, you can tell me his height and weight. As I said, we can't identify a tub full of bones."

"Five nine. One hundred and fifty," said the doctor.

Elena nodded. "That fits. It must be him."

The doctor then refused to answer any questions about Gus's affairs with students, and Elena refused to answer any questions about her birth control practices. She accepted, reluctantly, a handful of literature on birth control and venereal disease, stuffing the material into her handbag. Couldn't hurt to look it over, although she didn't have a sexual partner at present. It had got so you hated to take on anyone new, there being no way to be sure what beds he'd occupied before yours. Toward the end of her marriage, when Frank turned mean about her promotion and she started hearing rumors that he had slept with a snitch-addict who turned tricks on the side, Elena had infuriated him by insisting that he be tested. He'd knocked her down, and that had pretty much done their marriage in. Too bad. It had been good in the beginning.

She hiked across campus to an appointment with Charles Venner, Director of the Herbert Hobart Computer Center, casting a jaundiced glance, when she got to the center, at a sign that said the architecture was inspired by Mart and Eric's Variety Store in Miami Beach. The predominating colors were mauve, pink, and aqua, which didn't look even marginally hi-tech. Nor did the astonishingly well-endowed secretary who ushered Elena into Charles M. Venner's office.

"Here's the policelady, Charlie." The secretary smiled flirtatiously and received an answering look that was, in Elena's opinion, seriously lewd.

Embarrassed, Elena glanced away, and the office decor caught her attention. The room was dominated by a huge cherrywood desk with carved tassels at the corners and in the center a basket of flowers inlaid in multicolored woods. Behind the desk, an incongruous mismatch, sat Charles Venner, or Charlie as his nubile subordinates evidently called him; Elena hadn't seen any male employees.

"Welcome to the computer center, darlin'," said Charlie Venner.

"Thanks, *Mr.* Venner," Elena replied, none too pleased to be called darling by this short stranger, who roosted behind his ornate desk in his shirt sleeves, his muscles bulging, his brown hair curling energetically, and his brown eyes fastened on Elena's body.

"Call me Charlie," he insisted, staring at her breasts.

If she'd been headless, Charlie Venner wouldn't have noticed. "I'm Detective Elena Jarvis."

"Like that hair," said the computer expert. "Native American, huh? Hispanic and Indian stuff is big around here."

"It's a French braid," said Elena, wondering if everyone employed by the university was peculiar. Take Sarah, for instance. She seemed quite ordinary and proper, but if she really had tried to blow Gus up with a snail and later immersed him in unslaked lime, she wasn't the All-American Girl either. "Mr. Venner," she began.

"Charlie," he corrected.

She frowned at him. "I'm trying to trace an order for unslaked lime through the computer system. It was placed by Buildings and Grounds in early April." He'd gone back to staring at her breasts. "According to the company that processed the order, it was sent, but according to Buildings and Grounds, it never arrived." Elena had to resist the urge to hunch her shoulders. "They had to reorder to get their lime. Mr. Montes of Building and Grounds suggested that the computer center could run the trace for me, tell me where the stuff went." Now he was looking at her legs. She uncrossed them. "Are you listening to me?" she demanded.

"Well, sure," said Charlie. "You want us to trace some order that never showed up. Could take a few days."

"This is a murder investigation."

"No kidding? You got a great little figure there, you know."

"What?"

"The bod. Looks like you keep in shape. You run? Work out on the machines? Got some great machines here." He pointed to a stationary bicycle and a complicated exercise machine that crouched in front of his brocaded draperies. The place might have passed for a ladies' exercise club, but it certainly didn't look like a computer expert's office. His terminal was stuck off in a corner with a recliner stationed in front of it. "Wanna try one? People need to keep moving, do stuff to build the old muscles up."

"I'm into home improvement," she said.

"Home improvement?" Charlie Venner looked confused. "Like draperies and stuff?"

"Like gardening. Painting. Repairing my house." Elena thought of the adobe patching and the whitewashing she hadn't got to because of this case. "About the unslaked lime—"

"Oh sure. I'll put someone on it. Leave your number and what you want us to find out for you. You single or anything? Unattached?"

"I don't date people connected with a murder investigation."

"Well, hey," said Charlie, "it's not like I'm a suspect. I never murdered anyone, right? Who got murdered, anyway?"

"Angus McGlenlevie."

"Oh sure, the poet. I was never much on poetry, but I did like the title of his book."

You would, thought Elena.

"We're doing the grades right now. Takes up a lot of computer time."

"Murder takes up a lot of police time, so I'd appreciate that information as soon as possible. Like tomorrow morning."

Elena wrote out her problem but couldn't get Charlie to look at the request. She had a dreary feeling that Charlie Venner wasn't going to be a whole lot of help, and if the computer center wouldn't help, who would? Sarah came to mind—if she knew about computers. But she was gone, and even if she weren't, you couldn't very well ask the suspect to mess with

the evidence. If Charlie the Lech failed her, she'd have to call
I.D. & R.

Elena met Leo at the car. His initial description of the
remaining members of the English Department consisted
mostly of four-letter words.

"Right," said Elena, "but did they know anything about
McGlenlevie?"

"Everyone thought he was an asshole."

"Asshole? Was that the word they used?"

"Actually one guy used the term moral degenerate, and
another one called him a blot on the university's something or
other."

"Escutcheon?"

"Right. You college types are really impressive to us
barely-made-it-through-high-school guys. Are you ready for
the memorial service? They moved it to the presidential
reception hall—for easier access to the bar, I gather." He was
extracting a camera from the debris in the trunk of the car.

"I'm ready for lunch. It's almost two, and I'm starved." She
was disappointed that she wouldn't get to see the chapel.

"We can eat free at the post-funeral cocktail party. One of
the professors told me they have great food. He hated McGlenlevie, but he's going to the service to get in on the food and
booze afterward."

Elena groaned. "You really want to hear President S. pray
over a guy whose name he can't remember?"

"No, but maybe the murderer will show up and we can get
a picture."

Elena knew that happened sometimes and hoped Sarah
Tolland would stay away as a sign that she hadn't really killed
her ex-husband, no matter how it looked.

Twenty-five minutes later Elena was drinking a ginger ale,
much as she'd have preferred a margarita, and eating her
seventh canapé. President Sunnydale, who had indeed been
visited by a hard-nosed faculty committee that demanded food
and drink during the service, was still praying.

"Let us hope God has taken to his bosom our late brother,
Angus McClean," he said.

"McGlenlevie," Dr. Stanley murmured.

Elena snatched a toast round heaped with pâté from a passing waiter. She hated pâté but was hungry enough to eat anything.

"God has called our brother home and is even now, we trust, enjoying the beauty of—er—Angus' poetry."

From what Elena had heard, if God was *even now* reading Angus' poetry, Angus was about to get booted out of heaven.

"We can rest in the happy assurance that for all eternity our brother—er—Angus will be penning hymns of praise for the heavenly choir to . . ."

Elena spotted the tray that held little pastries filled with something delicious and creamy. She swept off three and shared one with Leo. This was the most cheerful memorial service she'd ever been to. Everyone hated the deceased and loved the refreshments.

13
..

"Two guys lookin' for a detective on the acid bath case,
Elena," shouted Harry Mosconi from the first cubicle on
Homicide Row.

Elena slapped her telephone back into its cradle after a futile
call to Charlie Venner at the computer center. Instead of
running the requested computer check, he had left town,
without leaving instructions for his staff. Elena looked up at the
two men approaching, both short, both wearing light-colored
suits.

"I'm Arturo Spengler, attorney for the Bonaventura family,"
said the skinny one. He had a little clipped mustache.

Part Cuban? she wondered and considered answering him in
Spanish just for the hell of it. Of course, New Mexican Spanish
might be no closer to Miami Cuban Spanish than it was to Los
Santos border Spanish. "Mr. Spengler." She rose and shook his
hand, noting the cut of his suit, which had probably cost twelve
hundred dollars.

"And this is Mr. William Spozzo, a friend of the family."

I'll bet, thought Elena, who pegged him as muscle. "Are you
a lawyer too, Mr. Spozzo?" she asked politely.

"Nah, and people call me Willie."

Elena nodded and withdrew her hand from Mr. Willie
Spozzo's gigantic, broken-knuckled paw. He snagged a chair
from across the aisle, and the two men sat down as she studied

Willie with surreptitious interest. His neck was thicker than his jaw, which was thicker than the top of his head. From the shoulders up he looked like a triangle with the point lopped off. "What can I do for you, gentlemen?"

Mr. Spengler adjusted the creases of his twelve-hundred-dollar, cream-colored suit. Mr. Spozzo forced his wide, muscular butt into the chair, and the trousers of his wrinkled fifty-five-dollar suit rode up at the cuffs, exposing socks so glowingly tangerine in color, Elena could hardly take her eyes away. If he made a hit and was seen doing it, the witnesses would remember those socks.

"Mr. Giuseppe Bonaventura—" Spengler began.

Miami Fat Joe, Elena amended silently.

"—wishes us to look into police harassment of his young daughter, Lili."

"Ms. Bonaventura has accused us of harassment?" asked Elena.

"She called her father—naturally—after the third or fourth contact from you people."

"Ms. Bonaventura discovered the body in an open murder investigation. Beyond her initial talk with us at the scene of the crime, she has refused to say anything. However, now that her lawyer is here, perhaps—"

"Miss Bonaventura has nothing further to reveal," Spengler interrupted smoothly. "The man was, after all, only her volleyball coach. She had stopped by his apartment, I believe, to pick up the game schedule for next year."

"That may be true," said Elena, "but she had a key to his apartment."

"Who says?" asked Willie.

"She dropped it on the table by the door, and her fingerprints were on it." They had lifted Lili's prints from the towelette packet for comparison. "There was no forced entry, and Mr. McGlenlevie was hardly in any condition to let her in himself."

"No doubt the murderer left the door open," said Mr. Spengler, "and she, worried when her coach did not answer, may have entered and picked up the key in passing. I hardly think that's evidence enough to implicate her."

"The fact is, Ms. Bonaventura was having biweekly trysts with her volleyball coach," said Elena.

The two men exchanged an alarmed glance. "Miss Bonaventura," said Arturo Spengler, "is known for her virtue."

"Well," said Elena, "you know how it is with the younger generation." She smiled tolerantly. "And girls away from home . . ." She let a friendly twinkle come to her eye. "We have several witnesses who are aware of Ms. Bonaventura's sexual relationship with the late Mr. McGlenlevie."

"You sayin' she's a suspect?" asked Willie. Spengler kicked him in the ankle.

"At this point, everyone connected with the late Mr. McGlenlevie is a suspect. Why, even you two gentlemen, now that you've appeared on the scene, would have to be added to my list."

"We don't consider that amusing, Detective," said Mr. Spengler.

"I wasn't joking, Counselor," said Elena. "After all, Mr. Bonaventura might have resented what he perceived as a seduction of his virtuous daughter. He might have sent a family friend"—she nodded in pyramidal Willie's direction—"to defend his daughter's virtue and reputation."

"Hey," said Willie, "I was in Miami."

"And you, Mr. Spengler?"

Mr. Spengler gave her a cold look.

"Well, we can check the airline records," said Elena, knowing full well that if Fat Joe Bonaventura had sent a hit man to put an end to Lili's affair, the fellow could have come in on any of a number of small drug-running planes that darted around on the border. He could have entered Mexico and come across on foot, on a bus, in a car, on a rubber raft, or even on the shoulders of one of the men who daily waded across the Rio Grande, their necks encased by the legs of short- or long-term immigrants. The possibilities for entering Los Santos unnoticed were almost limitless.

"Mr. Bonaventura wants his daughter back at home."

"I'm afraid that's impossible as long as the investigation is open and Ms. Bonaventura refuses to make a statement. Of course, she has a right to remain silent, as do you gentlemen, although we'd be delighted to take your statements as to where you were at the approximate time of death. Perhaps we could eliminate all three of you from our list. We always like to eliminate suspects in a murder investigation."

"Miss Bonaventura had nothing to do with the murder," said Arturo Spengler. "Mr. Spozzo and I have never been to this miserable town before."

Elena nodded. "Well, enjoy your visit, and do keep in mind that 'a policeman's lot is not a happy one.'" Elena was quoting Gilbert and Sullivan, which her father liked if he couldn't listen to *zarzuela,* Spain's contribution to light opera. "We always like evidence of where people were and weren't, as opposed to vague, unsubstantiated statements. If we don't get solid evidence, we keep digging."

The two visitors from Miami left, and Elena entered a report on them, called and left Fernie word of Bonaventuras in town, then considered what she could do to investigate the Herbert Hobart computer in the absence of any cooperation from Charlie Venner. The powers that be at H.H.U. had offered cooperation, but Elena herself, who wasn't by any means an active participant in the technological revolution, couldn't do a complicated search on an unfamiliar computer even with permission, which meant she needed an expert—which meant I.D. & R.

Some departmental gossip clicked in her head. The LSPD had just hired a new computer expert from Wyoming, a woman described to Leo by Pancho Rodriguez in Vice as a six-foot cowgirl with the world's best knockers. Elena decided that it was high time the department's minimal number of female police persons formed an old girls' network.

"Hey, Leo," she called to her partner. "What's the name of the new computer woman?"

"Daguerre," said Leo. "M.M. Daguerre." He never forgot a name, especially if it was attached to a memorable pair of breasts. "You wanna grab a bite at Tico's?"

"Nope. I plan to ask M.M. Daguerre to lunch."

"She's too tall for you. Just thought I'd tell you, in case Frank's turned you off men."

Elena made an obscene gesture, which he couldn't see

because he'd turned his back, then tried to find M.M. Daguerre's extension. It wasn't yet in the departmental phone listings. When Elena finally reached the woman, M.M. Daguerre sounded harassed, even over the telephone, and Elena had a hard time talking her into lunch.

"My God," said the computer expert, "if I put in eighteen hours a day for the next six months, I still wouldn't have this new system up and running."

"We're all in the same boat," said Elena. "Crime or computers—everyone in the LSPD needs three backups, which city council says they don't have the money to hire."

"Oh, what the hell," said M.M. Daguerre. "As long as we eat Mexican food, I'm willing to take the time."

Elena was surprised; she hadn't known Mexican food was popular in places like Wyoming—she hadn't even known they had computers, much less people, in Wyoming. Wasn't it a sheep and cow place? "I'll come downstairs and pick you up at noon."

14

Friday, May 22, 12:15 P.M.

In a welcome-to-Los-Santos spirit, Elena had offered to pay
for the lunch. Now she was regretting her generosity as she
listened to Maggie Daguerre ordering. Although the woman
was almost six feet tall, Elena didn't really believe anyone
could eat that much.

"I love Mexican food," said Maggie, closing her menu.
"That's why I came down here."

"Uh-huh." Elena was recalculating her monthly budget. The
woman had just ordered enough food to pay for the dwarf
apricot tree Elena had been planning to buy. "How'd you
happen to go into police work?" she asked after placing her
own, more modest order.

"My father and both my brothers are cops," said Maggie,
brushing aside somewhat ragged black hair that had fallen into
green cat's eyes.

She was a beautiful woman, Elena had to admit, and Leo
was right about the figure, tall and lush.

"On my father's side they've been cops way back to the
original immigrant Daguerre. He was a Basque shepherd who
came to Wyoming to make his fortune herding sheep." She was
scooping up salsa with tostados and eating them enthusiasti-
cally while she waited for her first course to arrive. "He'd
evidently just stepped off the train in Cheyenne when he saw
someone attacking a woman, so naturally he rescued her, and

72

she got him the job as police chief." Maggie pointed to herself when the waiter, who spoke only Spanish, arrived with the first dish. "Then he discovered that she was a madam, so he arrested her. How's that for gratitude?" said Maggie, grinning and stirring *pico de gallo* into her guacamole. "Great stuff," she said, nodding toward the salsa. "You don't get too much of this in Wyoming."

"And the computers?" prompted Elena, since that was the skill she was really interested in.

"Oh, I sort of fell into that. Hung out with some hackers in college, then started taking courses. When the department in Cheyenne needed a computer person, there I was, and it got me off the street where all my dad's old buddies thought they had to nursemaid me. They wouldn't even let me drive the patrol cars," said Maggie, and attacked a bowl of *chili con queso* and a plate of flour tortillas. "How about you? You're a real cop, a homicide detective!"

"My father's the sheriff in Chimayo, New Mexico," said Elena, "but I hadn't been planning on being a cop. I happened to fall in love with a guy on the Los Santos narcotics squad. I met him on a backpacking trip."

"No kidding," said Maggie. "I lost my virginity in a sleeping bag. Say, are you into canoeing?"

"Well, I've been rafting in the Rio Grande Box Canyon. That's up in New Mexico."

"Oh, right," said Maggie knowledgeably. "Good rapids. Can you canoe up there?"

"There are a few crazy people who do," admitted Elena.

Maggie pushed aside her empty bowl of *chili con queso* and dug into number twenty-one, which contained a sample of every type of Tex-Mex food served on the border. "So you're married to a cop?"

"Divorced," said Elena. "But by the time we fell out of love, I'd been to the Police Academy and even caught up with him in rank."

"Oh wow, that must have pissed him off."

"It did. Frank's good undercover, the original scruffy narc, but he doesn't do too well on the civil service tests. He still hasn't passed the sergeant's exam, and it took him four years to make detective."

Maggie nodded. "Lots of my dad's old buddies were like that. Screwed by the civil service exams. It's a real pain in the butt, not being able to drink beer with this, don't you think?"

Elena nodded, liking the woman, even if it was costing a fortune to get acquainted. She figured the bill might come to twelve or fifteen dollars. "Listen, I've got a favor to ask," she said as the last bite of refried beans disappeared from Maggie's plate.

"Sure, what is it?" Maggie hailed the waiter and asked if they had *flan*.

"*Sí.*" The waiter beamed approvingly and went off for the caramel custard.

Elena revised her monthly budget a second time. "I've got this murder case," she said, sipping her Diet Coke. "Maybe you read about it. Somebody dumped the body in unslaked lime and boiled off all the soft tissue. Now the Buildings and Grounds man at Herbert Hobart says he's missing a shipment of unslaked lime, which I ought to be able to trace through the computer system. The problem is I don't know any more about computers than I have to, and the head of the computer center not only didn't help, he left town."

"Is he a suspect?" asked Maggie.

"Not that I know of. Anyway, I wondered if you could trace that lime. The company that shipped it swears it was delivered. Central Receiving got it. Buildings and Grounds didn't."

"Well, I might be able to. Depends on how tight their security is and how cooperative they are."

"The president and vice-president have offered to do whatever's necessary."

"It's just that I've got all this work of my own, a whole new system to put in. It's a real bitch, and I don't have much help."

"Maybe some evening," suggested Elena.

"Well, O.K. It's not as if my social calendar is full."

"Listen, I really appreciate the help. Let me call the university and get back to you."

As they walked back to Police Headquarters, Elena thought

wistfully of Sarah, with whom she'd shared many pleasant meals. Even if Sarah came back to Los Santos, even if she wasn't tried for Gus's murder, she was a suspect, and Elena the investigating officer. Their friendship would never survive the acid bath case.

15
..

Wonder of wonders! Elena thought when Jaime Garcia told her that Lili Bonaventura was on the line. It would seem that the meeting with the Bonaventura representatives had brought results. Heretofore, Lili had refused to answer calls from Elena or Leo. Now she was doing the calling. Elena picked up the receiver and identified herself.

"What's the idea of telling my father's lawyer that I was getting it on with Gussie?" Lili demanded.

"That's what your teammates say," said Elena.

"They're just jealous."

"Right. Because you were getting it on with Gussie and they weren't, or at least not all of them."

"What's that supposed to mean?"

"Did it ever occur to you, Lili, that your father might have sent someone to put an end to the affair?"

"You mean Pop had Gussie whacked? No way. In the first place, he'd have got me out of town if he wanted to do that. And in the second place, he didn't know anything about it until you opened your big mouth."

Elena thought that was probably true, which moved Bonaventura and company further down on her list of suspects, not that she intended to forget about them. Fat Joe wouldn't necessarily have believed that Herbert Hobart University should be the sole protector of his daughter's virtue. On the

76

other hand, if he'd been keeping an eye on her, why had he allowed the affair to continue through two semesters? Lili was right; he hadn't known.

"And Gus wasn't sleeping with anyone but me," said Lili.

Uh-huh, Elena thought.

"And I didn't kill him. If you're looking for a suspect, how about his ex-wife? They couldn't stand each other."

"When was the last time you saw Mr. McGlenlevie alive?" Elena asked.

"I told you. Two weeks before I found his body."

"You didn't see him on campus or talk to anyone who had seen him?"

"Nope. Gussie and I were very discreet. With a father like mine, you have to be, and that's all I've got to say, except keep your mouth shut about my business. I could have *you* whacked, you know."

Lili Bonaventura slapped the phone down so hard that Elena had to whip it away from her ear to escape hearing damage.

"What was that all about?" Leo asked, wheeling his chair around the partition. He currently held the title in the rolling chair race held once a month on Homicide Row.

"An oversexed volleyball captain just threatened to have me assassinated," Elena grumbled. She typed in her I.D. number, the password, and a report on the telephone interview with Lili, including the threat.

16
..

"What's the matter?" asked Elena after the campus police-man let them into the computer center.

"The uniform," said Maggie and started to laugh.

Elena grinned. "That's art deco designer stuff. The women officers wear it too. I hear some of them even like it."

"Lavender cops! It has to be a first."

"Over here." Elena led her toward the computer station they'd been told they could use.

"This may be a waste of time, you know," said Maggie. "If they've got any kind of security, and us without the passwords, we're not going to discover anything."

Maggie sat down at the computer, logged in, and began to press keys, muttering to herself, while Elena lounged in a strange-looking fan-back chair and thought about her ex's latest visit—at least she assumed Frank was responsible. Someone had set off her truck alarm in the middle of the night, catapulting her out of a sound sleep. All the elderly neighbors who weren't hard of hearing came tottering out as usual, assuming it was Frank and saying they were going to call the police chief.

Of course there was no way to prove Frank had done it. Not when Los Santos lost thousands of cars to thieves who whisked the vehicles straight across the border, where they were absorbed into the Mexican economy, driven by the Federal

Judicial Police, local cops, businessmen, and politicians. That was another losing battle, but not one Elena had to fight.

"I don't believe this," said Maggie. "This system's got literally no security. I found all the passwords without even trying." She stared at the screen in amazement. "They must have hired Elmer Fudd to run their center."

"Worse," said Elena. "My bet is Charlie Venner's too busy sleeping with the employees to pay any attention to the computers."

"Uh-huh." Maggie went back to tapping and muttering as the letters and numbers streamed across the lighted screen. "Your missing unslaked lime ended up in"—she tapped once more—"the Electrical Engineering storeroom."

"Oh shit!" muttered Elena.

"Addressed to Sarah Tolland. You want me to see if I can find out when it got rerouted and by whom?"

"Yeah, do it." Elena had a very bad feeling that she knew who, if not when. But why would Sarah expose herself that way? Surely if she could delete her post-conference address, she could delete this stuff.

"Uh-huh." Tap tap tap. More information streaming across the screen. "Someone in Electrical Engineering did it. Sounds suspicious, huh? Unslaked lime isn't something you're likely to need in E.E."

"Not unless you want to dissolve a corpse," Elena muttered.

"The lime destination was changed on May first," said Maggie.

"Can you tell by whom?"

"Nope," said Maggie. "Just the station. There's no user code. It's on the departmental account. Anything else?"

"I guess that's it for now," said Elena morosely.

"Well, great. Let's go get a beer. I'm buying."

"Sounds good to me." As Detective Elena Jarvis watched Lieutenant Maggie Daguerre shut down the computer, she thought about the case. One thing for sure: If Sarah ever came home, she was in deep shit, and so was Elena for having let her go free the first time she tried to kill her husband. Or had someone else killed Gus and set Sarah up to take the rap?

"Say," said Maggie a half hour later, "you don't know

anyone tall, male, straight, and AIDS-free, do you? If you do, I wouldn't be opposed to a blind date."

"If I did, I'd be dating him myself," said Elena. "Unless you want to meet my ex, but I don't recommend him."

Maggie sighed. "When I came out here I didn't stop to think that everyone was going to be so short."

"It's those Hispanic genes," said Elena. "Frank's Anglo, and he's about your height, but he's no prize."

17

After a pleasant Memorial Day weekend spent working on her house, sharing a potluck barbeque with her elderly neighbors, and even ferrying some of those who didn't drive to local cemeteries, where they put plastic flowers on well-kept graves, Elena felt refreshed. She was ready to get back to work on the McGlenlevie murder, and determined to see that Sarah Tolland wasn't railroaded for something she was not likely to have done.

"All right," said Lieutenant Beltran, "what have we got on this acid bath case?" Because of the continuing newspaper coverage, he had asked for a report.

"Lime," said Elena.

"Huh?"

"I got a chemist to analyze the stuff in the tub. He says the liquid was unslaked lime and water. Like the stuff you use in whitewash."

"You would know about whitewash," said Beltran jovially. "I'll bet every adobe shack in your hometown got whitewashed once a year." He grinned and patted her on the shoulder. "How many people live in that town you come from, Elena? Sixty? Seventy?" His idea of a joke was to treat her like a country bumpkin.

"Oh, probably fifty, fifty-five," she replied amiably and untruthfully. Elena had long since learned to overcome her

81

irritation with Beltran's attitude. The man looked remarkably like her father—stocky, middle-aged, thickening waistline, cropped black hair sprinkled with gray, chin developing jowls. He also seemed to have appointed himself father *in absentia*. Which was O.K.; he was mostly on her side. When she dumped Frank, and the majority of her colleagues acted like she was a traitor to the uniform, Beltran had approved. And he was fair professionally, even though she knew he thought most of the women on the force were more decorative than useful.

"Most of what we've got," said Leo, "points to the corpse's ex-wife."

"If the corpse is McGlenlevie," Elena reminded him. Beltran wasn't going to be in her corner on this one, not if Sarah was the perp.

"Well, he was found in his own bathtub. Without dental records that's probably as close to an I.D. as we're going to get." Leo grinned and added, "Unless maybe Dr. Tolland tells us who she killed."

"That's it? You're identifying the bones as McGlenlevie's because they were in his bathtub?" Beltran looked less than pleased.

"Nah. We got a few more bits of evidence. Like the hair on the edge of the tub looks like the hair from the hairbrush in the bedroom, which is presumably McGlenlevie's. D.P.S. has the samples."

"'Bits' is the word for that piece of guesswork," muttered Elena.

"And there's a girls' volleyball championship ring on the finger bone," Leo persisted. "McGlenlevie was the coach of the championship team. The height and estimated weight match his in the one medical record we've got, which came from an employment physical at the university when he was hired. That, unfortunately, is it," he admitted.

"Elena?" Sergeant Escobedo had been sitting silently during the report. He must have assumed she had something to contribute, since she'd expressed reservations about Leo's evidence.

Elena wished now that she'd kept quiet. She didn't know who the corpse was if it wasn't Gus. The only useful information they'd turned up implicated Sarah, so Elena didn't want to mention it. Not that she believed Sarah had murdered anyone. And more important, to her personally at least, pointing a finger at Sarah Tolland was as good as saying, "I screwed up, Lieutenant." Elena decided morosely that she'd never make sergeant at this rate.

Beltran was grumbling about what a defense lawyer could do with that half-assed I.D. of the remains.

Leo repeated his own solution to the crime. "Everything we've got implicates the ex-wife."

"It's too pat," Elena protested. "Sarah Tolland is an intelligent woman. She wouldn't leave all kinds of evidence that implicates her."

"She's got a point," agreed the sergeant. "Seems kind of dumb for a college professor."

"If not her, then who?" Leo demanded.

"There's the Mafia girlfriend," said Elena, reduced to supporting less easily made cases. "She was in town. She could have returned to the apartment as many times as necessary to throw more lime into the tub. Then once she got him down to the bones, she put on the screaming act, and the neighbors called us."

"Lots of people can account for the girl's time between the last sighting of McGlenlevie and her discovery of the body. Classmates saw her in class or at finals. Roommates saw her at the dorm. The two other guys she was shacking up with account for the only nights she didn't sleep in her own bed." Leo looked smug.

Elena frowned, studied her fingernails. "There's the possibility that her father—that's Fat Joe Bonaventura from Miami," she added for Beltran's information—"that Fat Joe had McGlenlevie killed."

Beltran whistled silently.

"Organized Crime come up with anything?" asked Escobedo.

"Not yet," Elena admitted. "Fernie Duran's looking into it."

"If Fat Joe knew that much about her love life, why didn't he have the two college boys done? Sounds like they were getting more from her than McGlenlevie. She only visited the deceased every other week," said Leo. "Anyway, there's nothing on the flight records to show a hit man coming from Miami."

"Well, hell, Leo, they could come from anywhere and by any means," said Elena impatiently.

"The Bonaventuras are a long shot, and you know it."

"All right," said Elena. "There's the fiancée, Bimmie."

"Too dumb to have thought up the acid bath idea."

"Lime," snapped Elena. "You're worse than the newspapers."

"Yeah, yeah," said Leo. "What's your problem, babe? Is it that time of the month?" Then laughing, he put his hands over his head as if to ward off the forthcoming blow.

Beltran glared at him. Escobedo grinned, used to their verbal sparring.

Sighing dramatically, Elena held out a hand. "That's another quarter, Leo. Actually, that one's worth fifty cents." Leo was a hopeless tease. Ever since the department had sponsored sensitivity training for male officers, he had been saying outrageous things to her, claiming innocence, paying out quarters if she really got hard-nosed about it. He was the best partner she'd ever had—and the funniest. "Bimmie Kowolski," she reminded him.

"Right. She had a pretty heavy aerobics schedule during our time frame. Spent a lot of evenings partying by the pool with her neighbors. And most important, no one saw her at the faculty apartment house during our time frame."

"So tell me more about the ex-wife," said Beltran, having listened closely to their argument.

Elena knew she'd lost that round.

"Sarah Tolland," said Leo. "She tried to do him once before."

"Oh, come on, Leo," Elena protested.

"You remember Elena's exploding snail case, Lieutenant?"

Beltran frowned. "You're telling me that we're dealing with the exploding snail woman again?"

"Right. She's the chairman of Electrical Engineering at the university. Lives in the same building as McGlenlevie. Looks like she left town right around the time he might have died. Went to a meeting in Chicago, but she never came back.

Nobody knows where she is now. Her whereabouts are supposed to be in the computer, but they're gone. The secretary says *she* doesn't lose computer data."

Elena slouched down in her chair as Leo enumerated the damning evidence against Sarah.

"Then there's the unslaked lime. Because of it we can't pinpoint the time of death. So we want to know where it came from, right? Well, the head of Buildings and Grounds called us and said he'd ordered some but it never arrived. Turns out someone messed with the computer and rerouted it. The unslaked lime got sent to Electrical Engineering. Now why would they need unslaked lime in Electrical Engineering? What are they gonna do—whitewash their generators? Aberdeen, their storeroom man, remembers three big boxes coming in—about the right size. The shipment was marked for E.E., Sarah Tolland. But she never signed for it. It just disappeared overnight, like maybe she thought if she took it, he'd forget it ever came into his storeroom."

"Or maybe she never knew anything about it," suggested Elena. "I'm telling you, she's too smart to leave all that evidence behind."

"Smart just means she's smart enough to mess around with the computer and get the lime sent to her."

"Yeah, but she's not going to leave a trail."

"Maybe she thought we'd be too dumb to follow it," Leo retorted. "Anyway, the lime disappeared from the storeroom. Guess who had the keys?"

"Tolland," said Beltran.

Elena could see that he liked the case Leo was building. "Other people in the department had storeroom keys," Elena pointed out.

"Where'd you get that idea?" asked Leo. "The storeroom keeper said only Tolland and Bonnard—"

"I asked around," said Elena impatiently, "and most of them had duplicates, so it didn't necessarily have to be Sarah who—"

"Sarah?" Beltran's heavy black eyebrows shot up. "You're on a first name basis?"

Realizing that she'd made a mistake, Elena tried to look

casual about her connection with Sarah as she explained reluctantly, "After the exploding snail, I got her into my divorced woman's support group."

The look on Beltran's face said it all. How many times had she heard him tell someone that cops weren't social workers? She'd violated his first commandment. Also his second, by getting personally involved with a suspect.

"I'm disappointed in you, Elena," he said.

To her he looked more than disappointed. He looked pissed.

"Anyway, the lime came in and disappeared," said Leo quickly, as if to distract the lieutenant from Elena's admission.

"When was that?" asked Beltran.

"Wednesday, May sixth. The storeroom keeper meant to get a signature from Dr. Tolland. Instead he got sick and went home. The lime disappeared between then and Monday."

"Was Tolland still in town?"

"She'd left town by the time he checked his records and discovered he was missing a delivery. So he doesn't know for sure who took it. My guess would be—"

"Tolland," Beltran finished for him. He said the name like a sentence read in court. "Zero in on her. Question her colleagues. Find out if she actually attended this meeting in Chicago, where she went afterward, that sort of thing. And you, Elena, you screwed up. If you'd arrested her the first—"

"There was no case," Elena interrupted.

Her sergeant agreed.

"And I don't believe that she's the murderer this time either." *Just think what this is going to get you, Jarvis,* said the interior voice of the detective who wanted to be the youngest woman ever to make sergeant on the LSPD. *From now to retirement—no promotions, no raises, rotten assignments, all that good stuff.* Still, she defended herself—and Sarah. "It looks to me as if the evidence that points to her has been planted."

"Well, you would think that," said Beltran, "since the woman's a *friend* of yours. Maybe I ought to put someone else on the case—take you off."

Elena scowled at him. "If she's guilty, I can arrest her as fast as anyone." She said it, but she hated the idea.

"See that you do," said Beltran. "Track her down. It doesn't

look good, a case like this going unsolved after—what?—
eleven days. Especially such a high-profile case. Headlines
about bones in bathtubs. Acid baths."

"Lime," muttered Elena.

"The papers won't drop it until we make an arrest. I want to
be able to tell Captain Stollinger that we're close."

Back at her desk, Elena started making phone calls, calls she
should, admittedly, have made at least a week ago. Maybe
Beltran was right; maybe she should be taken off the case. First
she called the departmental secretary. Had she made Sarah's
airline reservations? No, she hadn't. Was it unusual for Sarah to
make her own? It depended on whether the trip was all
business; this one wasn't, so Dr. Tolland had arranged for her
own tickets, presumably paid the bill, and would submit a
reimbursement request for the business portion of the trip when
she got back. Did the secretary have any idea when she'd be
getting back? The secretary got huffy and said she couldn't
remember every little thing, and someone had tampered with
her computer. She'd like to get her hands on the guilty party.
Did the secretary know what travel agency Dr. Tolland used?
No, she didn't.

Elena started calling travel agencies. Leo came in and took
half. Forty-five minutes later she found one that had Dr. Sarah
Tolland on its customer list. Sarah had flown to Chicago on one
airline, from there to Boston on another. She was scheduled to
return to Los Santos via DFW on May 31. Would they know
whether she'd actually used the tickets? No, they wouldn't.

Elena sighed and called the first airline. Yes, Dr. Tolland, or
someone, had used the ticket to Chicago. Then Elena called the
American Association of Electrical Engineers, who had been
running the meeting. Yes, Dr. Tolland had given a talk on
Wednesday, May 13. They didn't know whether she'd attended
any other sessions. She had tickets for the banquet, but they
couldn't say whether she'd been there. Registration for the
meeting had started May 10.

Elena frowned, reminded again that Sarah had arrived in
Chicago two days early. Was that because she'd killed Gus and
wanted to get out of town? If so, it had definitely been a
premeditated murder because she'd made the airplane reserva-

tions a month in advance. But hell, if you wheeled in a barrel of unslaked lime, that took premeditation. It wasn't something people just carried around with them. Of course, Sarah might have killed him first and brought in the lime later. Directly from the storeroom? And where had she kept the extra barrels? In his apartment? No. An apartment tenant on Gus's floor had seen a uniformed delivery person wheeling in two large boxes on Sunday. Which was after Sarah left town—or when she returned.

But *three* large containers had been diverted to the Electrical Engineering Department and then disappeared. To where? Sarah's apartment? Had Sarah hoped one box would do it, then discovered there was some of Gus left, forcing her to fly back and use up one or two more boxes?

The whole scenario made Elena feel sick. And she couldn't imagine quiet, dignified Sarah doing any of the things that had been done. Sarah hauling around big boxes. Bashing Gus on the head. Dragging his body into the bathroom. Tumbling it into the bathtub. Running the water and then dumping in lime—whoosh, the lime hits the water and starts boiling, bubbling, while Sarah, tricked out in an ill-fitting messenger's uniform, judges the mixture, watches the flesh—ugh. That was *not* Sarah!

The second airline confirmed that Sarah had flown off to Boston. Why Boston? Elena wondered. Maybe they could get a search warrant, search her apartment, find out who she knew in Boston, whether she had another barrel of lime stashed in her closet. Waiting until May 31, almost a whole week away, to see if Sarah came home didn't seem like a good idea. Leo agreed and went after the search warrant when he got back from investigating a convenience store assault with Jaime Garcia, but the judge said they didn't have enough evidence. Elena shook her head and started checking the Boston phone book for Tollands. There were dozens. And then there were all the surrounding cities and towns, and they had Tollands too. Elena checked with Sergeant Escobedo to clear that many calls. Frowning, pouring himself a tablespoon of Maalox, he referred her to Lieutenant Beltran.

"My God," said Beltran when she reported to him on the

number of Tollands she'd have to call. "We've got three months to go on this year's budget, and we're almost out of money. I'm going to have to start cutting down on overtime unless the city council gives us an emergency appropriation. And we sure as hell can't afford that many long-distance calls." He glared at her—as if the number of Tollands in Boston was her fault.

What was going on here? Elena wondered. The Crimes Against Persons budget *never* ran dry. At least, not that she'd ever heard. "Then I guess we wait for May thirty-first." She kept her eye on him, expecting him to decide that maybe he could find the money for the calls after all.

Instead Beltran nodded gloomily. "You can make one call—to the Boston police. See if they'll help. In the meantime go talk to people at the university."

18
..

Leo, enamored with the idea of female engineers, had insisted that Elena take the male professors and he the female, which, as it turned out, gave her more or less everyone, and him more or less no one. Now she wasn't as irritated. None of her professors at the University of New Mexico in Albuquerque or the University of Texas at Los Santos had ever been as good-looking as Dr. Karl Bonnard, who had thick brown hair that looked as if it had been razor cut by an expensive hair stylist. Frank, when he'd got his hair cut at all, had gone to students at a barber college. He said the results added to his narc look. Elena had once thought the shaggy hair and stubble sexy. How did Sarah manage to keep the coeds from jumping Dr. Bonnard's bones? Elena wondered. Maybe she didn't care. The English Department obviously didn't.

Karl Bonnard responded to her question about the relationship between Sarah and Gus by saying, "He was a talented man, I gather, but not one a sensible woman like Sarah could remain married to for long." Bonnard gave Elena a smile so serious, so warm, that she felt a sudden avid curiosity about his marital status.

"McGlenlevie was given to pursuing women," Dr. Bonnard continued, "even girls. Naturally that was a problem for Sarah, but being an engineer, she solved it. We engineers, Detective,

90

are logical, problem-solving people. We see a problem, we solve it. Logically."

"Perhaps you could elaborate on that, Dr. Bonnard. Dr. Tolland's solution, I mean."

"Well, it wasn't by attempting to blow him up with a snail, if that's what you're thinking. Engineers are not given to bizarre solutions. I realize your files will show that McGlen-levie accused her of attempting to murder him with a snail, but I think you can attribute that to bad conscience on his part. Having been such a deplorable husband, he probably *expected* her to retaliate. Being a poet, he might expect bizarre solutions, passionate retaliations, that sort of thing. But let me assure you that Sarah Tolland, as any of her colleagues will tell you, is not the sort of woman to murder an ex-husband, no matter what the provocation. She did the sensible thing and divorced him. It's just unfortunate that McGlenlevie stayed on here at the university."

The man seemed downright indignant on Sarah's behalf, which was decent of him, considering that they were colleagues, not family. Elena could remember Frank laughing when she complained about her first partner in C.A.P., who hadn't wanted to work with a woman and took pains to make her life miserable. "You wanted to be a detective," Frank had said. "Get used to it." Fortunately for her, she hadn't had to. She'd moved to Escobedo's squad and worked so well with Leo that the sergeant paired them off more often than not.

Elena smiled at Bonnard, who smiled back. And what a smile! She'd be willing to bet he'd broken some hearts in his time. And he had great cheekbones and teeth. Elena always noticed teeth, probably because one of hers was a little crooked. Nobody'd ever had orthodontia in Chimayo while she was growing up. You'd have had to go into Santa Fe. And no one had the money, anyway. When Josie, Elena's younger sister, had wanted her teeth straightened, their father, the sheriff, had said, "You got 'em all. What's the problem?"

"Sarah," Bonnard added, "is a fine woman and a distinguished electrical engineer."

Loyal, thought Elena. *Especially considering he works for her.* Elena tried to imagine how Lieutenant Beltran would act if she were the lieutenant and he the detective. "Could you give me any idea of Dr. Tolland's schedule during the last few weeks?"

"Why?"

"Well, the information might eliminate her from suspicion."

Dr. Bonnard considered her request. "As I am acting chair, I do happen to have information, and I suppose it's my responsibility as a citizen, as well as Sarah's friend and colleague." He flipped a few pages back on his desk calendar. "Her last final was May eleventh. I would assume that she left the next day because——"

"Wait a minute. May eleventh?"

"Yes, Monday, May eleventh."

"She was here in Los Santos on May eleventh?"

"She would have to have been." Dr. Bonnard gave Elena such a charming smile that she almost lost her train of thought—that the ticketing in Sarah's name showed her to have left on Friday, May 8.

"Sarah is not the type to ask someone else to conduct and grade her final, much less assign her grades for the semester. So as I was saying, I assume that she turned her grades in and left on the twelfth. On the thirteenth, Wednesday, she was to present a paper at the national meeting. She'd hardly miss that."

Elena's head was whirling. Sarah in town on Monday, maybe Tuesday? That gave her plenty of time to keep the lime boiling. "And *after* the conference?" Elena asked.

Bonnard looked further in his calendar, stared in thought at a framed photograph on his desk. Elena couldn't see the picture, although she wanted to.

"Perhaps she stayed over in Chicago."

"She didn't."

"Well then, the secretary can certainly provide information. Sarah always leaves word where she can be contacted when she is out of the city."

"Unfortunately, this time there is no such information in the secretary's computer," said Elena.

Dr. Bonnard's handsome face registered disbelief. "No address? No telephone number?"

Elena shook her head.

"Well, that does surprise me," he mused, "because Virginia would have tackled her, if necessary, to get the information. Virginia is very strict with us," he added wryly. "Of course, it's easy enough to delete something from the computer—deliberately or inadvertently—if you have the access code, but Sarah would have no reason to do that, and as efficient as Virginia is—well, it would be almost impossible for *her* to make that kind of mistake, not that the most efficient of us don't make mistakes." A quick smile flashed across his face.

Elena smiled back. She liked Bonnard. He was a little stuffy, but he had a good word for everyone—even grumpy Virginia. "Does Dr. Tolland have the access code to the computer in which that information would have been entered?"

"Of course. She's the chairwoman."

"Do you know of any confrontations between Dr. Tolland and her ex-husband after the snail incident you just mentioned?"

Dr. Bonnard looked uncomfortable. "Just rumors," he murmured. "Nothing from my own knowledge."

"I'd be interested in hearing the rumors," said Elena with a sinking heart. This man, who was obviously on Sarah's side, must know something incriminating.

"I'm sorry, Detective Jarvis, but I don't deal in rumors, and I hardly think you can expect me to. This is a close-knit department."

"I see." Elena minded less than he probably thought. "Well, if you think of anything that might be relevant, here's my card. Don't hesitate to call." She passed the card across the desk to him and noted that he touched her fingers as he took it. The contact took her by surprise.

"If it's not out of line," he said, looking a little embarrassed, "I think you have beautiful hair." Then he added with wry humor, "Is that overstepping the bounds between police officer and interrogatee?"

Elena had to laugh. "Well, I don't usually receive compliments during the course of a murder investigation," she admitted.

"No?" He looked flatteringly surprised. "Well, then if I may further overstep the line, Detective, are you married or seriously involved with anyone?"

I'll be damned, thought Elena. *He wants to ask me for a date.* She'd never dated a college professor. In fact, she'd never dated anyone quite as handsome as Karl Bonnard. Frank looked pretty good when he didn't have that drug-dealer, dirty-blond stubble on his chin, but he was no movie star. "I'm divorced," said Elena, knowing she ought to put a stop to this turn in the conversation as she had with Charlie Venner.

"I, I must admit, am separated from my wife," said Dr. Bonnard. "It's a difficult period in one's life."

He looked depressed, and Elena's heart went out to him as she remembered the miserable end to her marriage with Frank. "Well, it gets easier," she said sympathetically.

"I don't suppose—" He looked touchingly hesitant. "I don't suppose you'd care to have dinner with me? I mean if it's not professionally improper. I'm not a suspect, am I?" he asked. Again the wry smile.

"No, of course not," said Elena. Her mind skittered in momentary confusion. Would it be improper? She'd love to go out for a change with someone who wasn't the beer and bowling type. Someone who'd never played a practical joke on anyone in his life. And they did have something in common— failed marriages. She glanced at him. He looked so handsome. And dignified. He was probably lonely; she'd certainly been lonely those first months after she kicked Frank out. She glanced at Bonnard again and thought, Why not? As he said, he wasn't a suspect. "I guess we could," she said.

"Tonight?" he asked eagerly. "There's an excellent new restaurant across the river. Santa Maria del Valle."

Elena's eyes widened. She'd read a review of it in her morning paper that said it was very good and *very* expensive. When had anyone ever taken her to an expensive restaurant? "Why not?" she said. She didn't have to tell Leo.

Karl Bonnard glanced at her card, evidently looking for an address. "Shall I pick you up at seven?" he asked.

Elena reached across the desk for the card and wrote her address on the back. "The neighborhood's not too dangerous," she said. "Most of the residents are over seventy, and there are

enough house alarms to discourage the rougher element."
Except Frank, she added to herself.

"I know the area," he said. "Very interesting homes. Well-built, I should think. I'll look forward to seeing yours, Detective Jarvis." He glanced at the card again. "Or perhaps you'll permit me to call you Elena?"

"Sure," she replied, and then wished she'd said something more sophisticated, like, "I'd be delighted" or "Please do, dear Karl." She almost laughed aloud at the idea of ever saying, "Please do, dear Karl." Karl Bonnard, obviously thinking himself the target of her smile, gave her another view of his perfect teeth.

19
⠢

"Leo, I'm onto something." She couldn't bear to tell him yet that Sarah might have been back in Los Santos after her Friday departure. Determined to look into it herself, she handed the remaining names on her list of engineering professors to Leo. "You see these people. I've got to talk to the secretary." And Elena, who had hardly been able to concentrate on the interview that followed her visit to Karl Bonnard's office, went off to talk to Virginia Pargetter, went off to find another piece of evidence to bolster the case they were building against Sarah Tolland.

"Didn't you tell me that Dr. Tolland left on Friday?"

"I did," said the secretary.

"But she returned Monday."

"Not that I know of."

"Dr. Bonnard says she had a final on Monday."

"That's right."

"What did she do about it?"

"I didn't ask her."

Elena wanted to scream at the woman, who had been uncooperative throughout the investigation.

"You mean she may have left the students sitting there in the examination room, wondering why no one came to give the exam, wondering whether they'd get a grade in the course?"

"If that had happened, I would have heard about it."

"Then what did happen?"

"You'll have to ask Dr. Tolland."

Elena gave Virginia Pargetter a look of extreme frustration. Ask Dr. Tolland, who had conveniently disappeared? "I call the registrar's office to see if she turned in grades? Right?"

"You could do that."

Without asking, Elena dragged Mrs. Pargetter's telephone across the desk and picked up the receiver. "What's the number?" Mrs. Pargetter, with slow deliberation, took a university telephone directory from the lower left-hand drawer of her desk and passed it to Elena. Elena ascertained within minutes that grades had been turned in on Monday for all the students in Dr. Tolland's class, but that the clerk could not say whether or not a final had been given. "I'll need the names, addresses, and telephone numbers of those students—here, or at home if they've left town," said Elena, asking herself whether Sarah had to be in town for the registrar to show a Monday turn-in. There might be other ways. Maybe the grades arrived through the mail. No, that didn't make sense. The final itself had been on Monday. Or maybe it hadn't. Well, maybe someone else turned the grades in—a professor, a student, a—oh, hell—didn't it take a while to grade the final, average the grades, fill in some—

"We close at five," said the clerk. "I couldn't prepare the list that quickly."

Elena glanced at the office clock, which read 4:57. Ignoring Mrs. Pargetter's smug look, she snapped at the clerk: "So stay open. This is a homicide investigation. Do I have to call President Sunnydale and have him call you?"

"President Sunnydale will have gone home for the day," Mrs. Pargetter murmured.

Evidently the registrar's clerk didn't know that, because she succumbed to the threat of presidential intervention. Fifteen minutes later Elena picked up the information at the administration building, after a walk across the campus in 98-degree heat. She discovered that all the students in Sarah's class lived out of town and had gone home. "Foiled again," she muttered, knowing that there was no money in the department's budget for even one long-distance call to see whether Sarah had actually given a final on Monday. In fact, having just put in an hour of overtime on her eight-to-four shift, Elena wondered about the status of the overtime budget.

20
..

Tuesday, May 26, 6:37 P.M.

Listening to the evening news as she was driving home, Elena heard the chief of police tell a reporter inquiring about the acid bath case that there wasn't enough money in the departmental budget to make the phone calls necessary to track a suspect. By mid-June the overtime budget would be gone unless the city council made an emergency appropriation. "Fighting crime costs money," said the chief, "and money's what we lack—money and manpower."

So that's why Beltran wouldn't O.K. the telephone calls, she thought, glowering at a Honda that had just whipped into her lane, nearly clipping her fender. They—Beltran, the chief, and the rest of the brass—were playing politics. Showing the city council that heinous crimes would go unsolved without an extra appropriation.

With only fifteen minutes to dress, Elena decided that she had nothing suitable to wear to a very expensive restaurant in Mexico. Bonnard would probably show up in a tuxedo, making her look like the little match girl by comparison. And why had he chosen such an expensive place? To impress her? Make her feel uncomfortable?

Elena took a deep, calming breath and yanked from its hanger the dress she'd worn three years in a row to the policeman's ball—not because she thought it a wonderful

choice; it was her only choice. And if Bonnard didn't like it,
too bad! She was a small-town girl from northern New Mexico,
not a big-city fashion model. And why was she getting mad at
Karl Bonnard, poor man? All he'd done was ask her out to
dinner. Like her, he was feeling lonely after the breakup of his
marriage.

She noticed with dismay that the restaurant had valet
parking. Karl turned his car, a very sedate, exquisitely cared-
for family sedan, over to a young man who looked like a
hundred young men she'd interviewed in gang shootings. She
wondered if the car would reappear when they had finished
dinner. But then, this kid, if he was moonlighting as a car thief,
probably pursued his second occupation in Los Santos.

They mounted the steps to a Mediterranean-style mansion,
white stucco with wrought-iron filigree and a lush yard. It had,
no doubt, belonged to some Mexican millionaire who sold it
when the neighborhood became too commercial. Inside, the
decor was traditional Hispanic, dark carved furniture of much
better quality than anything Elena owned. And the other diners,
including her escort, were better dressed than she. Elena
sighed. *Maybe I ought to forgo a few home improvement
projects and spring for some clothes,* she thought, *especially if
I'm going to be dating Bonnard.* She smiled across the table at
him as she was handed a menu big enough to wallpaper her
bathroom. Of course, after tonight they might never have
another date. He might have noticed the dress she was wearing.

Then she thought of Sarah. If she had to arrest Sarah, it
wouldn't look good to be dating a member of Sarah's department. *I should have stayed home,* Elena thought gloomily, but
allowed herself to be distracted as Bonnard began to tell her
the tale of his failed marriage.

"My wife's a delightful woman," he said over avocado soup.
"Well, she *was* a delightful woman. About six months ago she
fell into some sort of—how shall I describe it?—religious
frenzy. She joined one of these charismatic sects where they
speak in tongues."

Elena stuck her fork into a piece of marinated *jícama* and
tried to imagine the wife of the handsome and dignified Dr.

Bonnard speaking in tongues, perhaps rolling around on the floor of some little storefront church.

"I am an engineer, after all. I found the whole thing inexplicable and embarrassing. Mary Ellen even told my friends and colleagues about her religious eccentricities." He stopped talking about his wife to break off and eat a small piece of crusty roll, murmuring, "To clear the palate." Elena wondered if she was supposed to clear hers too. Evidently not. Karl took a judgmental sip from the miniscule amount of wine the waiter had poured for him.

Elena understood the purpose of the wine-tasting ritual, not that Frank had ever drunk wine, except for the Tattinger anniversary bottle he had suggested as a substitute for marriage counseling. What she didn't understand was how the taster, should he be dissatisfied, was expected to respond. For instance, did he spit the test mouthful out somewhere? On the tablecloth? She pictured Karl Bonnard doing that and suppressed a grin. In fact, he seemed to be satisfied. One waiter was now pouring wine into her glass while another prepared her flaming tournedos. With appreciation she watched the blue flame leap from the copper pan that held her dinner. This was living!

"I have to admit that I find creation scientism, which is a tenet of their belief, not only intellectually unacceptable, but personally distasteful," said Karl before she could get the first bite of beef in brandy sauce to her mouth. She was trying out French food again. Sarah had been crazy about it.

Elena realized that she should have anticipated this conversation, but why was it that divorced and separated men always wanted to talk about their ex-wives? She could have told Bonnard stories about Frank that would have curled his hair, but she was too considerate to do it. Still, Karl was very handsome, and the beef was *wonderful*.

"Our arguments," said Karl, as if Elena were hanging on to his every word, "became increasingly acrimonious. She seemed quite a different person from the amiable woman I once loved."

Frank had changed a lot too, Elena thought. From a cheerful, practical joker to a guy who couldn't stand it when she did better on the civil service exams than he had. Who wanted her to transfer to Narcotics so he could show her he was the better cop, who slugged her when she accused him of infidelity.

"She's gone off to some religious retreat from which I fully expect she will not be returning."

If she is planning to return, thought Elena with dismay, *I'm dating a married man.* The monologue continued in the same vein through the main course and the salad that followed—one long parade of bewildered complaints about the absent Mrs. Bonnard. If Karl had done as much complaining while his wife was in residence as he was doing in her absence, Elena wasn't surprised that the woman had left. Not that Elena couldn't sympathize with him. It wasn't much fun to see the person you married turn into an unpleasant stranger. Still, she'd rather have talked about something else. To get through the next round of bitching, she ordered Cherries Jubilee for dessert, having been so happy with her arsonist's entree. She did wonder, as the cherries went up in flames, whether the restaurant had sufficient fire extinguishers to protect the diners should the whole place follow suit.

Then Karl took her by surprise. "I've been a long-winded bore," he admitted. "You're probably thinking, 'No wonder the poor woman left him.'"

Elena, who had learned to control her expression in a hundred cutthroat poker games with Frank and his buddies, didn't reveal by so much as a flicker of the eye that he'd guessed exactly what she was thinking. Instead she gave him a noncommittal smile.

"You've been a good sport," he said, taking her by surprise again. "I imagine this has happened to you before—I mean a divorced or separated man telling you his marital problems."

Elena shrugged and said in an attempt to be tactful, "Since men don't talk to each other, they have to talk to someone sometime."

"That's an interesting point of view. Are you saying you think men are more repressed than women?"

"Emotionally?" Elena thought about it. "Sure. Men ignore whatever's bothering them as long as they can. Then they hit someone." She was thinking of Frank, but she knew other men like that.

"And you think women don't repress their emotions, then lash out?"

"Women are certainly less given to violence. A look at any police blotter shows that. But to take an example closer to home, look at Sarah Tolland. From what you said about Gus McGlenlevie, she'd certainly have reason to build up a lot of resentment, yet she seems more amused by her ex than resentful."

"I didn't realize you knew Sarah."

"I investigated the snail thing. She was perfectly calm. He was the one tossing accusations around. In fact, can you imagine Sarah Tolland lashing out at anyone?"

There was a fractional hesitation. Then Bonnard shrugged and said, "As I told you, engineers seek logical solutions."

"Murder's hardly that," said Elena.

"One wouldn't think so." Then he smiled. "I hope you didn't accept my invitation to dinner in order to talk about my chairwoman."

"No, of course not." Elena felt a little guilty. She poked at a brandy-soaked cherry with her spoon. Why had he hesitated when she said, "Can you imagine Sarah lashing out?" Had he seen Sarah as anything but calm and precise? He'd replied by saying, "Engineers seek logical solutions." And murder sure wasn't a logical solution to an irritating ex. So why had that sounded like an evasion? The answer was that it wasn't evasive. He'd said that before. About engineers.

". . . pretty lady end up on the homicide squad?"

"I beg your pardon?" She tuned back in at the end of a sentence that tended to raise her feminist hackles.

"I asked how such a pretty lady managed to end up on the homicide squad?"

As opposed to what? Ending up barefoot and pregnant in the kitchen where I belong? asked the Mrs. Frank Jarvis voice in her head. Frank had suddenly wanted to be a father when she made detective and he didn't make sergeant, although when she'd finished school and suggested that they have a baby, he'd said, "Narcs make lousy fathers."

"Crimes Against Persons," she corrected Bonnard, "not homicide. The victim doesn't have to die to get our attention."

He must have caught a hint of asperity in her response because he said, "You'll have to admit there's probably a very low percentage of women detectives, yet you made it. And not only that, but you've taken your unusual position and success in stride."

Elena turned that remark over in her head. He seemed to be paying her straightforward compliments, yet she could have sworn that the what's-a-pretty-girl-like-you garbage had been sexist.

"Not all women adjust to responsibility so sensibly, you know. Ah—" He looked as if he were searching for an example. "Well, no matter."

"Who were you thinking of?" she pressed.

"No one in particular. Just some women in positions of authority tend to overreact to stress—completely lose it, as the students say." He smiled and took a sip of his espresso.

Completely lose it? Was he talking about Sarah? She was the woman in a position of authority that he'd see the most of. Elena had never seen Sarah completely lose it. Did that mean Sarah was capable of losing control and—say—murdering someone? *Dear God,* thought Elena, *have I been ignoring evidence because my assumptions about her were all wrong? Did I discount the snail episode because even then she didn't seem like a murderer to me?*

"My point is that you defy the stereotype of the overemotional female in charge."

He'd been talking stereotypes. Not Sarah Tolland. *I'm getting paranoid about this case,* Elena thought.

"I know we're supposed to support classes, as opposed to individuals. I should be advocating that homicide squads all over the country reflect the general population in gender, race, whatnot, but the truth is that I'm more interested in individuals. You've worked your way into a position that, I'm sure, was hard to achieve, and I admire you for it. Even more, I admire the way you handle it now that you've got it. I don't doubt that you'll do more to pave the way for other women in police departments than any radical feminist could ever do."

Elena didn't know whether she cared for the remark about radical feminists, but she could hardly fault him on a personal level. He'd paid her a very nice compliment, and she gave him a warm smile over her last spoonful of cherries.

"How about a brandy?" he asked, returning her smile.

"Why not?" she said. She seemed to be in need of it. Her nerves were still on edge. And all because he'd been talking about stereotypes. Not Sarah. In his office, he'd said flat out that Sarah wouldn't have killed McGlenlevie, and Karl Bonnard ought to know Sarah a lot better than Elena did. Sarah and Bonnard had been colleagues for three years. After only six weeks acquaintance, Elena didn't think Sarah had done it either, but she was happy to have her own opinion corroborated by someone who should know.

21

Wednesday, May 27, 4:40 P.M.

Sarah tugged her bags aboard the airport shuttle, wondering how things had gone in the department during her absence. There had been no calls for help from Virginia or from Karl Bonnard, to whom Sarah delegated authority in her absence. He was the only other tenured full professor in the department and, therefore, had a seniority equivalent to hers, if anyone could be said to have seniority in a university that was only three years old. Of course, Sarah wouldn't have expected any calls from Bonnard, who held his own abilities in high regard. She sighed, climbed off the shuttle bus, and pulled her wheeled suitcase four parking spaces down the line to her car, wishing she regarded Bonnard as highly as he regarded himself.

Well, perhaps nothing had gone wrong. Hard to believe, when she'd left with finals week still in progress, but the ever vigilant Virginia hadn't called—not even to complain about Bonnard, whom she detested, although Sarah had never been sure quite why. Virginia *did* tend to be opinionated. To be on the safe side, Sarah decided to stop by the department before going home. There was time, but only because her bag had been spewed off the plane with unusual speed. She threaded through the heavy afternoon traffic on the interstate, her air conditioner running full blast. After the cool late spring weather in Boston, Los Santos' dry heat felt like full summer.

During her drive south around the mountain, her mind wandered to Colin Stuart, an electrical engineering professor from the University of Washington whom she'd met in Chicago. He was well known in the field and a charming man, forty-five or so, with a slender body, a fine craggy Scots face, and hair of a distinguished gray, although not perhaps as gray as her own. With her the original blond color disguised the aging process.

She and Colin Stuart had met for cocktails and dinner Wednesday night and dinner Thursday, having become acquainted after her own talk. He had come forward, afire with interest, which was always flattering, and whisked her off to the hotel cocktail lounge for a discussion of her paper. She had also discovered during that first evening that Stuart was looking to make a move because of escalating allergy problems in Washington.

Sarah had suggested during their second dinner that he might like to spend a semester at Herbert Hobart to get away from northwestern pollen. The delicately stated offer included the inference that, should he find Herbert Hobart to his liking, a permanent position would be available. She warned him about the students, who were not always impressively bright. Some were very good, she said, and "with a big endowment and lots of money in our budget—"

"Enough to take on visiting professors at a whim?" he broke in, smiling. "I envy you the financial independence. State institutions all over the country, as you probably know, are facing yearly budget cuts."

Sarah nodded and went on to say that there was money to hire good postdoctoral fellows or bring several along with him if he wanted. "It facilitates the research," she explained and added, "We do have our better undergraduates in research programs, although that takes up more of the professor's time and poses certain limitations to the difficulty of the work."

"I think I could live with it," said Dr. Stuart. "May I get back to you?"

"Yes, certainly. You'll want to discuss it with your wife."

"Unhappily, my wife and I divorced recently," said Dr. Stuart.

"I'm so sorry to hear it," Sarah replied.

"Thank you. My allergist surmises that the stress of our breakup may have brought on my problems, which had been mild to nonexistent before."

"Perhaps you'd find the desert kinder to your health," said Sarah, "and the change of scene might help with the post-divorce stress."

"You're very thoughtful," he said, and Sarah at that point had felt a frisson of interest that went beyond the professional. Now she had to wonder how smart it was to hire, even temporarily, a man she found attractive. She'd been off men entirely since Gus, and at age forty-two really thought that she might not try marriage again, that she was quite happy single, ecstatic really, since she'd put Gus out of her life. Even intelligent women could be exceedingly foolish where men were concerned. An electrical engineer had no business being swept away by a poet, no matter how amusingly eccentric or how adept in the bedroom.

Sarah sighed and pulled over into a slower lane because some redneck in a pickup truck was honking. "Oaf," she muttered. The only person who drove a pickup truck that Sarah had ever found socially interesting was Elena Jarvis, and she did suppose that Elena, with her amazing number of fix-up projects on that charming if disintegrating adobe, needed a pickup truck. Sarah herself was very happy that the university furnished her with an apartment. She'd have to see about getting one for Colin Stuart if he accepted her offer. If he didn't—well, that might be for the best, although she knew that she'd be disappointed.

She slowed and turned off onto the Herbert Hobart exit, heading toward the campus, which was tucked between arroyos on the west side of the mountain. She could have sworn the temperature dropped thirty degrees, but no doubt it was an illusion created by the oasis of green which Herbert Hobart maintained, as if the campus were situated in Miami Beach, its architectural and landscaping mentor. Every building was a copy of some art deco delight from the historic district, every inch of the ground lushly landscaped with tropical grasses, bushes, palm trees, flowers.

In a town whose water resources were dwindling alarmingly, Sarah wondered how long the university could maintain this green enclave in the desert. Surely the environmentalists, if not the water district, would complain when the rest of the city was turning brown under water rationing, and Herbert Hobart, because of its huge endowment and private wells, was sprinkling madly and blooming.

In her reserved chairman's space, Sarah parked her BMW, which she had bought as a sort of congratulatory gift to herself on the occasion of her divorce. She turned off the ignition, edged out, skirt tucked decorously around her knees, locked the door, and strode into the Engineering building.

"Virginia." She smiled at her secretary. "I haven't heard a word from you. Have things been going so smoothly? Bonnard been cooperating, has he?"

Virginia's lips, never given to wide or even minor smiles, tightened into a grim line. "I had no telephone number for you after you left Chicago. I didn't even know when you'd be returning."

"Of course you did," said Sarah. "I left you my brother's Boston number—and my date of return, although I'm back early."

"The information is gone," said Virginia, "and no matter what anyone says, I didn't accidentally delete it from the computer."

"Well, goodness, unless every hard disk in the department crashed, the loss of a telephone number and date is no major disaster. What was the problem?"

"We're being sued," said Virginia.

"Sued?" Sarah's eyebrows rose. The average annual income of a Herbert Hobart parent was above six hundred thousand dollars. The parents could afford to, and did, sue on occasion, but Harley Stanley, the world's most tactful and enthusiastic vice-president for academic affairs, had been known to turn a law suit into an endowment. "Did you call the vice-president's office?"

"I did, but these parents are being particularly unpleasant. They say that Dr. Radna Ramakrishna unfairly gave their daughter a D in the main-frame course."

Sarah nodded. "Is Dr. Ramakrishna in the building?"

"No, she's in India. Do you want her telephone number?"

"Not really," said Sarah. "Why should I bother the poor woman because some not-too-bright spoiled rich girl got a D in main-frame? Did Radna leave her grade books and make a deposition to the university attorney before she left?"

"She did."

"Good. Any more departmental problems? No? Is this my mail?" Sarah had scooted into her office to pick up the waiting pile, which she stuffed into her briefcase. "I'm going home now, Virginia," she said, already anticipating a long soak in her bathtub. "Anything else can wait until tomorrow."

"But Dr. Tolland," Virginia called after her, "this Detective Jarvis has been calling. They made me promise—"

"I'll call her when I get home," Sarah interrupted as the office door closed behind her. Air travel made her feel grimy and out of sorts. She'd have a bath, a light dinner, and an early night. It sounded heavenly.

22

Sarah took a leisurely bath, then microwaved a pasta salad which she ate with French bread and a glass of white wine while she looked through her office mail and listened to messages on her answering machine: six click-offs, two aluminum-siding salesmen, several out-of-work gardeners (didn't any of these people know she lived in an apartment?), and a light-bulb salesman for the blind; one call from Gus, the first on the machine, two calls from Elena, and one from Virginia telling her to get in touch with the office because they needed her post-Chicago telephone number. *Damn,* thought Sarah, *why didn't I call to check the machine?* The only call she returned was Elena's.

"Hi. This is Sarah. You wanted to get hold of me?" There was a silence into which Sarah asked, puzzled, "Did you want me to pick you up for the support group tomorrow?"

"Sure." Another pause at Elena's end. "Listen, Sarah, you mind if I come over tonight?"

Sarah was surprised. "Well, not if you make it fast. I was planning to go to bed. I find air travel exhausting, and the trip from Boston is a long one."

"Boston?"

"Yes, I was visiting my brother. I'm sure I mentioned it."

"No, I don't think so," said Elena. "Look, I'll be over in twenty minutes, O.K.?"

111

"All right," said Sarah, glancing at her watch. It was seven. If Elena didn't stay too long, she could be in bed by eight.

"You heard about Gus?"

"Gus? No. What's he done now?"

"Oh, well, I'll tell you about it later."

Sarah hung up, briefly considered staying in her bathrobe, rejected the idea, and went into the bedroom. Within five minutes she was wearing pleated slacks, a narrow leather belt, and a silk blouse. She combed her hair and returned to the living room to go through the mail she'd collected from her box downstairs—bills, catalogues from computer companies, the usual array of solicitations from NOW and Planned Parenthood. She could make out the checks tomorrow. Magazines. Opening a copy of the *New Yorker*, she settled down to wait for Elena.

23
..

Elena felt a moment of acute discomfort as she punched in Leo's telephone number. She hadn't faced until now just how terrible she was going to feel when Sarah realized that Elena viewed her as a suspect in Gus's murder. *I as good as lied to her,* Elena thought. *I'm not going over there for a friendly chat. I'm not even going by myself.* "Leo, she's back."

"Listen, I got two steaks on the grill, one I paid for, and two hungry neighbors salivating on the patio, not to mention my wife. Who's so important—?"

"Sarah Tolland. I think we should get over to her place right now."

"Well, shit," said Leo.

Elena could hear Concepcion in the background, making remarks about how much steak would be left if he took off before he finished cooking it.

"The one steak we'll have this month," he muttered, "and I won't get a bite."

"I'll buy you a taco after we've had our conversation with Sarah."

"Yeah, thanks," said Leo. "I'll pick you up."

"O.K., but hurry. I told her I'd be there in twenty minutes. She said she wanted to get to bed."

"So we'll roust her out."

After thirty minutes, which Elena spent dreading the con-

113

frontation to come, and Leo complaining about missing his own B.Y.O.S., bring-your-own-steak, party, the two detectives pulled into the parking lot of the faculty apartments. Here she'd parked to investigate the exploding snail and later when she'd been an invited guest at Sarah's place. Here she'd parked the night they found Gus's bones in the tub. Elena sighed as the red doors of the elevator slid closed.

Two minutes later Sarah opened the door, laughing. "You've got to look at this," she said, handing over a *New Yorker* cartoon. Then she noticed Leo, looming behind Elena. "New boyfriend?" she asked.

Sarah seemed almost lighthearted, and Elena found the mood disconcerting. "This is my partner, Leo Weizell," she mumbled.

A little frown flitted across Sarah's smooth forehead, but she shook hands with Leo and invited the two of them in. "Well, look at the cartoon," she said. "You'll love it."

Dutifully Elena looked at the cartoon, which was funny, although she didn't feel much like laughing. "Sarah, Gus is dead."

Sarah looked at her blankly. "Gus McGlenlevie?"

"Right."

"I don't believe it," said Sarah, her voice now level and matter-of-fact, her smile gone. "The one thing you can say for Gus, maybe the only thing, is that he's healthy."

"He was murdered." They were both watching her closely.

"You're not serious!"

To Elena, Sarah looked convincingly flabbergasted as she dropped into one of her brown silk chairs. "Murdered? By whom? Some husband? Or an irate boyfriend?"

"Or an ex-wife?" said Leo.

"What ex-wife? I'm the only—" Sarah turned pale. "You can't think—" She turned to Elena. "I haven't even—I've been out of town."

"He's been dead for some time." Elena hated this. Sarah looked so bewildered.

"But he's on my answering machine." Sarah gestured toward the machine on the end table. Leo immediately went to take the tape out.

"Look, Sarah, we're going to have to ask you to come down to headquarters."

"Am I really a suspect?" she asked wonderingly.

"At this point, ma'am, everyone connected with the late Mr. McGlenlevie is," said Leo.

Sarah stared at him searchingly. "Do I need a lawyer?"

"If you want a lawyer, ma'am, we can certainly wait while you call one."

"But do I *need* a lawyer? Are you, for instance, going to read me my rights?"

"At this point," said Elena, "we just want to ask you some questions, Sarah. You can understand that we have to, given that snail complaint on our books."

"Snail? Surely he wasn't killed by a snail!" she exclaimed. "You haven't said how he was killed. And I haven't said how bizarre I find this visit. I don't understand why your questions can't be asked here."

The questions couldn't be asked in Sarah's apartment because Leo had called Lieutenant Beltran, who wanted to observe the interrogation from behind the one-way glass at the station. *Because he doesn't trust me, not on this case,* Elena reflected gloomily. *Maybe not ever. And if my superiors don't trust me, my career is down the toilet.* Everything she'd been afraid of was coming down on her because she was a cop with divided loyalties. And because the thought of doing her duty made her miserable.

"It's better to do it at headquarters, ma'am," said Leo. "If you don't mind."

"I do mind," said Sarah wearily. "I don't even understand." She rose and picked up her handbag. "How long do you think this is going to take?"

Leo shrugged, and Elena hunched her shoulders uncomfortably as Sarah gave her an accusing look, which Leo caught. "I'd better take my own car," Sarah muttered, poking through the mail on the coffee table in search of her keys.

"You can ride with us," said Elena.

Sarah glanced at her quickly, alarmed.

"And of course, you'll be given a ride home."

"Ah." Having located the keys, Sarah put them in her purse, and they left. "You haven't said how he died."

"A blow to the head."

"And when?"

"Let's just wait till we get to headquarters." After that the ride continued in silence, Sarah sitting in the back seat, Elena in front, Leo driving. The two attempts Sarah made at normal conversation had to be met with reticence because Elena was afraid that anything she said would anger Sarah or raise Leo's suspicions.

They took her through the side door and into C.A.P.'s nonthreatening lineup and interrogation room. Sarah glanced around and headed for the blue polka-dot Early American sofa. She sat, leaning against the arm, her back almost turned to the one-way window on the right side of the room. Elena and Leo exchanged glances.

"Why don't we sit here around the desk, Mrs. McGlenlevie?" Leo suggested.

Sarah gave him a cool look. "Dr. Tolland or Professor Tolland will do," she said. "I never took Gus's name during the marriage, certainly not afterward. Are suspects not allowed to sit on the comfortable furniture?" The rest of the room was utilitarian, a desk, a number of armless brown vinyl chairs, two wall-mounted blackboards, and the large dark window that concealed a narrow room where officers could see and hear a suspect being questioned or victims could view a lineup.

"It's just that that sofa gives me the creeps," said Elena. "I used to sit there interviewing poor little kids who'd been raped by their stepfathers and—well, you know. Bad memories."

Before Elena had finished her speech, Sarah shot up off the sofa and took a brown chair held out for her by Leo. The chair placed her facing Beltran behind the window.

Once they were sitting around the desk, the questions began. "Just for the record," said Leo, "we'd appreciate it if you could account for your whereabouts during the last three weeks."

"*Three* weeks!" Sarah exclaimed. "If you wanted that, you should have asked me at home. I have an engagement calendar."

"Do the best you can, Sar—Dr. Tolland," said Elena, very

conscious of Lieutenant Beltran behind the glass. Sarah hadn't missed the "Dr. Tolland." Her face went blank when Elena said it. "We can pick up the calendar when we take you back," Elena finished. She felt as if there were a stone in her diaphragm pushing up, keeping her from breathing deeply enough.

Sarah shrugged. "Three weeks. Well, I spent a week doing the usual end-of-the-term departmental business and holding finals. After my last final I flew to Chicago for a meeting. I was giving a paper."

"On what day did you leave for Chicago?" asked Leo.

"May eighth—Friday. Registration for the meeting was Sunday, first sessions Monday. I had—"

"Let me interrupt you for a minute," said Elena. "When did you come back to Los Santos from Chicago?"

"Today," said Sarah, surprised. "Well, not from Chicago. I went from Chicago to Boston and then home from there."

"And you didn't return to Los Santos from Chicago—even briefly?"

"No. Why would I do that?"

"What about your Monday final?" asked Elena.

"Oh." Sarah smiled in relief. "I couldn't imagine why you'd think I returned, but I see now. The administration of the final was the last problem assigned to my students. They had to figure a way that the final could be given in my absence by computer, graded, the final grade used to produce the semester grade, and those grades turned in to the registrar.

"It's not really that difficult a problem, but they enjoyed solving it. And it worked beautifully. We even factored in what a failure in the program would do to the final grades of those who proposed it, although that part wasn't necessary, as it happened. When I called the registrar's office Tuesday, the grades were on record and sounded reasonable to me. Of course, I'll check all the data tomorrow."

Elena and Leo exchanged glances. The explanation sounded bizarre to Elena, although she knew that she couldn't discount it.

"Is that kind of stuff part of electrical engineering?" asked Leo.

"Our course list has a heavy computer science component," said Sarah.

"So you know a lot about computers?"

Say no, thought Elena, although she knew, after the description of the final, that the answer was yes—yes, Sarah could have tampered with the lime-routing and with her travel information. But wait. Why delete Boston and the date of return if she was going to come back—and early at that? Sarah was saying that certainly she knew a lot about computers. Leo looked smug.

"Did you have any evening appointments during the last week while you were still here in Los Santos, Dr. Tolland?" asked Leo.

"No. Well, I went to the support group on—no, actually I—"

"What support group would that be, ma'am?"

"Why don't you ask Elena?" suggested Sarah tartly. Then when he stared at Sarah, waiting, she added, "Oh, for heaven sake, it's a divorced woman's support group. She was the one who got me into it—after the infamous snail episode."

"Maybe we'd better go back to that. Do you have any explanation of how Mr. McGlenlevie's snail happened to explode?" The corners of Leo's mouth twitched.

"I'm glad you find it amusing, Detective," said Sarah. "Since that seems to be a factor in your suspicion that I may have murdered my ex-husband, I don't think I'll talk about it."

"That's certainly your privilege, ma'am."

"You mentioned the support group," Elena interrupted. "But you didn't attend that last Thursday."

"Well, for heaven sake, Elena, I left you a message. My plane took off at five-thirty the next morning. I had to pack."

And murder your husband, Elena thought, testing out the idea when Sarah was actually in front of her. It didn't seem at all convincing.

"And Gus was alive when I left. There's a call from him on my machine, from Sunday evening I think it was. You can listen to it if you don't believe me."

Leo nodded and patted his pocket where the tape resided.

"Is there a date on the tape?" asked Elena. "I mean given by the machine or Gus?"

Sarah frowned. "The machine gives only the day of the week and time, but you can extrapolate the date from the other messages. I was gone—ah—three Sundays, and the messages are scattered over that time."

Elena thought the telephone message from Gus could be a wonderful alibi. As an electrical engineer Sarah would know how to fiddle with the tape or the machine, and they might never be able to prove the tampering, any more than they could fix an approximate time of death beyond the evidence the murderer meant them to have. The unslaked lime had wiped out all possibility of using the body to provide that information. Or if Sarah had been at home, not picking up the phone, the message might have taken her to Gus's apartment, where she killed him. The messenger with the two gift-wrapped boxes had been seen Sunday night. Could Sarah have dissolved him in the time she had between Sunday and her paper on Wednesday?

The biggest problem was that Elena couldn't believe Sarah had done any of it. She was smart enough, certainly, and knowledgeable enough, just not vicious enough—at least Elena didn't think so. Uneasily she remembered Bonnard's remark about women "losing it." But he hadn't been talking about Sarah. Necessarily. *Maybe I should be reassigned,* Elena thought. *I'm not a disinterested party.*

"You were saying you flew to Chicago on May eighth," Leo was saying. "What flight would that have been?"

"I don't know," said Sarah, "but I've got the plane tickets." She fished through her purse and slapped them down in front of him. Leo started to pocket them. "Just take down the information," said Sarah. "After all, I might need them as part of my defense." Her voice was low and angry.

Elena, watching Sarah's hostility grow, felt worse and worse about the situation. Sarah's attitude wouldn't make a good impression on Lieutenant Beltran, who liked pleasant women in subordinate positions, not hostile, self-possessed women in positions of authority, women who made better money than he and wore better clothes. Leo was copying down the ticket information. "The convention didn't begin until May tenth," Elena pointed out. "And you didn't give your paper until May thirteenth." She could see that Sarah was taken aback by the detailed information they had assembled. "How is it you happened to go two days early?"

"Because I'd been invited to give a seminar at the University of Illinois, Chicago. You can check that with Brett Harlingen of the E.E. Department. I was their guest for the two days in question." Then she stopped talking for a moment, frowning. "And won't that look wonderful," she burst out, "if the police call a noted colleague to verify my whereabouts?" The calm, delicate lines of her mouth tightened.

"And then?" Elena prompted.

"And then I registered on Sunday, attended meetings, seminars, gave a talk myself on Wednesday—my God, have you been questioning conference officials about my where-abouts? What must they think?" She took a deep breath, striving for control. "I had meals with colleagues, cocktails, did a little shopping, all the usual things one does at a—"

"Did you at any time leave Chicago during this period, ma'am?" asked Leo.

"No, I did not."

Elena was thinking that Sarah might have been able to hobnob at the University of Illinois Friday and Saturday and fly home Sunday to kill Gus. She might even have pre-registered so she didn't have to be there Sunday at all, and she didn't *have* to show up until her paper on Wednesday. There was plenty of time to dissolve him.

"Do you think you could locate people to verify your presence on the days you've mentioned?" Leo asked.

"Yes, I suppose I could," said Sarah. "But I'll be damned if I'll do it," she added. "Unless you're arresting me. Are you?"

She ought to be anxious to clear herself, Elena thought. Cooperative, not surly. Maybe the whole alibi was fictitious.

"We're not arresting you, ma'am," said Leo. "This is just a routine interrogation. So when did you leave Chicago?"

"It's on the ticket. You've already written it down."

He checked the date. "And then you went to Boston?"

"To visit my brother, Dr. Mansard Tolland; I've already told

Elena—before I realized I was a suspect in a murder. When I thought I was chatting with a friend."

Leo frowned. Elena had to keep herself from glancing at the window, behind which Lieutenant Beltran was sitting, listening, hearing the suspect call an investigating detective her friend. Well, the friendship was undoubtedly a thing of the past, Elena thought sadly. Sarah would never speak to her again—either because she'd end up behind bars or because she'd remain free—and furious.

"And I was with him—my brother—the whole time—well, when he wasn't attending to his practice, but then I was with his fiancée, as well as with colleagues at Boston University and Harvard. Oh, and I had lunch with some people at M.I.T."

"We could get verification from all these people?"

"Certainly—if I gave you their names—which *at this point,*" she said, sarcastically echoing his words, "I don't intend to do. Why bother them when you're just conducting a routine interrogation?"

"There's been a change made in your tickets, ma'am."

"Certainly. I came home early. Does that seem like the action of a murderer?"

Good point, thought Elena.

"Could you explain why you did that?" Leo asked. "Like maybe you received a call from Los Santos. Phone records are available."

"Well, check them," snapped Sarah.

"Maybe you could just answer the question," prodded Elena gently.

"No, I didn't receive any phone calls. I came home because my brother had to fly to Brazil to do an operation on some soccer player—Evono—Evana—"

"Valenzuela?" asked Leo.

"Right."

Leo was an avid soccer fan and watched games on Mexican TV. "I hope your brother's good," he said fervently.

"He is," said Sarah.

"So you came back to Los Santos?" Elena pressed.

"Yes. I was supposed to return on Sunday, next Sunday. I came back today because there wasn't any particular reason to stay on in Boston. My brother's fiancée wanted to go to Brazil with him, and I didn't want her to stay in Boston on my account."

"Wouldn't you have to pay a penalty to change your tickets?"

"I flew first-class. First-class tickets can be changed or refunded."

"Must be nice," said Leo, glancing at the expensive wrinkle-free cream-silk blouse and tailored beige slacks she'd evidently put on when Elena asked to come over.

Sarah said nothing.

"Have you any idea why your ex-husband called you?"

Sarah shrugged. "He said he had a favor to ask and he'd call me back."

"Has he asked you many favors since the divorce?"

"Several," said Sarah coldly. "Although I can't imagine why. I certainly didn't encourage him."

"So your post-divorce relationship was not friendly?"

"It wasn't unfriendly. There was no relationship."

"Yet in March you invited him and Ms.—ah—Kowolski, his fiancée, over to dinner."

"With every intention of never seeing him again," said Sarah sharply.

"Because you planned to kill him in what looked like a bizarre accident."

"I did not plan to kill him, and I don't intend to say any more about the snail incident, so don't ask me. Aren't you violating my rights by—"

"You're here voluntarily, Dr. Tolland," Leo reminded her.

Because it looked as if Sarah was about to insist on leaving, Elena asked quickly, "Did you see or talk to Mr. McGlenlevie after the snail incident, Dr. Tolland?"

"Except for that message on my answering machine, I haven't heard from him, which, *as you know,* is just fine with me."

As you know—Elena understood the emphasis. Sarah wasn't letting her deny the friendship. And she did know that Sarah preferred not to hear from Gus, or at least she knew what Sarah had told her—at those dinners and meetings the last couple of months.

What would Sarah's attitude have been during that time if she had, in fact, tried to kill Gus and planned to try again? She would have thought Elena an idiot to be taken in by a would-be murderer, to be providing group therapy for a woman who was using it as cover for a second murder attempt. Was Sarah that manipulative? Elena wondered uneasily. Was she even now counting on Elena to sidetrack the investigation? "So you didn't see Mr. McGlenlevie after the snail incident?" Elena asked.

"Oh, of course, I *saw* him," Sarah replied. "To say hello to on campus. I didn't have a conversation with him—or kill him—or go to his office or his apartment or his fiancée's apartment—or wherever he was when he was killed. You still haven't said."

"In his apartment," said Elena, thinking of Sarah's finger-prints, which had been found on a framed photograph in Gus's apartment. Sarah had lied.

Leo was frowning at her, but what did he expect? Elena wondered irritably. All Sarah had to do was ask someone or look up back issues of the newspapers, which had published about as much information as the police had obtained.

"In his apartment?" Sarah exclaimed, looking pale. "That's right upstairs!"

"Yes, ma'am," said Leo. "Now we'd like to ask you for some information about your husband."

"Ex-husband," she corrected.

Leo nodded. "What can you tell us about his health?"

"His health?"

"Did he have a doctor?"

"Not during the time we were married. Gus was disgustingly healthy." She stopped, looking to Elena very tired. "I guess that's not a sensible way for the suspect to talk about the victim."

"He didn't have a bone disease?"

Sarah looked puzzled. "I don't think so."

"What about his teeth? Did he have a dentist?"

"Not unless he acquired one since the divorce. I never knew

him to have any trouble with his teeth. In fact, I remember him bragging that he'd never had a cavity."

Elena and Leo exchanged glances, realizing that this was the second time Sarah had told an identifiable lie. "No cavities," said Elena, writing that down. The remains in the bathtub had fillings. That's why Elena had called all those dentists, assuming the work would be on record somewhere.

"Well, I suppose he might have acquired some since the divorce. I wouldn't know."

Not *that* many, Elena thought. Why would Sarah lie about his teeth? Unless she wanted to further confuse the issue by raising doubts about who had died in that bathtub. If it wasn't Gus, Sarah's motive disappeared. But it had to be Gus. If not him, who else? There would have been a missing person report by now, and Elena had someone checking those both locally and nationally—just to be on the safe side. She didn't doubt that the bones were those of Gus McGlenlevie. She did doubt that Sarah had killed him. Still, the killer had been so devious. A defense attorney would have a ball with the case once they'd made an arrest. And Sarah—well, Sarah was smart enough to have planned the whole thing.

"So as far as you know, there's nothing wrong with his teeth or bones?" Leo prodded.

Sarah frowned. "Is this some calcium-related thing?" she asked.

"Now, Dr. Tolland," said Leo, ignoring her question, "about the unslaked lime you ordered."

"The what?"

"Unslaked lime. It was delivered to the storeroom of your department, addressed to you, and picked up—I've forgotten the dates."

"I don't know what you're talking about. I don't even know what unslaked lime is, but it's certainly not something we use in electrical engineering."

"Computer records show it was shipped to your department. Your man Aberdeen logged it in."

"Well—" Sarah ran trembling fingers through her short blond graying hair. "Who signed it out?"

"It wasn't signed for. Someone who had a key just took it out of the storeroom. Who has keys, Dr. Tolland?"

Sarah leaned her head against her hand. "Aberdeen does. And I do," she admitted. "Karl Bonnard does. He's acting chairman when I'm out of town."

Elena shifted uncomfortably on her utilitarian brown seat, thinking hard. She couldn't scrape up any solid reason to connect Karl Bonnard to the case. What would his motive have been? Granted he was probably next in line for Sarah's job, but killing your chair's ex-husband and framing her seemed an extreme measure to advance yourself professionally, not a "logical" solution to a problem, which Karl maintained was an engineer's way of handling things.

"Actually, there may be other keys floating around. All of us lend them," said Sarah. "They could have been copied. What is unslaked lime, anyway, and what does it have to do with Gus?"

"One last question, ma'am. You must realize that we wanted to get hold of you as soon as his—ah—body was discovered, but your secretary had no telephone number for you after you left Chicago."

"So she told me, but you can be quite sure I gave her that information. I even watched her type it into the computer, and she's not one to erase data through carelessness. She's a very efficient woman."

"She told us," said Leo, a smile almost breaking through. Elena assumed that he was remembering a conversation with the formidable Virginia. "So if she didn't erase it, maybe someone else did." He stared at Sarah hard.

"Well, I didn't," she said, straightening and replying firmly. "And we can certainly find out when it was done, maybe even by whom. In fact, if you want to go over to the university now, I can find that out for you, along with more information on this unslaked lime business."

"I'm afraid, ma'am," said Leo, "that we couldn't allow you to go into that computer system."

Sarah looked at him blankly for a moment. "I'm the chairman of Electrical Engineering, and you're telling me that I can't use the computers until you find out who killed Gus? That's crazy."

"That's the way it is," said Leo. "We can't allow a suspect to tamper with what might be evidence in our case."

"So I *am* a suspect."

"As I said, ma'am, there are lots of them."

Elena was thinking, with alarm, that it might be hard to keep Sarah out of the university computer. If she was guilty, she might be able to erase evidence, from her house, for instance. People accessed computers by telephone, didn't they? Jesus, what were they supposed to do? Arrest her on the spot to keep her away from the computer system? Rip out her telephones?

Sarah looked amused for the first time since the interrogation had begun, bitterly amused. "I can see what you're thinking, Elena. Rather than allowing myself to be put in jail, perhaps it would be easier on all of us if you confiscated my modem and then called Charlie Venner, who is head of the computer center. He can cancel my access code."

Leo looked at her suspiciously. "I thought you were worried about not being able to conduct business."

"I'd rather retire for a week than go to jail," said Sarah. "Charlie's number is in the book. Call him. He'll tell you it's possible to freeze me out of the system."

Elena and Leo looked at each other. They didn't know what the hell they were doing, not on security measures, and Charlie Venner seemed to be held in wide contempt. Was Sarah suggesting that they rely on Charlie because she knew he'd botch the job?

"Daguerre," Elena murmured, and Leo nodded. Elena left the room, called Charlie Venner's number, and realized immediately that she'd caught him in bed with some female. She told him what they wanted and asked if it was possible, doubting all the time that he'd actually know. She then insisted that he meet Leo at the computer center and perform the operation in Leo's presence. "We want her frozen out of the system within the next half hour," said Elena, thinking, *Before she can get home and use her telephone.* Charlie didn't want to leave his apartment and had to be threatened. Elena then called Maggie Daguerre and asked her to meet Leo and Charlie to see that it was done correctly.

"I've got two days off starting tomorrow," Maggie wailed.

"At four in the morning I'm heading out to backpack in the Gila."

"Well, don't get engaged to any Los Santos cops while you're there," Elena advised. Maggie laughed, grumbled some more, and finally agreed to meet Leo at the computer center.

"If you don't have any more questions, Leo, I'll call for a squad car and take Sarah home," said Elena after she'd returned to the interrogation room and whispered the computer arrangements to her partner.

"I have some questions," said Sarah. "I don't understand any of this. You seem to suspect me because of that exploding snail, which you know yourself, Elena, is something that happens occasionally, and because of some unslaked lime, but I have no idea what that has to do with anything."

Leo and Elena stared at one another for a minute. "Everything but his bones was dissolved by unslaked lime and water," said Elena expressionlessly.

Sarah turned dead-white, and at that moment Elena was sure that Sarah was innocent.

"Dissolved," Sarah echoed weakly. "You mean he—" She looked too sick to continue.

"Nothing left but the bones," said Leo.

Sarah leaned her elbows on the desk and ran trembling fingers into her hair. Then she looked up. "Have you had an anthropologist look at the skull? They can reconstruct how the person looked in life. Otherwise, I don't see how you know that the remains you found were Gus."

"We'd have to send it to the FBI," said Elena. "It would take eight months or so before it came back."

"There's an anthropologist at H.H.U."

"That would cost money," said Sergeant Escobedo, entering from the hall. Elena hadn't realized that he was in the other room with Beltran.

"He'd probably do it for the fun of it," said Sarah wearily. "He couldn't stand my ex-husband, who evidently had an affair with his wife."

"What's his name?" asked Elena.

Escobedo shook his head and said, "He wouldn't exactly make an unbiased expert witness." He introduced himself to

Sarah, then reminded Elena of her earlier plan to get a patrol car to escort Sarah home.

"This is like a nightmare," said Sarah as they climbed into the squad car.

"I know it seems that way," Elena replied, wondering whether the driver was listening, whether this conversation would, by tomorrow, have passed through the ranks at Five Points and then leapfrogged to substations on the Westside and over in the far Northeast and the East Valley. "But I'm a Crimes-Against-Persons detective, and Gus died a violent death. Investigating it is my responsibility."

"But surely you know I wouldn't—" Sarah stopped. "Oh, never mind," she muttered, and that was the last thing she said to Elena until she had to point out her modem so Elena could confiscate it.

"Maybe, if you don't mind," said Elena, "I'll have the telephone company cut off your service for a few hours until we figure out what we're doing."

"Oh, marvelous," said Sarah. "You do that."

The telephone rang. Elena, knowing she didn't really have the right to say what she was going to say, murmured, "Only if I'm listening on an extension."

Sarah, mouth in a straight, angry line, gestured toward the livingroom telephone and strode into the bedroom. Elena heard her saying hello, then a male voice replying cheerfully, "Colin Stuart here. You're a hard lady to get hold of, Sarah. I'm afraid I've assumed that your offer to come down and take a look at Herbert Hobart is still open. When your secretary told me late this afternoon that you'd got back to Los Santos early, I went ahead and made reservations."

"Oh." Sarah sounded disconcerted, and Elena wondered if Colin Stuart was a male friend, or even a lover. "For when?" Sarah asked.

"Early tomorrow morning. I ought to be in before noon."

"I see. Well, I guess I could pick you up at the airport." Elena scooted to the door and shook her head. Sarah scowled and rescinded her offer. "Perhaps it would be better if you took a cab straight out to the department. I'll arrange hotel accommodations for you."

"Fine," said Stuart. There was a short silence. Then he added, "Or had you changed your mind?"

"No. No, of course not. The offer's still open."

"I think I've caught you at a bad time."

"Not at all," said Sarah, frowning at Elena, who still stood in the doorway listening, the cordless telephone in her hand. "I'm just tired—from a long day flying," Sarah added.

"Of course. Well, I'll see you tomorrow."

Sarah hung up. "A departmental visitor," she muttered. "So I'm not allowed near either computers or airports?"

"Look Sarah, I'm sorry about this. I really am, but Gus is dead, and he did accuse you of trying to kill him."

"That's ridiculous. I never wanted Gus dead."

Elena remembered the horrified expression on Sarah's face when she heard what had been done to her ex-husband's body. "I believe you," she said, "but there are other people involved in the investigation now." Elena watched as her friend's mouth tightened. "Also there's evidence pointing in your direction."

"So you say. No one's explained anything to me."

"I'd better be going," said Elena. She was supposed to be eliciting information from Sarah, not providing it. "I'll be in touch."

"I wish you wouldn't," said Sarah grimly. "And if you're going to cut off my telephone, you'll have to stay until I've made reservations for him."

Elena monitored that call, then took the elevator to the ground floor, feeling depressed. On the basis of evidence, Sarah was the best suspect they had. She could have done it. All the things that had been done to conceal the identity of the killer were clever enough to have been Sarah's doing. Yet Elena didn't believe Sarah was guilty.

And why? Gut feeling. The expression of horror on Sarah's face when she heard about Gus's remains. A belief in Sarah's basic decency, but that was based on an acquaintance amounting to six or seven evenings spent together, one of them when Sarah was the suspect in an attempted murder investigation. Reluctance to lose a friend, although it might be too late to remedy that. Elena knew her reasons wouldn't impress Leo or Manny Escobedo or Beltran. And against these weak arguments stood her reluctance to ruin her chances for advancement in the department, although she might already have done that too.

This case was a no-win situation from which she couldn't extricate herself. Days ago she had let that opportunity slip because she thought that admitting personal involvement with Sarah would call into question her judgment on the snail incident. No win, she thought glumly. It had been no win since she stepped into the apartment that held Gus, Bimmie, Sarah, and the snails in garlic butter.

She climbed into the front seat of the squad car and slammed the door.

24

Wednesday, May 27, 10:39 P.M.

Once she had the apartment to herself, Sarah huddled in a corner of her sofa. Elena had said a blow to the head. Detective Weizell had said the murderer dissolved everything but the bones. And they thought *she* might have done it. Sarah couldn't recall ever hitting anyone, much less hard enough to kill him. As for dissolving someone, anyone, especially a man with whom she'd once been intimate—well, the very concept was outrageous. It was too bizarre, too macabre, for a sane person to contend with.

Shivering, she decided to concentrate on practical, ordinary things, the visit tomorrow of Colin Stuart, for instance. Sarah tried to plan his itinerary at H.H.U. and couldn't get beyond the impression of the university he'd receive if she were arrested in the middle of the job interview or during the mandatory tour of the department.

Compulsively her mind returned to the interrogation. She went over the whole event, question by question, to assess her impression that she was indeed the prime suspect in Gus's murder. What other conclusion could she come to? All their questions were designed to incriminate her. Sarah did what she now felt she should have done initially; she went downstairs, found a pay phone, and called her lawyer, who said, "You can't be serious," and went on to explain that he never handled criminal cases. "I could put you in touch with a good criminal lawyer, although I can't believe you're really going to need one, Sarah."

"Let's hope," she responded grimly, hung up, returned to her apartment, and went to bed. Sleep would be an escape; the evening that preceded it was the nightmare. How could they think she had killed Gus? Elena especially. How could Elena even entertain such a possibility? She'd said she didn't believe Sarah guilty, but she had asked as many questions as Detective Weizell.

Then that sergeant had come in. It suddenly occurred to Sarah that the long window on the far side of the interrogation room had been one of those with someone lurking behind it, invisible to the person on the other side. The sergeant, maybe others, must have been listening, watching her. That's why Elena didn't want her to sit on the sofa. The watchers couldn't have seen her face that way. And Elena had said there was other evidence. What possible evidence could there be when she was innocent?

Perhaps Elena had always suspected her, had stayed in touch in order to keep an eye on her, suggested that Sarah join the support group as a way of foiling another murder attempt. Sarah tried to remember what she'd said about Gus and the marriage in casual conversation or at the group. Had she said, in the meaningless way people do, that she felt like killing him when he totaled her car? How could she have been so naive about Elena?

Sarah had thought she'd made a friend, someone different from her academic acquaintances, someone who didn't want to talk campus politics or compare publication lists. Someone who talked about things that seemed both alien and fascinating. Instead, she'd exposed herself to sporadic surveillance.

And all because she couldn't resist the impulse to teach Gus a lesson. Why in God's name had she ever indulged herself in that snail trick?

25
..

Wednesday, May 27, 10:42 P.M.

"Lieutenant Beltran wants to see you at headquarters," said the patrolman while Elena was fastening her seat belt.

"Oh, shit," Elena muttered. By the time they'd got toward the end of the interview with Sarah, Elena had forgotten about Beltran, concealed behind the one-way glass. Sarah's hostility and defensiveness would have made a bad impression on him, an impression Elena would somehow have to counteract, preferably without getting herself fired.

"We're waiting for Leo and Daguerre," said Beltran when Elena arrived at his office. "I don't suppose you've met Daguerre."

Manny Escobedo nodded to her. He was eating peanuts from a snack machine.

"Yes, I have," said Elena, smiling at Manny, giving Beltran her best responsible-detective look. "She went with me on her own time to the university to look through their computer files." Elena was glad that Manny, who didn't seem so convinced of Sarah's guilt, had stayed. Her sergeant was at least keeping an open mind.

"Discovering what?" asked Beltran.

"Discovering that a shipment of unslaked lime meant for Buildings and Grounds was rerouted by someone in Electrical Engineering, addressed to Sarah Tolland, then taken out of the storeroom when the storekeeper wasn't there to get a signature."

"Oh yeah, I remember. Tolland had the keys to the storeroom."

"Tolland, the assistant chairman, the storeroom keeper, probably others."

"Just how friendly *are* you with this woman?" Beltran demanded. "You didn't push during the interrogation."

"You know Leo and I switch off—good guy, bad guy—and, depending on the suspect, I'm usually the good guy."

"Well, don't good-guy us out of an arrest because you like her. You brought her into your support group; isn't that what she said? You ought to know better, Elena. We're not some do-good social-work organization. We arrest 'em. We don't reform 'em. She should have been busted the first time she tried to kill him."

"Snails explode on their own, Lieutenant. You can be sure the defense would have pointed that out," said Elena. "And can you imagine what the papers would have done with a charge of attempted murder by exploding snail? At trial we'd have had to depend on the testimony of Angus McGlenlevie, who was wearing a sweat shirt that said 'Poets Do It In Iambic Pentameter.' The man's a total flake."

"The man's dead," Beltran retorted, "and if we'd arrested her the first time, he'd still be alive. Just because you didn't like him doesn't excuse allowing him to be killed."

"That wasn't why I—"

"Lieutenant," interrupted Escobedo, "I read Jarvis' report. The screening attorney in the D.A.'s office would have thrown the case out." Manny crumpled his peanut bag and dropped it in the lieutenant's wastebasket.

"Then he'd have been wrong, wouldn't he? Damnedest thing I ever heard of." Beltran shook his head. "Only a woman would think of killing her husband with a snail."

"There was no real evidence that she tried to kill him," Elena protested.

"Why the hell do you say that? She had motive and opportunity," said Beltran. "I suppose your feminine intuition told you she was innocent."

"My feminine intuition told me we'd look like assholes if we busted her. Probably get hit with a suit for false arrest."

"Assholes?" muttered Beltran. "I don't like to hear that kind of language from a woman."

"Well, just think of me as one of the guys." Elena tried a jaunty grin. "Their language is certainly worse than mine." She didn't want to get into it with Beltran.

"Obviously we've got a female perp. Worrying about a messy, decaying corpse. Housewife reaction."

Elena gritted her teeth and was saved from retorting by Leo's entrance with Maggie.

"O.K., Leo, what have you got?" asked Beltran.

"I haven't got anything." Leo looked surprised. "Lieutenant Daguerre here saw to it that the suspect's access code was canceled, but she said any third-grade hacker could get into that system."

"I've been in it twice now," said Maggie, "and the longer you look at it, the more security holes you find." She turned to Elena. "Pretty exciting, huh? A female criminal. Using a computer to hide her crime. Son of a gun!"

"Maybe we ought to send it in to that 'You've-come-a-long-way-baby' commercial on TV," suggested Escobedo and introduced himself to Maggie since no one else had. Maggie grinned and shook his hand.

Beltran glared at both of them.

"Well, I just meant," Maggie continued, seemingly quite unaffected by his disapproval, "that what with feminism and all, you hate to think women are missing the boat on crime when they're making such strides in other fields—medicine, law, police work, garbage collection. I saw just the other day that the city's hired its first garbage woman. Or would you call her a garbage person? I'm not really up on feminist—"

A warning rumble of impatience issued from Beltran's barrel chest. Manny Escobedo was laughing.

"I thought you were here to report on computer stuff, Lieutenant," said Beltran grimly.

Maggie swerved nimbly back to the crime. "Anyway," she said, "the only way you can be sure of keeping your suspect out of the university computer system is to have her watched night and day."

"I took her modem," said Elena, fishing it out of her large handbag. "And I had her phone service shut down."

"Big deal. There are computer stations all over that campus, and she probably has friends with modems. Or she could go buy another one. Use a public telephone. How are you going to combat that?"

"We'll arrest her," said Beltran.

Elena's heart missed a beat.

"We've got motive, we've probably got opportunity—as much as we could for anyone—and we've got fingerprints at the scene where she denies ever having been."

Elena cursed herself for bringing in that birthday-gift box.

"We've got the computer evidence that points to her. Leo, you write up the affidavit and warrant. Elena, you sign with him. Then bring it back to me. I'll get in touch with the judge myself."

"There you go." Maggie hooked the strap of her bag over her shoulder and rose. "O.K. if I head for home now?"

Beltran jerked a thumb toward the door in answer, and Maggie left. Elena could see that he disliked the computer expert. Which wasn't surprising. She'd used the F-word, feminism, and she was at least six inches taller than Beltran.

"Lieutenant, I don't think arresting Tolland is—"

"Your problem is you're not thinking at all, Jarvis. You've never arrested a woman for murder, have you? Maybe you think a woman can't commit murder—unlike your beanpole buddy, Daguerre, who seems to think women criminals are some great new invention. Well, there *are* female murderers. They're nothing new. And we've got one on our hands, one you're going to arrest first thing tomorrow morning.

"*You,* Jarvis, are going to arrest her." Beltran stabbed a thick finger in her direction. "Because if you can't arrest a woman, I want to know it before you take the sergeant's exam. You're lucky I'm not putting you in front of a review board for failing in your duty the last time."

Elena bit her lip and tried not to look as anxious as she felt.

Escobedo shook his head. "She was right to ignore those charges, Lieutenant. There wasn't—"

"Furthermore," Beltran interrupted, "you're going to bring the woman in in cuffs like you would any other murderer. And you're not going to offer her any special consideration because you've been stupid enough to make a buddy of her. You got that, *niña*?"

Elena nodded. Beltran calling her *niña*, which meant little girl, was a demotion in itself.

"Assign a man to Tolland's apartment tonight, Leo."

Having put her down, Beltran was now acting as if she were invisible—or unreliable. As if she'd allow Sarah to get away. Maybe even help her escape.

"See that she doesn't leave; keep her under surveillance until you've made the arrest. I want those affidavits tonight."

"He's gonna use his judicial buddy," said Elena wanly as they left Beltran's office and headed for Homicide Row.

"Yeah, but he's not gonna roust a judge out at this time of night. Probably won't be able to arrest her till noon."

Escobedo told Elena to cheer up and asked how tall she thought Lieutenant Daguerre was. When Elena said, "A good five inches taller than you, Sarge," he sighed, said good night, and left the department.

As soon as he got to his own cubicle, Leo made a call to set up the surveillance Beltran had ordered, after which he grumbled, "I don't see why he couldn't have had you do the warrant. You know how to type." Two-fingered, he was putting in his I.D. number, then the password.

"Yeah, but he doesn't trust me," said Elena, dropping into her chair across the aisle. She had just begun to picture how awful it was going to be—handcuffing Sarah, marching her off to jail. "It's a mistake—this arrest."

Leo shrugged. "So it's a mistake. He's the one who's making it. Not me. Not you, which is good, 'cause you don't need any mistakes. You need to concentrate on getting off his shit list. He can do you a lotta damage."

Elena knew it. Beltran, if he demanded a hearing, could get her canned or demoted. She'd hate to end up back on patrol. Frank, on the other hand, would love to see it happen.

"Hey, don't look so down. He'll forget about it in a year or so."

Leo guffawed, and Elena glared at him. She knew Leo was on her side, but he could be a real pain. He had a sense of humor only slightly less raucous than Frank's. She just didn't mind it so much in Leo, but then she wasn't married to him. If the warrant came through in time, maybe he'd agree to come in early so they could arrest Sarah at home rather than at her office where her colleagues would see it.

"You gotta admit she's the best suspect we have," said Leo. "Everything points her way. Motive, opportunity, and the acid bath."

"Lime. We don't know about opportunity because we don't know when he was killed. She could have been out of town, probably was."

"You're too mixed up in this personally, Elena; Beltran's right about that."

"Hey." Maggie Daguerre strolled up the aisle from the other end. "You *know* this murderer, Elena?"

Both Leo and Elena turned in surprise. "Sure, she knows her," Leo replied. "Elena let her go the first time she tried to do in her old man."

"Oh, come on," drawled Elena. "An exploding snail? That's an attempted murder?"

"An exploding snail?" Maggie started to laugh. "Well, since you're going off duty, how about a beer and a taco? Is that sergeant still here? He can come along."

"He's too short for you, Maggie," said Elena. "And I thought you wanted to get home to bed, get a good night's sleep before your four A.M. backpacking date."

"Jesus, that sounds awful," said Leo, looking up from his computer terminal. He took the minimalist approach to exercise. His one stab at nonprofessional physical activity in recent years had been tap dancing—classes, videos, sudden bouts of exuberant tip-tapping when the impulse overcame him. He called it soft shoe when he didn't have his taps on. Leo took his dancing seriously.

"What I wanted was to get out of that office," said Maggie

fervently. "Man, that Beltran transmits hostility like vacuum cleaners radiate magnetic rays."

"I didn't know a vacuum cleaner had magnets," said Leo, turning on his printer. "I'm always fixing Concepcion's. Where's the magnet?"

"Damned if I know," said Maggie. "I've never had an apartment with carpets, but a vacuum cleaner will screw up your floppy disks. Now how about that beer?"

"Sounds good to me," Leo agreed. "Just give me a minute."

"I'm dead beat," said Elena, who was depressed about her relations with Beltran and sick at the prospect of arresting Sarah the next morning.

"Tough," said Leo. "You promised me a taco. Even if you threw in a beer, it wouldn't add up to the steak I missed." Having pulled the printout from the computer, he put an arm around Elena, bent down, and whispered in her ear, "A drink might cheer you up, kiddo."

True, she thought. Four might be even better. They both signed the affidavit, and Leo took it in to the lieutenant.

Sarah was as good as arrested, Elena thought despondently.

26
..

Elena waved cheerfully to Leo and Maggie, who were hanging out the windows of the squad car, shouting and waving back. She waved to the patrolman who was taking them home because they were all too drunk to drive. Four margaritas had a bigger effect than she would have imagined—or had she drunk six—or eight? She hoped Beltran never heard about this. Flagging down the squad car had been bad enough. But flagging down a squad car when you were drunk and staggering around in the middle of the street down near the bridge from Mexico made a bad impression on the brass—and on the general public, who, fortunately, had been in bed, and on your fellow fuzz. Fellow fuzz—Elena started to giggle. "Bad, bad impression," she mumbled, trying to take the evening's transgressions to heart.

Still giggling, she attempted to fit her key in the keyhole. No luck. The keyhole wouldn't stop dodging. Maggie was going to be sorry tomorrow, Maggie was. She was *very* drunk, so drunk she'd probably barf on her hiking boots—much to the disgust— Elena made another stab at the keyhole—much to the disgust of her fellow—fellow what? Fellow who? She tried the key again, and it tumbled out of her hand and clinked onto the doorstep. Oh lord, how was she going to find it when the lights weren't on—why weren't they? Elena always left the outside lights on.

140

Well, it didn't matter. She pulled out her flashlight and played it on the cement while she leaned her head against the door and stared at the beam, following it by rolling her head, which, she found, caused a similar rolling sensation in her stomach. She spotted the brass twinkle of the key in the moving light and dropped quickly to her knees, as if the key might hop away from her.

"Gotcha!" she exclaimed, her knees stinging from the rough cement. "And good-bye to another pair of hose." She consoled herself by remembering that pantyhose were cheaper than slacks. She could have scraped a hole in the slacks that matched her jacket. Nodding solemnly at that piece of budget-ary wisdom, she weaved into an upright position, key in one fist, flashlight in the other. Considering the way her stomach felt, she decided that Maggie might not be the only one barfing on her hiking boots, only—suddenly Elena remembered Sarah, her good friend and fellow divorcée. Both married to assholes. Only Sarah's asshole was dead. Deceased. Croaked. And tomorrow she had to arrest Sarah. And handcuff her. Because Beltran said she had to.

Blinking hard against tears of self-pity, she focused the flashlight on the lock and pushed the key into the pool of light. The next moment she was stumbling into the house, the flashlight rolling on the tiles, casting a looping beam on the living room floor. The hair on Elena's neck rose. Things were on the floor that shouldn't be. Before the flashlight stopped rolling, she'd pulled her gun and flicked the light switch with her left hand.

The sight of her living room—upholstery woven by her mother slashed, books torn and pitched everywhere, a big jagged hole knocked into the TV screen, the brass and wood chandelier lying twisted and broken among the crazily tilted springs of the sofa—the malicious violence of it all made her want to weep. Everything. Everything had been trashed. Her comfortable room that she'd accumulated piece by piece was gone.

Grasping the gun firmly in both hands, she moved from room to room in the house, her arms in position to shoot. She took the corners and the doors with care, just as she'd

been taught, just as she and Leo did on a case when they
anticipated the presence of someone dangerous. She covered
every inch of the house, but no one was there.

Hell no, no one was here. He was home in bed. Elena hurled
herself into the living room, found the telephone buried under
the wreckage, plugged it back into the wall, and called him. He
sounded sleepy when he answered.

"You son of a bitch," she screamed. "I'm calling the police.
Do you understand? This is the last time—"

"What happened?"

"You know what happened, you bastard. You sick, twisted—"

"Ellie, I haven't done anything. I swear—"

"I hope they throw you in jail forever. I hope they kick your
butt off the force. I hope—" She choked on the tears as they
began to flow.

"I'm coming over there."

"Try it. Just try it, you scumbag. I'll shoot you. That's a
promise, Frank, you—you—" Unable to think of anything
else to call him, she slammed down the receiver, took two
quick breaths, wiped the escaping hair away from her forehead,
and called headquarters.

"Look, Detective Jarvis," said the young cop who arrived in
response to the call, "if it was Frank Jarvis, why would he leave
that message?"

"What message?" asked Elena, who felt terrible—tired to
death, nauseated, trembling.

"On the mirror." The patrol officer looked at her peculiarly.

Elena looked at the message and wondered how she could
have missed it. In sloppy lipstick letters if said, "Quit it, bitch,
or you'll be sorry." Elena blinked. Frank, even at his most
angry, had never called her "bitch." He'd knock her down, but
he wouldn't call her a dirty name. And quit what? Who had
written it, and why? Elena took a mental fumble through her
cases, itemized what she'd been doing the last few days. She
couldn't think of anyone who would do this sort of thing—
unless it was that she had been trying to tie the Bonaventuras
to Gus's death.

Would Fat Joe order this, thinking that Elena was about to

arrest his daughter or because Elena was getting close to one of his henchmen, some Willie-Spozzo type? They were mad as hell that Lili hadn't been given permission to leave Los Santos, but there had been no active investigation of them until the last few days. Should she call Beltran and tell him about this? Could she stall Sarah's arrest by—Elena shook her head wearily.

She knew Beltran. Only positive proof that someone else had killed Gus would change his mind. And she didn't have it. Even tonight's vandalism couldn't be tied to the Bonaventuras. If they'd done it, they'd be too professional to leave finger-prints, just as there was no evidence of forced entry. Elena was sure the Bonaventuras could get into any house they wanted, but then so could Frank, and he'd know enough not to leave prints.

"Ah, Detective Jarvis—" The young patrolman interrupted her thoughts. "Your ex-husband is outside. He wants to—"

"Arrest him," Elena snarled. "He's been playing games for months. No matter what the message says." She nodded her head toward the mirror. "He could have done it. He's a narc. Didn't you know that?"

"Yes, ma'am," said the kid, backing up.

How long had he been out of the academy?" she wondered. Two weeks?

Some fun drunk, she thought bitterly when everyone had gone—the burglary detective on night duty, the I.D. & R. people taking pictures and dusting for prints. Tomorrow she'd feel worse than she did today, and tomorrow she'd have to— Elena gulped back tears again. No use to think about Sarah. Elena trailed into her bedroom, which was untouched. Why? she wondered. Did the Bonaventuras respect a lady's bedroom? Did Frank think he could get into her bed if he left it intact? She stripped down to her underwear, didn't bother with nightclothes, and slept with her gun under her pillow, just in case someone came back to trash the rest of the house.

Just before sleep overcame her, Elena remembered Karl Bonnard talking about women "losing it." Could tonight's interrogation have tipped Sarah over the edge? Could the chaos in the living room—No, that was crazy. For one thing, "bitch" probably wasn't in Sarah's vocabulary. For another, how could Sarah have known that Elena wouldn't be home? Anyway, Sarah was under surveillance until the warrant came through. No one could accuse her of vandalism, just murder.

27
..

"Colin, welcome to Herbert Hobart." Sarah rose from her desk to shake his hand, hoping hers wasn't clammy. She'd been terrified all morning that the police would come for her. Maybe the fact that they hadn't, meant they weren't going to. Maybe they'd found the murderer. Oh God, she hoped so. Here was Colin looking so handsome, intelligent, and likable, and how was she to concentrate on his visit?

Sarah couldn't believe this was happening to her. It was like those morning nightmares that were interrupted by the alarm before they got too awful. However, this one seemed determined to drag on past its time. She took a deep breath and smiled at Colin. "I've—ah—registered you at the Camino Real—downtown, which should be pleasant if—if you're fond of mildly historic places." *Get hold of yourself, Sarah.* She clenched her teeth hard and concentrated on serenity.

"Just so they have hard beds," Colin replied, smiling and holding her hand a second or two longer than necessary.

Sarah waved him to a chair and returned to hers, tucking into her purse the name and telephone number of a criminal attorney which she'd just got from her lawyer. "Have you had a chance to look over the H.H.U. brochure?" she asked.

"Yes, very impressive, except that it doesn't mention the average S.A.T. score."

"We try to look at each student as an individual," said Sarah

145

dryly, feeling better as she settled into her role as job interviewer.

"That low, is it?"

"It's about 950," she admitted. "As I said, we have the money to hire post-docs, and some of our students are actually very bright."

"Which means their reason for coming here was . . . ?"

"Looking for plush living and a good time. Getting kicked out somewhere else. Not for cheating; we don't take cheaters. But if they're rich enough, we'll accept the intelligent but excessively—ah—lecherous, or—mischievous."

"O.K., I get the picture. Just how much money is there for postdoctoral fellows? And what are the chances for a graduate program in the near future?"

"It's been discussed, but not implemented. Maybe you'd like to see our equipment. It's more impressive than the student body, although there's one thing you can say for them. They're well-dressed."

"And well-housed, and well-served. I didn't miss that bit about the best maid-to-student ratio in the country."

As they rose to leave the office, Sarah remarked, "You must have left in the middle of the night to get here before noon."

"I don't sleep much anyway." He opened the door for Sarah, and they confronted Elena Jarvis and Leo Weizell.

Sarah felt the blood drain from her face.

Elena, looking rather haggard, glanced at Colin, and Leo said, in a very formal tone, "Dr. Tolland, we have a warrant for your arrest for the murder of Angus McGlenlevie."

From the corner of her eye Sarah saw Colin Stuart's mouth drop open.

Elena read Sarah her rights while Leo took out the hand-cuffs. "You have the right to remain silent . . ."

It was all going too fast, and she'd been taken by surprise, after all. Panic-stricken, Sarah glanced at her secretary's desk. Dear God, Virginia was out. Pulling away from the handcuffs, she opened her purse to retrieve the slip of paper. Detective Weizell grabbed her hand, his grip rough and forceful, as if she'd threatened him.

"I'm getting my lawyer's name and address," she said, "not

a weapon." He took the purse away from her. "In the zip pocket," she said anxiously. Surely they wouldn't keep her from contacting a lawyer? She couldn't even remember the man's name.

Detective Weizell ran the short zipper and fished out the note that read "From the desk of Sarah Tolland," then the name and telephone number in her neat, legible script. Sarah turned to Colin Stuart and, not meeting his eyes, murmured, "I'm terribly sorry about this, but could you call the number on that slip of paper, explain the situation to the lawyer, and ask him to meet me—where are we going, Detective Weizell?" Sarah couldn't bear to look at Elena. She hoped her sometime friend had spent as bad a night as her face indicated.

"Headquarters at Five Points," Elena replied.

Sarah didn't acknowledge her by look or voice. "Ask him to meet me at Police Headquarters at Five Points," she said to Colin.

"What the hell *is* the situation?" asked Colin, looking completely dumbfounded.

"I'm being arrested for the murder of my ex-husband, a crime I didn't commit." Sarah raised her chin, controlled the tendency of her lips to tremble, and widened her eyes at the corners because she knew that controlled tears. She also knew how she looked—cool and calm. People were always telling her that. "How can you be so calm, Sarah, when the lab is in a shambles?" "You have no feelings, Sarah. Here John may die, and you're as cool as ice." Much they knew, she thought bitterly.

"In fact, the murder probably occurred while I was sitting in the hotel cocktail lounge in Chicago with you," she continued to Colin Stuart, "or while I was giving my paper—who knows? They don't seem to." She shot a resentful glance at Leo and Elena. How could they do this? They had to know she wouldn't kill Gus. Elena, at least, had to. Maybe Elena looked so terrible because she did know but had been overruled by a superior. On the other hand, maybe she was hung over. Maybe last night she'd been out celebrating the upcoming arrest.

"Anyway, could you make the call? Virginia ought to be back any minute. Have her contact Karl Bonnard, and he'll take over your visit." By that time Sarah was in handcuffs and leaving the office. They were delayed only momentarily by Virginia's arrival in the doorway.

"What in the world?" she exclaimed, looking from Sarah's face to the detectives.

"I've been arrested. Get hold of Karl," Sarah instructed. "Have him take over the schedule I've set up for Dr. Stuart. Dr. Stuart has the telephone number of a lawyer. Perhaps you could make that call for me, Virginia. No use embarrassing our guest any more than necessary." *See Mother,* Sarah thought, *even in handcuffs I've taken care of all the social amenities.*

"Sarah, we have to go now," said Elena, and they went.

28

Thursday, May 28, 11:20 A.M.

"If you're hoping for a confession, you won't get one because I did not kill Angus," said Sarah as Leo put his hand on her head and ushered her into the caged back seat of the car. Ordinarily they would have taken her to headquarters for interrogation first, but she told them pointedly that she would say nothing further without her lawyer present. Students on the sidewalk stared as the car pulled away from the building.

Leo drove directly downtown to the Los Santos County Detention Facility, parked across the street, and they walked Sarah down the ramp into the cage where they would have parked if they'd had a violent prisoner under arrest instead of Sarah. Handcuffed behind her back, looking much less controlled, Sarah complained that her lawyer would not know where she was, since she had, on their assurance, left a message that she would be at Police Headquarters.

"It was your choice to go directly to jail, ma'am," said Leo. He was taking his gun from its holster and depositing it in a lock box.

"None of this was my choice," she cried.

"We'll call Five Points to tell them where you are," said Elena soothingly. She kept her back turned and divested herself of her own firearm, unable to watch as Sarah's nerves frayed.

Then they took her inside to the jail magistrate, where the bailiff instructed her to stand on the brass plate in front of the bench after she'd sat waiting impatiently on a chair to the side while bail-reduction hearings were conducted in a small courtroom crowded with prisoners, attorneys, A.D.A.'s, security personnel, and witnesses.

When the judge started to advise Sarah of her rights, she told him stiffly that she had already been Mirandized.

"Don't interrupt me, madam," said the magistrate. "There are other rights you may not know about," and he went on to mention a bond-reduction hearing.

Sarah said, "Good. I'll certainly want one of those."

The judge nodded. "The state is entitled to three days notice on homicide cases, so you can wait the three days—"

"In jail?" she asked, horrified.

"In jail," he replied. "Or you can bond out on the bail already set. If you pay cash, a bond-reduction hearing might be worth your while. You could get some of your money back before you stand trial—that's providing I reduce the bond. If you use a corporate bond, which is to say a bail bondsman, you won't get your money back, so a reduction hearing would be a waste of time. Now, if I may go on to other rights, madam."

Sarah interrupted him again when he listed an examining trial. "What's that?" she asked.

He squinted at her. "Examination of the evidence in case some judge wants to dismiss the charges."

"I want one of those," said Sarah. "Since I didn't kill Angus McGlenlevie, there's bound to be a lack of evidence."

"It's your right, madam," said the judge, "although dismissal of charges is unusual, and of course, the police can recharge you. Also an examining trial is held only if you're not indicted within thirty days. The District Attorney's office will give your attorney access to their files anyway, so you'll know what evidence they have against you."

"That should be instructional," Sarah muttered bitterly. Her face set as she listened to the rest of what he had to say. Then Elena touched her elbow and guided her to Booking on the second floor, over blue floors molded with endless small circles, past blue doors, through a brown door on the right.

"Damn," Elena muttered under her breath when she saw

how many arrestees there were to be processed. She motioned Sarah through an orange door and told her to wait there.

"There are no chairs," said Sarah, eyeing the other occupants of the room nervously. None of them looked even marginally respectable in comparison to Sarah's conservative, well-groomed, suited figure.

"It's O.K. They're all handcuffed," Elena murmured.

"So am I," said Sarah, giving Elena an indignant look, then turning her back.

Elena stood outside with Leo, thinking about how Sarah would take the booking procedure. She almost wished she didn't have to stay. On the other hand, as upset as Sarah was, the presence of someone she knew might make the process a little easier for her. An hour passed before they could present Sarah at the property window, where her handcuffs were removed, her purse handed over by Leo, and all the contents inventoried. The sheriff's officer told her to take off her jewelry, her high heels, even her suit jacket. She was asked if she had anything in her pockets and replied that her pockets were in the jacket. Sarah asked to have her eyeglasses returned, and the officer said, "You see those signs?" She looked at the red signs hanging beside the window. "Read them for me please, ma'am."

"Keep hands off counter." "Officers must stay for the end of booking."

The officer nodded. "You don't need the glasses," and he listed them on the inventory and continued, "One yellow metal watch."

"Gold," said Sarah.

"Well, we don't know that. One white metal ring with clear stones."

"Platinum and diamonds," said Sarah.

The officer finished listing her possessions. "Now ma'am, if you'll step to the left side, put your hands against the wall and move your feet back and out, we have to do a search."

Sarah looked at him in horrified astonishment. Elena swallowed as a female officer was called from behind the long, dark red counter. Sarah had to be coached into the position and turned her head sharply, starting to move when the officer ran her hands up under Sarah's skirt.

"Face the wall, ma'am," said the woman. "I'm almost through here."

Elena could see the muscles tensing in Sarah's jaw. Then she was led to the right side of the property window and her small nyloned feet placed within the large outlines of feet painted on the floor. "Look at the jailbird, ma'am," said the photographer and snapped the four-shot Polaroid which produced four small color photos of a wild-eyed Sarah in a businesslike blouse, every gray-blond hair in place. "Nice picture," said the photographer. "If it's any consolation, you don't look like a murderer." Sarah looked like a woman on the edge.

Elena watched nervously as another sheriff's officer turned Sarah away from the camera and walked her to the curve in the dark red counter where he rolled ink onto a pad that looked like black linoleum and pressed each of her fingers onto the inked surface, then onto the fingerprint form. "There you go, ma'am," he said, and walked her toward a line of holding cells that faced the long, high counter.

Elena stepped forward. "Maybe she could sit out here on the bench," Elena suggested, having glanced at the four women in the holding cell. Several of them looked as if they might have murdered someone, one in self-defense if her battered condition was any indication.

"Why, she want to make a phone call now?"

"Why don't you call your lawyer, Sarah," said Elena.

Panic flashed in Sarah's eyes. "I can't remember his name. If I call my regular lawyer, will that mean I can't call the criminal lawyer later?"

"No, of course not. Go ahead and make your call."

Sarah punched out the number on the wall phone between holding cells and then dropped down on the bench with the receiver pressed to her ear. Elena watched the alarm spread over her face. Evidently the lawyer was in court, and his secretary didn't seem to know the name of the criminal attorney he had recommended. Sarah's hands were shaking when she stood to hang up the wall phone.

"You could call a bail bondsman," said Elena. "You'll want to bond out."

"I don't know any."

"There's a list there on the wall."

"What was my bail set at? Maybe I have enough to pay it myself."

Elena glanced uneasily at Leo. "Two hundred thousand dollars, ma'am," said Leo.

"Two hundred *thousand*?" Sarah echoed. "Good lord, you must think I'm a danger to the public."

"We don't set the bail, ma'am. And you'd have to put up cash if you're going to do it yourself."

"It can't be because you think I'm a flight risk. I came *back*." Her voice sounded almost plaintive.

"It's no use worrying about it right now," said Elena soothingly. "I imagine your lawyer can get it reduced."

"If I can ever find him—and then I'd have to stay here three days. Isn't that what the judge said? The state has a right to three days notification on a bond-reduction hearing in a homicide case?"

"Maybe he's downstairs right now. You told them at your office to call him."

"Oh." Sarah exhaled slowly. "Then ask him to come up here right—"

"He can't until the booking procedure is over."

Sarah, hands twisting at her waist, asked, "What does a bail bondsman charge to guarantee that sort of bond?"

"Ten to fifteen percent."

Again Sarah's eyes widened. "That's twenty to thirty thousand dollars. Do I get *any* of that back?"

Elena shook her head.

"It's unconscionable," Sarah muttered, and dropped back onto the bench, looking pale. "Thirty thousand dollars just to get out of jail for something I didn't do."

"You'll have to go into the holding cell now, ma'am, if you're through making calls," said the sheriff's officer.

"There's a collect phone over there," said Elena quickly, pointing to some blue telephones on the wall down the length of the counter. "You can call friends or family."

"Family? My brother's in Brazil. And my mother would have a heart attack if she knew I'm in jail."

The officer, in light tan trousers and a short-sleeved shirt with a red, blue, and silver sheriff's emblem on the shoulder, unlocked and slid back an orange door, motioning Sarah into a large room with cement-block walls, the lower half of which were painted brown and the upper half white. Jail-style wainscoting, Elena had always thought. Wooden benches jutted out from the walls. There were four other women in the room. Elena, watching outside the door, could hear one of the women ask Sarah what she was in for.

"Homicide," said Sarah and sat down on the only empty bench, turning her face away from her cell mates.

The woman, who had long black hair and was wearing a miniskirt and boots said, "She-it. What'd you do? Kill someone with snobbery?" and she click-clacked across the cell to sit by a sad-looking Hispanic girl in a limp flowered dress. It was an hour before Sarah was called to stand on the wooden platform in front of the red counter and give information—height, weight, date of birth, tattoos. She looked so astounded when she was asked if she had tattoos that Leo had to put his hand over his mouth to keep from laughing. Elena glared at him. She had never been more anxious to escape from the county jail.

Sarah was asked her driver's license number, which she didn't know because the property room had her billfold, her social security number, which she did know, and any numbers she might have from previous brushes with the law, to which she replied, "I once had a traffic ticket, but I have no idea of its number. That was my sole experience with the police."

Once the computer had produced the booking sheet to which her picture was attached, she was taken around the far end of the counter and directed again to position herself on huge footprints in front of a sign at chest level that gave her booking number, date of booking, and the words, "Police Department, Los Santos, TX." They took a front view and a side-angled view, after which she was again fingerprinted, each print put on a card with red lines and type that fit in a frame on the white marble counter.

"These go to the FBI, to Austin, and to both Los Santos' departments," said the officer fingerprinting her.

"Wonderful," said Sarah. "Now I'll be in every criminal computer in the country."

"That's right, ma'am," said the officer. "These are called patent prints. They're used to compare with latent prints from the crime scene."

"I was never *at* the crime scene," Sarah protested.

Elena and Leo, who were standing back at the end of the red counter, heard this and exchanged glances. Elena shook her head. She already knew that Sarah's prints had been found in Gus's apartment.

Then Sarah was led back the way she had come, along the high red counter, around the corner. "That's it," said the sheriff's officer to Elena and Leo. "Booking's completed. You all can take off."

Sarah cast one desperate glance at Elena before the officer led her across the hall to another large room.

"Wanna go get drunk again?" Elena muttered to Leo.

"I'd hate to think this is turning you into an alcoholic."

"If anything could, this is it."

They took the elevator downstairs and went out to retrieve their weapons.

"You know what? I feel like a traitor leaving her here."

"Oh, come on," said Leo. "There's probably a high-priced lawyer waiting for her downstairs right now."

"Yeah. But that bond—it's ridiculous. Sarah's not a flight risk."

"Well, you know Beltran and his friendly judge. He could probably get a million-dollar bond set on Mother Teresa."

"Yeah." Elena opened the locker and slipped her 9-millimeter into the shoulder holster while waiting for the door to rise, then walked up the ramp with Leo to the car across the street.

29
..

Elena fretted that evening until she finally gave in to her anxiety and called to find out who was on duty at the jail. Luck was with her. Sergeant Pete Dominguez said he'd be glad to check up on her prisoner. "Still here," he announced after a couple of minutes.

Elena groaned silently. It was after nine o'clock, so there was little likelihood that Sarah would bond out tonight. "Has she seen a bail bondsman or her lawyer?"

"Hold on." Another short wait. "Yeah, the lady's had four visitors. Pretty good for a first night in jail. Let's see. She saw someone from Expert Bonding Company at five, before she ever went upstairs."

Elena tried to imagine Sarah in that little booth on Two, trying to sit on the round silver plate that jutted out on a rod from the wall in front of the window through which prisoners could talk to lawyers and bail bondsmen. There was no way to do it in a ladylike or comfortable way, especially in a straight skirt, and Sarah might still have been in her suit skirt, probably was. She'd have had to hike up her skirt or sit sideways and twist around to face the window. "No bond, huh?" she asked Pete.

"Well, she's still inside. Maybe Expert is checking her out, but jeez, it says here the bond is two hundred thousand. With the banks closed, how's she going to come up with twenty or

156

thirty thou in cash, not to mention collateral for the rest? Does she own a house?"

"No house," said Elena, and she had no idea whether Sarah had that kind of money or would want to spend it—at least, not before she found out what it was like to stay in jail.

"O.K., let's see. Then she had a civilian visitor, Karl Bonnard, a professor at H.H.U."

Elena breathed a sigh of relief. Thank God Sarah was getting support from her colleagues. Sometimes in cases like this, the family and friends dived for cover. It was damn nice of Karl to go down to the jail and visit. And he had a house; maybe he'd offer to co-sign for the rest of the bond. Elena felt like calling and thanking him, but she didn't. She had to stay out of it now.

"Her attorney showed up at—ah—let's see. Bonnard came at six. Her attorney showed up at seven."

"Well, hell, he took his time."

"Hey listen, it's Oliver Formalee. If I were charged with murder and could afford him, that's who I'd want—even if he did show up late."

Elena nodded. If Sarah could afford Formalee, who was the best in town, one of the best in the state, maybe she could afford the bond.

"You can bet Formalee will get that bond reduced if she's willing to wait the three days. Your lady will be out on the street pretty quick either way. That's my take."

Elena nodded. Pete was right. Formalee wouldn't let that ridiculous bond stand if Sarah wanted to wait the three days for a bond-reduction hearing.

"And then she had one last visit, about nine o'clock. Guy named—ah—Colin Stuart. Listed as friend of the prisoner. So that's two of the four she's allowed to list."

Stuart? Of course. That was the man who had been in the office when they arrested her. The man who had called her the night she got home to say he was coming to Los Santos the next day. The man that Sarah had so bitterly indicated a personal interest in—if it hadn't been derailed by Gus's murder and the investigation. Well, it looked like the guy still had that personal interest. And Sarah, with no family in town, could use all the friends she could get. Maybe Stuart would be her co-signer. "Can you tell me who's in the cell block with her?"

"Hey, you're really taking an interest in this broad."

"Well, she's not the kind that would know what to do with most of the maggots who check into your establishment."

"Maggots?" Pete laughed. "Good word for them. Well, let's see what maggots we've got in with Dr. Sarah Tolland. There's a parole violator waiting on a parole board hearing. Ah—an agg assault. Prostitute assaulted a john who evidently decided not to pay. Ah—one robbery, second offense. Get this—she robbed a newsstand, stuck a deodorant tube in the owner's back. One aggravated robbery, woman who was begging, using a knife. Down on the plaza. Had a two-year-old with her. One kidnapping—husband had custody of the kid. Mother snatched it. You probably read about that one in the paper."

"Oh, sure. Nadine arrested the woman. Poor thing."

"Poor thing, my butt," said Pete. "She was convicted of child abuse. Got a suspended sentence."

"I didn't know that."

"Woman in for agg assault on a police officer. Member of Mujer Obrera. They were picketing one of those little sweat-shops where the boss hadn't paid 'em in a couple of weeks. Boss called the cops to get the trucks in and out of the lot. Woman hit the cop with her picket sign. Aggravated assault against an officer."

"Yeah," said Elena. "I wish we didn't have to get into that kind of stuff."

"I agree with you there," said Pete. "You gotta feel sorry for those women. They make little enough even when they do get paid. Then those sleaze fly-by-night companies come in, hire some people, operate for a couple of months while the contract lasts, quit paying the operators, and try to get outa town before the shit hits the fan. Cop was lucky she didn't hit him with a sewing machine."

"Too bad she didn't hit the owner instead of the cop," said Elena. "Any more?"

"Just *your* maggot, hon. Dr. Sarah Tolland, homicide."

"An empty cell in the block," marveled Elena.

"If we go empty, which isn't too often, it's usually on Eleven."

"Thanks, Pete."

"No *problema*."

Elena hung up and went out onto her patio to trim the vines she was growing on a trellis for shade on the west side of the house. As she snipped industriously, she tried to imagine her friend Sarah up there on Eleven, eating dinner at a table bolted to the floor with the women Pete had described, sitting in a six by twelve cell with a window in the metal door, having to use the stainless steel john where anyone could look in on her.

She probably wouldn't be using one of the two community showers in the cell block that night. They'd have made her shower before they put her into jail clothes and sent her upstairs. Elena hoped they'd had sense enough not to insist on de-licing her. She could just imagine how Sarah would feel about a suggestion that she had lice.

And the clothes. Elena shook her head and twined an errant section of the vine into the trellis. Sarah in one of those red smocks with the elasticized waist and the slip-on blue tennis shoes, probably all of it too big for her. She'd look like a concentration camp inmate. Elena whacked off a section of the vine she hadn't meant to cut and then swore under her breath. She'd be sorry about this gardening project come next spring.

Oh boy, she hoped Oliver Formalee got his client out before Sarah had to spend another night on one of those hard bunks that jutted out from the wall in a tiny cell on the eleventh floor. With her gourmet tastes she probably wouldn't eat from the time she went in to the time she got out. They'd have a real hunger strike on their hands, not the usual kind where the prisoner announced that he or she was on a hunger strike and then consumed Twinkies and Cokes from the commissary. Most of the hunger strikes involved giving up jail food, not all food. At least Sarah had been lucky, if you could call it that. She'd been arrested on Thursday, which was one of the three visitor's days on the women's floor. Tuesday, Thursday, and Sunday. Pray God Sarah wasn't in long enough to see a second one.

Elena had just finished bagging the trimmings and dragging

them to the alley when Karl Bonnard called and mentioned his visit to Sarah, saying that he'd understand if Elena refused to see him until the case was resolved. The man had a finely tuned sense of propriety, she thought, better than hers. "I offered to put up my house as collateral for part of her bond," he added, "but I'm afraid she was too proud to accept." Elena was so touched that she accepted his invitation to dinner. Which wasn't maybe the best idea. On the other hand, she didn't have to tell him anything if he seemed to be pumping her for information on Sarah's behalf, and she did like his company— once he'd apologized for talking endlessly about his soon-to-be-ex-wife—and his loyalty to Sarah. Maybe she could learn something from him that would help Sarah.

30
··

"Got news for you," said Leo, sitting down across the aisle from Elena. "She's bonding out. She'll be on the streets in time for lunch."

"On the streets?" said Elena grumpily. "That's not really a term that applies to Sarah Tolland."

"Your prejudice is showing," said Leo. "Oliver Formalee's her lawyer, and he's already filed a bunch of motions. Must have stayed up all night."

Elena nodded. Sounded like he was doing his job. God knows what he was charging Sarah for it. Of course, the screening officer at the D.A.'s office had to agree to take the case and assign it. The whole thing could disappear there or be sent back for more evidence. There were lots of possibilities that would keep Sarah from standing trial.

Elena noticed for the first time how glum Leo looked. "What's wrong with you?" she asked. "You're not still hung over, are you?"

"I gotta wife who says she ain't sleeping with any *borrachos* or whatever the Spanish word for drunk is. That's night before last. I told her I was drinking with two very nice policewomen, and she didn't like that either."

"Can't blame her there. Easy to see you were taken with Maggie Daguerre."

"The hell I was. What are you talkin' about? Me an' the

161

cowgirl? Don't ever let Concepcion hear you say that. Anyway, it was Escobedo who was taken with Daguerre. He asked me this morning if I thought she'd go out with someone shorter than she was. So just watch what you say around my wife."

"Hey, Leo. I was just kidding. Concepcion's not really mad at you, is she?"

"Nah. It's just that she turned up not pregnant for the zillionth time."

"Well, for God's sake, go to a doctor and find out why."

"She did. No reason."

"So you go."

"Jeez, Elena, do you know what they're going to expect me to do?"

"Sure."

"No, you don't."

"A quarter says I do."

"Done."

"Jack off in a paper cup."

Leo groaned and handed her the quarter. "Don't tell me you and Frank wanted to have a kid, and he had to—"

"Frank didn't even want a dog unless it could sniff out drugs and was at least moderately vicious—that's except for the time he wanted me to quit the force and couldn't think of any way to talk me into it unless he got me pregnant. The s.o.b."

"Which means you're still pissed, huh? Is that in general? Or about your house?"

"Both. And especially with Beltran. I hope someone trashes *his* house," she muttered. "Then he'll see how easy it is to *get over it.*"

"Face it, kiddo. If your mother was over at Providence Memorial being given the last rites by the bishop, Beltran would have made you bust Sarah Tolland. He figured he was teaching you a lesson."

"I know it. I guess I should be glad he didn't hear about our night on the town."

"Yeah. Think positive. He's really riding the tails of the guys investigating the break-in at your place."

"He probably thinks they'll find Sarah's prints."

"Right. He looks for Sarah's and finds Frank's."

Elena shook her head. "Frank wouldn't leave prints. I'm not even sure he's mean enough to slash my mother's upholstery, not when I haven't done anything spectacular to set him off."

"What then? Random break-in?"

"With that message? And nothing stolen? I realize I don't have much, but ordinary thieves would have taken the TV and the hi-fi stuff instead of destroying them. My money's on the Bonaventuras. Fernie's asking around."

"Jeez, honey, I hope you're wrong. Fat Joe Bonaventura's probably got more high-paid thugs on his payroll than we have cops in the whole city. You seen Beltran since we arrested your buddy?"

Elena shook her head. "You know we don't have that great a case. Makes me wonder whether Beltran really did push for Sarah's arrest to teach me a lesson about getting involved with suspects."

"I was kidding about that. Beltran just wants this mess off the books—fast." Leo leaned back in his chair, his face serious, and said, "Basically the man's got a soft spot for you, Elena. If he'd had a daughter instead of four worthless sons, you'd be his choice."

"Oh, right. He's gonna hold up my promotion. Bring me before a review board. Real fatherly."

"So, some fathers are hard-nosed. Stay out of it, babe. You're in enough hot water for being friends with a ferocious, cold-blooded poet-whapper. If it weren't for our brilliant police work, she'd probably have gone on killing poets for years—decades—"

"Oh, shut up." Elena grinned at the idea of Sarah Tolland, serial poet-killer. Leo was such an endearing fool. "Sarah's no more guilty than you are."

"Well, I'm not much on poetry. If I was actually forced to listen to some, I might snuff the poet."

"For two weeks I've been feeling bad because I thought maybe she killed him," said Elena, "but did you see the expression on her face when she heard about the bones in the tub? She didn't kill anyone."

31
..

Friday, May 29, 11:15 A.M.

Sarah had a meeting with her lawyer at mid-morning. She had authorized her bank to deposit twenty thousand dollars with the bonding company and had put up stocks and bonds as collateral to cover the rest, using her inheritance from her father to finance her release, which Oliver Formalee assured her would occur by noon. Much to her surprise, Karl Bonnard had come to visit her the night before, offering to co-sign her bond with his house as collateral. Of course, Sarah had refused to let him do that, but she considered the offer extraordinarily kind and felt conscience-stricken that she hadn't liked the man better over the three years of their association.

Formalee, a slender man in his middle years with gray hair and eyes, wearing a gray suit and tie, had already sent an associate to the District Attorney's office to look at the police and case files. "This D.A.'s more open with information than most," he told Sarah and pointed out that he'd begin by calling into question the identification of the remains.

Sarah nodded. "They asked me about dentists and fillings. Gus didn't have either."

Formalee made a note. "They have computer evidence that this unslaked lime was rerouted on the evening of May first around nine o'clock, but they can't tie that absolutely to you."

Sarah nodded. "In fact, I can probably account for my time

that night. I think I was giving a speech, but I'd have to check my calendar."

"They have it. I'll send my associate back for the information. Then they say your address in Boston was deleted."

Before he could check his notes for the date, Sarah pointed out that she'd come back to town early. "So the deletion means nothing."

Formalee agreed. "Then there's the snail thing, but it's not very impressive. The detective didn't take it seriously enough to pursue the case at the time, and I doubt they can get it admitted at trial."

Sarah was relieved that he wasn't going to ask her about the snail.

"Various people think you had reason to kill him, but that hardly means you did. The most damaging piece of evidence relates to your presence at the scene of the crime."

"I've never been in his apartment."

Formalee's eyes narrowed. "They found your fingerprints there."

"That's impossible!" cried Sarah, her heart starting to race.

"On a framed photograph."

"But—" How could that be? "A photograph of what?"

"I don't know, but I suppose I can find out. The point is, they have evidence that you were there, although you've told them you never were. *That* looks bad."

"The wedding picture!" said Sarah. "When we were dividing up the property, he asked who got the wedding picture, and I handed it to him. But—but surely, it must have been dusted since then. It's been forever."

Formalee frowned. "Weak. I'll have to see if he had a maid. How rigorous she was about cleaning. The fingerprints can hurt us. The jury will think you wiped off other prints and forgot those."

"I can't believe this is happening to me."

Colin Stuart met her on the first floor after the interminable bonding-out process. Sarah was amazed at how many times they checked to be sure they were really releasing Sarah Tolland and not some other person. They checked her face against the photos, her fingerprints; they asked questions only she could answer. They checked out every single item they'd taken from her during booking, including three bobby pins from her handbag. It took so long, she was trembling with weariness and hunger by the time she emerged on the first floor and saw Colin waiting for her. And she was touched by his support. The man hardly knew her, yet he'd visited her last night and come again this afternoon.

"Did Karl take good care of you yesterday?" Sarah asked, trying to resume a mantle of professional dignity as they walked across the lobby.

"Actually, last night at dinner," said Stuart, "he seemed more interested in what I could do for him than what he could do for me. Yesterday afternoon he was in a big hurry to see the dean. He interrupted the tour every ten minutes to try again for an appointment." Stuart held the door for her, and they went down the ramp to the street. "Once he got one, he turned me over to someone in Physics, who was pretty surprised to find himself recruiting for E.E." Stuart took her arm as they stopped at the street corner for the traffic light. "I suppose he could be serious about wanting to free you to defend yourself, but I'm usually suspicious of people who advance their own interests while claiming to be doing the loser a favor."

"What are you talking about?"

"Bonnard suggesting to the dean that he be appointed chair, whether or not you got out on bail."

"But he offered to put his house up as collateral so I could get out."

"Did you accept?" asked Stuart, looking puzzled.

"No, of course not."

"Well, your secretary was in a flat-out fury about his conversation with the dean. She was going to call you about it, but I gather she didn't get through."

Sarah sighed. Virginia had probably expected to make the call to Sarah's apartment. Maybe you couldn't call people in jail. Probably not. And Bonnard. Offering to co-sign her bond while he was going after her job.

"Bonnard probably knows you well enough to know you

wouldn't accept the offer. I wouldn't be too grateful to him if I were you."

"What did the dean say?" she asked, overcome with a sense of bleak premonition. Already this was interfering with the most important thing in her life, her career.

"Nothing, I gather. He's thinking it over. Bonnard got quite defensive at dinner last night when I asked him about it. He hadn't counted on the dean's secretary passing the news to your secretary."

"Then he should have known better. The secretaries' grapevine knows everything. The English Department secretary probably knows who killed Gus," Sarah added bitterly. They had walked along Overland and now took an elevator to the seventh floor of the County Courthouse Parking Garage.

"I hope you don't mind," said Colin. "Virginia gave me your car keys so I could pick you up."

"Good heavens, she must like you!"

"Is that good or bad?"

"Just unusual," Sarah murmured as she started her BMW and began the slow, circular roll to the pay booth on the first floor. "Do you know anything else about Bonnard and the dean?"

"Bonnard *says* he's doing it for your sake, because you'll need to devote your time and resources to a strong defense. I gather he suggested that you be given a leave of absence."

Bonnard had said nothing about any of this to her. Had that omission been a kindness? Or an attempt to grab her job before she could protect herself? Colin leaned across and paid the parking fee because the jail had returned her money in check form instead of cash. She shook her head at the impression all of this must be making on him.

Initially she had felt sadness over Gus's death. Now, as her troubles multiplied, she felt the old anger reviving. What the devil had he done to get himself killed, and why did the messes in his life have to spill over into hers? Divorce was supposed to prevent that.

"I'm sorry Karl treated you so cavalierly," she said to Colin. "I just don't understand him."

"It's pretty simple. He wants your job."

"Well, we both applied for the chairmanship initially," she mused. "Although he's never *said* anything to indicate that he resented my being chosen."

"Given the kind of man he is, he must have been and probably still is resentful."

"What sort of man do you take him to be?" Sarah asked.

"Arrogant."

That's what Virginia said once—that Karl Bonnard was an arrogant stuffed shirt.

"How about it?"

Sarah turned to Colin, unsure of what he was asking.

"Lunch," he prompted.

"Are you sure you want to be seen with a person accused of murder?" She asked the question with a smile, but behind her question lay the fear that he might prefer to have her decline. Maybe he was counting on it, as Karl Bonnard had counted on her refusing his offer to co-sign her bond. She stopped at a traffic light and turned to study Colin's face.

He grinned and replied, "Maybe I'm one of those people who get off on violence and sensationalist court cases." Sarah's smile died. "Bad joke, huh? I'd still like to take you to lunch."

Sarah, who hadn't really eaten anything since breakfast the day before, accepted. But she'd pay; she had credit cards even if she didn't have cash.

32

Friday, May 29, 3 P.M.

"It boils down to whether you think I killed Gus," said
Sarah. "Do you?" She felt too grim and too anxious to put the
question more tactfully to the dean.

"Well, I've certainly felt like killing him a time or two
myself," said the dean wryly, "but, no, I don't think you killed
McGlenlevie."

"And I am, as they say, innocent until proven guilty, which
puts the question of my competence to continue as department
chair right back into your court." Sarah had made the appointment with Dean Neil Brumbaugh as soon as she got back from
lunch with Colin. "If it's any help, I anticipate no problems in
carrying on—no matter what Karl Bonnard would like you to
believe."

"Now, Sarah, Karl tells me he brought the matter up out of
concern for you and for the department," the dean pointed out
mildly.

If that was true, why hadn't he told her when he came to the
jail offering to co-sign her bond? "More likely he wants to be
chair and sees my problems as an unexpected stroke of luck,"
said Sarah. She was more inclined to believe Colin about
Bonnard's motives than any self-serving explanations Bonnard
offered to cover his tracks. "My lawyer tells me the District
Attorney's office could refuse to prosecute or the grand jury
could refuse to indict. But Karl went after my job before I've

even *been* indicted. If that isn't opportunism, I don't know what is."

The dean appeared to be pondering her statement. Then he nodded. "I rather imagine you're right about that," Brumbaugh agreed. "What's your assessment of his administrative skills?"

"Good grief, Neil, are you asking me to recommend my own replacement?"

"No, Sarah. Not at all, and I do realize how resentful Karl has been ever since he found out he wasn't going to be chair."

"He has?"

"He complained bitterly when your appointment was announced. Even threatened not to come here. As I remember, he had doubts about a woman's ability to carry out administrative duties."

"I never knew that." Karl was a good actor, she thought. Maybe that's why he'd always made her uneasy. "I hope you're not going to give him the position."

"Well, I'm getting pressure from Harley. You know how much he worries about the university's image. If he could, he'd make you disappear, but I think in this case I'll have to ignore him—"

"Thank you, Neil."

"—until such time, if it comes, when you really are too overcome by your personal problems to carry out your duties."

Sarah paled.

"Now, I'm not saying that will happen, Sarah. Let's hope this mess just goes away."

"Yes, let's hope."

"As for Bonnard, if I have to relieve you, I think I'll appoint myself temporary chair. That might teach him the value of loyalty."

Sarah was surprised and touched, and she went on to her 4:30 appointment with her lawyer feeling a bit heartened.

She had a thing or two to tell him as well. One was a description of Gus's sexual liaisons. "I think you should let me talk to the police," she said. "There had to be dozens of people who had a better reason for killing him than I."

"The police won't see it that way," said Formalee. "You go in and talk about his infidelities, you'll be putting arrows in their quiver." Formalee was well known as a bow-and-arrow deer hunter, one of the few who actually got a deer on rare occasions. "You'll look like the stereotypical jealous wife— excuse me, ex-wife. At any rate, I don't want you saying a word to them, Sarah. If we go to trial, I probably won't even put you on the stand."

"Are you saying that I'm not at all credible?"

"Sarah, if you take the stand, the prosecution might find a way to ask you about the snail. Otherwise, I've got a shot at keeping it off the record." He stared at her reproachfully, having asked about and been told the story. "Plastique, for God's sake! That's terrorist stuff. Where did you get it, anyway?" Oliver Formalee ran a distracted hand through his dignified hair. "No, don't tell me. It makes me damned uneasy to realize that there are women around who can turn on a blender and blow up an apartment house."

"You're overreacting, Oliver. I blew up a snail shell, not an apartment house."

Sarah had forgotten about the snail—momentarily. "But *someone* killed him and then tried to make it look as if I had. How are we going to find out who if we don't force the police to continue the investigation?"

"If you can afford it, we'll hire a private detective."

"It's going to cost me my life savings to defend myself against something I didn't do."

"Better than going to jail," said Formalee. "You want me to find a detective?"

"Let me think about it. Have you got the information from my engagement calendar?"

"We only talked about that this morning," said Formalee dryly.

"And I can't use the computers. I could have retrieved the information that way."

She left the lawyer's office and drove to the Camino Real, where she was meeting Colin for a drink under the hotel's historic Tiffany dome. The deep, soft lounge chairs and low tables, discreetly separated from one another, plus Colin's relaxed company, were very soothing to her frazzled nerves. However, she felt a tinge of conscience regarding him. Colin would be leaving on Monday, and because she had been pursuing her own problems, she had palmed him off on other faculty members for extensive tours of the campus and the city.

"Why don't you have dinner with me?" he suggested. "There's an excellent restaurant not fifty yards from us."

She shifted in her squashy leather chair and thought, *If I spend the evening with him, I could end up in his bed, just for the reassurance of a human touch. And I hardly know the man.* "I'd better go home, Colin, and think through my problems."

"You know," he said reassuringly, "that it's got to turn out right in the end."

"Just the fact that I've been arrested makes me question that," said Sarah, "and I don't want to wait for the end, as you put it. Formalee said homicide trials sometimes take as much as three years to get to court." She shuddered to think of spending three years with her future at risk. She'd go crazy.

"Do you want me to stay?"

She glanced at him in surprise. "I'm sure you've better things to do with your summer."

"Professionally speaking I do, but the few days I've been here have improved my health and outlook."

"Have they? Well, I'm glad something good has happened. Are you seriously considering our offer then?"

"As long as you're going to be chair."

"Well, I'm still chair at the moment. I had a talk with the dean. He's not going for Bonnard's let's-all-take-care-of-Sarah-by-dumping-her pitch. If I start going to pieces, Dean Brumbaugh will appoint himself chairman."

Colin Stuart chuckled. "I'd like to meet that man."

"I assumed you had," said Sarah and glanced at her watch. "Unfortunately, it may be too late now." She finished her drink, refused with regret his offer to stay in Los Santos—how could she enlist that sort of extensive support from a man she'd only known a few days?—explained that several of the E.E. faculty would pick him up for dinner at seven, and went back to her apartment to sort through everything she knew about the case.

The police had given her little information, but she had photocopies from the local papers, which she'd made at the library before her appointment with the dean. She read the stories over and over, astonished at the details. Someone had hit Gus on the head and then put his body in a bathtub full of unslaked lime. Why? Why the attack? Why the lime? And whatever the motive, the police couldn't be sure it was Gus.

Elena's question about fillings nagged at her. Gus didn't have cavities. And bone disease. What was that about? The man never even caught colds. He'd thought being spattered with hot garlic butter was a major medical emergency. Yet obviously no one believed her about his teeth.

Then there was the lime. They said someone rerouted the unslaked lime by computer on May 1. After thinking for a minute, she looked up the number of Jaime Esposito, president of the local engineers' society, and called him.

"Jaime, this is Sarah Tolland, and before you hang up, I didn't kill him."

"Jesus, Sarah, I never thought you did. What can I do for you?"

"Do you know the date of that speech I gave?"

He was gone briefly, then returned with the date. "Thank you, Jaime!" she exclaimed. "You may have saved my life, or at least my sanity. Do you remember what time I arrived at the banquet?"

"Sure, you got there before me, and I got there around quarter to seven."

"Right, and you can vouch that I was there the whole time?"

"Well, of course I can. I sat beside you."

"And I left when?"

"I don't know. Must have been ten o'clock. No, wait a minute. We went down to the bar and had a couple of drinks—you and I and Marta, and let's see, the Bigelows, and Nacho. Nacho was with us. We were all together until quarter after eleven, eleven-thirty."

"Yes!" said Sarah, her arm rising in the clenched fist sign of triumph, a gesture she'd never made in her life. "Thanks again, Jaime. I've got to get off."

"Sure, Sarah."

Eleven-fifteen or eleven-thirty. She could account for her time from six forty-five to eleven-fifteen that evening. She thought back to her conversation with Formalee. The rerouting had been logged in around nine according to information from the D.A.'s files. She'd have been talking in front of a hundred people or so when someone—the murderer, no doubt—made that change from a computer in the library. It could have been anyone. She thought a minute, Formalee's insistence that she was not to talk to the police going through her mind. Then she punched out Elena's number. No one answered.

33
..

As Elena dressed for her dinner date with Karl Bonnard, she thought about Beltran, who wouldn't let her pursue the acid bath case any longer. He had been angry at her suggestion that the Bonaventuras might have trashed her living room, accusing her of trying to sabotage the case. So she could only wonder in her few spare moments that afternoon: Had that clotheshorse Bonaventura lawyer and thick-neck Willie Spozzo left town? Had they been in Los Santos before they showed up at her desk? Had they or their people wrecked her house?

She hadn't touched the living room. The crime scene unit had finished with it. The insurance adjuster came and went, assuring her that a check would be in the mail. But Elena made no move to clean up. When she left the house, she stared at the room as she threaded her way among the wreckage; when she returned, she looked at it again, her anger at the vandals and at Beltran hardening.

Shaking her head, as if to eject the bitterness, she combed and redid her French braid, thinking about Sarah. Had she gone straight back to work once she bonded out? Were people at the university edging away from her because she'd been accused of murder? Were students whispering, dropping the one course she taught in the summer? Frustrated because she couldn't call Sarah, angry because Beltran had her road-blocked, Elena turned her attention to the case on which she'd worked all afternoon with Leo—a dead man who had beaten his wife and a wife who had disappeared after the murder. Beltran wanted the woman found. Elena suddenly realized that she hoped the woman was a thousand miles away, deep in the interior of Mexico, safe for the first time in years, staying with family who loved her and didn't show their affection with clenched fists.

Elena had suggested to Karl that they eat somewhere casual, not because she didn't appreciate eating in expensive restaurants, but because she didn't have time to go out and buy a dress. He might, after all, notice if she wore the same dress two dates in a row. She settled for the pants suit she wore to court.

His idea of casual turned out to be the dining room at the Camino Real, where during the whole meal she had to listen to harp music. It sounded like running water and induced a need to visit the ladies' room after two glasses of wine. Worse, over by a giant potted plant sat the man who had been with Sarah in court and when she was arrested. He ignored his companions and stared at Elena, making her feel guilty and restless. When she came back from the second trip to the powder room, worried that Karl might think she had some embarrassing bladder problem, she took a different seat so her back would be to the starer.

"How's the McGlenlevie case going?" Karl asked.

"I'm not really at liberty to discuss that," said Elena.

"Well, you can understand that I'd be concerned. Not only is Sarah a friend and colleague of three years, but I may well be stuck with the chairman's duties if the administration decides that the scandal and the time she'll have to spend defending herself will lessen her effectiveness as our chairwoman."

"You mean they're going to fire her?" asked Elena, horrified.

"No, no, she's tenured. That's how they got her to come here, that and the chairmanship, for which she really had no prior experience. But they may relieve her of the chairmanship."

"That's terrible. People are innocent until they're proven guilty."

"I'm glad to hear that you feel that way," said Karl.

Elena eyed him sharply. He'd said he might "get stuck with" the chairmanship, but the truth was that he was going to profit from Sarah's misfortune. "Don't you?"

"What?"

"Think she's innocent?"

"Of course. Although I realize that she may have had a motive. Considering everything I've heard about McGlenlevie, it's a wonder she didn't kill him while they were married."

"What was your personal experience with him?" Elena asked.

"Actually, I never met the man."

"Never? He and Sarah were married for—what?—two years?"

Bonnard shrugged. "They didn't mix socially with the department. Perhaps she was ashamed of him—or afraid he might try to strike up an acquaintance with one of the wives or with Dr. Ramakrishna."

"I think I met her." *That would be the little Indian lady who was having a nervous breakdown.*

"Well, she's not the best professor we've got," said Karl. "But she tries," he added hastily. "Of course, all that's beside the point. No matter how much evidence you have against Sarah, and I assume it's considerable"—he looked at Elena questioningly but got no response— "I simply can't believe that Sarah killed him. And then treated the body with such— vindictiveness. The newspaper description would indicate a—well—intense hatred. Of course, one never knows what lies in the human heart, especially a heart that has been wounded—But Sarah? No, no, she'd never do what—well, what happened."

Intense hatred? Was that the explanation of the unslaked lime? To erase from existence as much of Gus as could be done away with? Elena and Leo had been thinking mostly in terms of the lime being used to disguise the time of death and eliminate odor so the body wouldn't be discovered. But hatred? It made sense. Not in connection with Sarah, but . . . or was she underestimating Sarah's resentment of Gus? Was Sarah so good an actress that she could fake that mildly irritated detachment that had seemed to characterize her feelings for her ex-husband and the horror she'd shown on hearing how he died?

And why was Karl spending the whole evening talking about Sarah? It wasn't very flattering. But then Elena had to admit that she'd been pumping him. Maybe he was wondering why *she* kept talking about Sarah.

"I hope you'll let me order dessert and a liqueur for you," he said.

Elena gritted her teeth. She liked to do her own ordering.

"You'll love this combination," Karl assured her. "Calvados and apple tart."

"What's Calvados?" she asked suspiciously.

"Apple brandy. It's the perfect complement for the tart."

When the order arrived, Elena tasted the apple tart—good. Then she took a sip of Calvados. It tasted like kerosene. Obviously there were drawbacks to associating with gourmet types, no matter how handsome.

In fact, that had been a problem between her and Sarah. Sarah claimed Mexican food gave her indigestion. Elena thought most French food was the pits. But Sarah had never insisted that Elena imbibe kerosene with dessert. On the other hand, French food was often covered with some gunk, so you couldn't be sure what they'd put underneath, probably cow's spleen or something disgusting from a goose, which seemed to be a French favorite. Sarah had once ordered goose liver as a first course. The memory of that evening made Elena want to laugh out loud, but Karl was looking terribly serious, worrying about Sarah evidently.

"If you want to know about Gus McGlenlevie, you ought to ask Virginia," he said. "She may have been the first person in the department to suggest that someone kill him. This is just gossip, of course."

Jesus, thought Elena, *Shut up about it, will you?* "What happened?" she asked like the good detective she was.

"Oh, McGlenlevie's girlfriends kept calling the department. If they couldn't get him at English, they'd try E.E."

Elena remembered the conversation on the exploding snail evening. About Gus's girlfriends calling the house and how angry he had been because Sarah wouldn't relay messages, because she threw out the answering machine, and finally because she arranged for an unlisted number.

Karl might mean well, but everything he said was like another nail in Sarah's coffin.

"And then there was the time he wrecked her car." Bonnard chuckled. "Sarah's a remarkable woman. She has as much appreciation for a fine car as a man. Now, I hope you won't take that as a chauvinist remark." He smiled engagingly at Elena. "I guess I'm remembering my own wife, who thinks that a car is on the same level as a washing machine. If it works, who cares about the rest?" He was swirling his Calvados in the brandy snifter, sipping as if he actually enjoyed the stuff.

"But I was talking about Sarah," Karl resumed. "McGlenlevie took the car without her permission, got drunk, and then he didn't *run* a stop sign; he ran into it, so I guess you could say he stopped. She had a Mercedes at that time. Sarah had to bail him out of jail and retrieve what was left of her car from the impound lot. She evidently said that if he ever touched another car of hers, she'd run him over. I believe she instituted divorce proceedings immediately thereafter."

Wonderful, thought Elena. *We're going to have to subpoena this man to testify.* Later when she got home, she made notes on the conversation and called Leo.

"Bingo," said Leo. "She threatened to kill him and tried to kill him. Even with the shaky evidence on the actual murder, those two tidbits ought to give the jury plenty to think about."

Elena nodded glumly. She felt like a traitor, using Sarah's friends and colleagues to convict her.

"That computer rerouting you used to get me indicted?"

"Sarah?" Elena had been putting on an old T-shirt of Frank's when the telephone rang.

"That's right—Sarah. Well, there are a hundred engineers who can tell you I was giving a talk right here in Los Santos at the time that happened, people who were with me at the Marriott from quarter of seven to eleven-thirty that night, not just a few people, lots."

"Thank God," said Elena.

"Thank God? What's that supposed to mean?"

"I hope you don't think I'm enjoying this."

"You don't think I killed him?"

"I wondered about it when we found him. I couldn't help thinking about the snail thing, but Lord no, I don't think you killed him. As Bonnard pointed out, it would take a crazy person to do what was done to the body."

"Bonnard? Why were you talking with him?"

Jesus, Elena thought, *I should have kept my mouth shut about Karl.* "I met him during the investigation. Nice guy."

"Oh yes, he's a wonderful person," said Sarah bitterly. "While I was in jail, he was telling the dean that he should be appointed chairman in my place."

"Listen, I'm sure you've got that wrong, Sarah. I know he could end up with the job, but I don't think he wants it."

"He wanted it three years ago when I got it, and he's asked for it again. Actually—" Sarah paused. "I'd never realized it before, but I don't think Karl likes women."

"But he said flat out the first time I met him that you couldn't have killed Gus."

"He did?"

"Well, who can figure men?" said Elena. "They can be sweet as pie personally and complete bastards on the job. Anyway, thanks for the information about the computer."

"You're welcome. My lawyer will probably shoot me for calling."

"I don't see why. Anything that blows our case is good for you."

"Maybe." Sarah sounded doubtful. "Has it occurred to you that someone is going to a great deal of trouble to make it look like I killed Gus?"

There was a long silence; then Elena said, "Well, yes, now that you mention it. Can you think of anyone who has it in for both of you?"

"I don't think I have any enemies, but Gus must have had dozens." There was a pause. "Well, I'll hang up now."

"Wait, wait. What was the name of the engineer's society?"

"American Association of Engineers. Los Santos chapter. Jaime Esposito's the president. Do you want his number?"

"Sure."

Sarah gave it to her and hung up.

Elena finished getting ready for bed and turned out her light, thinking about Sarah and Karl. Sarah had sounded genuinely shocked to hear that Bonnard had stuck up for her on the matter of McGlenlevie's death. On the other hand, Elena had been shocked to hear that Bonnard was going after Sarah's job. She shouldn't have been. That's the way men operated. Frank had turned into a real bastard as soon as Elena caught up with him in rank, although he still claimed to love her. Go figure. Maybe she'd just expected too much of university professors, thought they were above professional back-stabbing. Bonnard obviously wasn't. In fact, he wasn't at all the loyal department member he'd made himself out to be. He had acted as if becoming chairman in Sarah's place would be a pain, not something he wanted. Why? She thought about it and decided that if he really liked her, he wouldn't want her to know he was a sneak. But did he like her?

Sarah said he disliked women. He'd certainly been nice to Elena—all those complimentary things he'd said about her becoming a detective, paving the way for other women.

But what had he said about other women? He couldn't stand his wife because she'd turned religious and embarrassed him in front of his colleagues. He'd been condescending about the Indian professor, said she wasn't the best, although she tried. And Sarah—what did he really think of her? That she was unqualified when appointed chair. Elena shook her head, hating to think that any man that handsome could be as underhanded as Frank. Frank had once blown a case of hers when she was new in C.A.P.—deliberately blown it, she'd always thought.

Then shrugging away the perplexing problem of men and their motivations, Elena turned the light back on and called Maggie Daguerre. Maggie might be able to give her some answers—not about Karl, but about that speech of Sarah's.

"Sarah said she was giving a talk to an engineering society

during the time that unslaked lime was being rerouted. Any way she could have done both?" Elena asked.

"Well—let's see." There was a silence, then: "There are a couple of possibilities. For instance, she could have excused herself to go to the john and logged into the university system on a pay phone. I could maybe trace that back, but the rerouting seemed to be done from a library terminal. I'd have to think about that. Also people would probably have noticed if she trotted off to the ladies' room in the middle of her speech. Another possibility—she fooled around with the date and time on the computer. Changed it for the entry, then changed it back. Again I may be able to trace it."

"I thought her access code was canceled."

"Yeah, but not when this happened."

"So you think what she told me may not be significant?"

"Oh, hell, I don't know, Elena. You really want her cleared, don't you?"

"Yes, I do. On the other hand, I don't want to be made a fool of."

"Tough spot to be in. I can search the computer files again."

"I'd appreciate it."

34
..

Friday, May 29, 10:15 P.M.

I hope I did the right thing, Sarah thought after her conversation with Elena. She went into the kitchen and poured herself a glass of wine, regretting the dinner she could have had with Colin Stuart. But if she'd done herself any good by getting in touch with Elena, it was worth it. Should she call her lawyer? Not tonight, she decided. She wanted to feel good about her action, or at least ambivalent, for a little while. And Bonnard sticking up for her with Elena. That was a surprise. But then he'd also offered to put up his house as bail collateral. As Elena so eloquently put it, "Go figure."

Sarah picked up the recent issue of a professional journal and began to read, forcing herself to concentrate. Colin had an article in it. Very good too. She'd probably never see him again after the weekend.

Or maybe she would. In a burst of defiant optimism, she called the dean to invite him and his wife to dinner, then called the Camino Real and left a message extending the invitation to Colin. Now where should she take them? She certainly wasn't going to cook. In fact, given the exploding snail incident, she doubted that any sensible person would want to risk having dinner at her table.

35
..

Monday, June 1, 10:40 A.M.

In low spirits Sarah drove back to the university after putting
Colin Stuart on a flight to Denver where he would change
planes and return to Seattle. Given her situation and the
possibility of Bonnard becoming chairman, she doubted that
Colin would accept the offer of a visiting professorship,
although the dean had liked him. She entered her office at the
university to find Bonnard seated with a pseudo-casual air on
the corner of Virginia's desk.

"My dear Sarah," he said, looking insufferably sympathetic,
"your legal troubles are obviously taking their toll. If there's
anything at all that I can do—"

A scowling Virginia shoved the corner of the Out box into
his haunch. As he shot off the desk with a surprised yelp, Sarah
murmured coolly, "I expect to be able to function as usual,
although, of course, I appreciate the offer, Karl." What a
hypocrite he was! They both were.

"You're very brave, but I'd have to point out," he replied,
hand hovering over the injured side of his buttock, "that it's
nearly eleven. You're always in your office earlier than this."

"I've been entertaining a potential member of the department," she retorted.

"Over breakfast? Over the whole weekend?"

Sarah experienced a flash of such anger that she could
almost imagine wanting to kill someone. "I picked Professor

Stuart up at the Camino Real, took him to breakfast, and put him on a plane. Are you suggesting that we spent the night together?" Her voice became colder and marginally louder. "Have you ever known me to indulge in such behavior? Or even heard rumors to that effect?"

Karl, looking mildly offended, protested, "You misunderstood me, Sarah."

"Did I misunderstand your visit to the dean, about which I heard in detail?"

"My offer was made out of consideration for you, Sarah, not any desire for your job," he said stiffly as she whirled into her office and slammed the door. However, she then felt horrified at her own loss of control and wondered if what he said could be true and she was suffering from paranoia. She'd better go to the library, she decided. A few quiet, undisturbed hours in a carrel, working on her latest article might rid her of the uncomfortable emotions spawned by the conversation with Bonnard. Sarah prized a calm and orderly life, which was one reason that she had divorced Gus, the late master of emotional and psychic disorder. She took out the wide-brimmed hat that she always wore around the campus as protection against the intense, high-altitude sunlight of Los Santos, placed it carefully on her head, tucked a notebook computer into her briefcase, and reentered Virginia's office.

"I'll be at the library for the next two hours," she said, her voice quiet and controlled once more.

"Right," said Virginia. "I won't tell Bonnard where you are."

"I don't need protection from my own faculty, Virginia."

"Everyone needs protection from the knife-in-the-back types," said Virginia.

Briefcase firmly clutched in her right hand, Sarah walked down the hall, a new light in her eyes, for a vengeful and absolutely sound idea had occurred to her. She might, as her trial approached, actually become unable to fulfill her duties as chair. She might even be convicted. Justice did misfire occasionally, she conceded gloomily, and she could hardly run the department then, but Colin could. He'd make an excellent chairman, temporary or permanent. Excellent. She'd suggest that to the dean, if it became necessary. If Karl really wasn't after her job, he wouldn't mind. If he was, he'd hate it. He'd seethe with anger and frustration, which was just what he deserved.

Sarah blinked, appalled at herself. She was turning into a person she hardly knew, much less liked. Vengefulness, paranoia—those were hardly qualities she admired. She'd have to weed them out. With that resolution foremost in her mind, she strode out of the building and made her way to the library, dodging busy sprinklers. Buildings and Grounds kept that St. Augustine grass, so foreign to west Texas soil, green and lush. Ridiculous. Desert landscaping would have been ecologically sound, but President Sunnydale insisted that they remain faithful to the vision of their benefactor, Herbert Hobart, late video-game king, who had left his entire fortune to found a university that looked like Miami Beach, yet faced, across the river, a Mexican city where he claimed to have enjoyed the best week of his life. Rumor indicated that part of that best week had been spent in a Mexican jail.

There was certainly no accounting for taste, thought Sarah, but then no one had ever said the late Herbert Hobart wasn't a full-blown eccentric, perhaps even certifiably insane. Any man who wanted to be remembered as having endowed a university whose avowed mission was the education of the very wealthy and only marginally intellectual was, at best, strange. While lost in these thoughts, she turned up the steps that led to the neo-Egyptian library, avoiding the braided-asp handrail and a cluster of students conducting a caviar-tossing contest, which involved pitching the oily roe into each others' mouths. Sarah shuddered and increased her pace. Fortunately, she thought, brushing an errant fish egg from the lapel of her suit, one could count on finding few students inside the library. When she glanced up to favor the young contestants with a scowl, an apparition appeared before her, a bearded apparition carrying a backpack. Sarah pulled up in mid-stride, her legs beginning to tremble, her heart pounding.

"Morning, Sarah," said the apparition.

Sarah Tolland, for the first time in her life, fainted.

•   •   •

She came to with the confused impression that she was being kidnapped—tied to a cot and loaded into a van while onlookers gawked but failed to come to her rescue as the doors to freedom slammed shut. Sirens whooped into an unbearable clamor, increasing exponentially the dull pain in her head, the vehicle lurched forward, and a sinister person who looked like Geronimo clad in white began to fiddle with bottles and needles, further adding to Sarah's alarm.

"Do you have any sort of heart problem, ma'am?" he asked in prosaic tones, relieving her mind somewhat, for she now realized that she was in an ambulance, not a kidnapper's getaway vehicle.

"I have a ghost problem," said Sarah, her voice faltering as she remembered the cause of her fainting spell. She watched the medic exchange raised-eyebrow glances with another attendant, and then they mumbled between themselves about the administration of a sedative.

"I do not need to be medicated," she said. "I need to talk to the police."

"The police? Were you attacked, ma'am?"

"Only psychologically. I need to speak to Elena Jarvis. She's a detective in the Crimes Against Persons Division. If she's not on shift at present, her home number is—are you taking this down, young man?"

"No, ma'am. Maybe you could tell it to someone when you get to the hospital."

Sarah knew an uncooperative person when she saw one, and subsided, protesting only when they wanted to stick a needle in her arm. "Get away from me," she snapped.

"We'll have to tell your family that you refused treatment," Geronimo warned.

"I have no family in Los Santos, and I don't need treatment. I need to talk to Elena Jarvis." She was whisked from the ambulance into the public hospital, complaining that, as she had insurance, she should have been taken to a private hospital—not that she needed treatment, just an aspirin and access to a telephone. No one paid the slightest attention to anything she said except the part about having insurance.

"Herbert Hobart insurance," she replied in answer to suspicious prodding. Evidently this hospital saw few patients who even claimed to have insurance. "National American Health Association. Where's my telephone?"

It was an hour and a half before they finished administering tests she tried to refuse. Then they installed her in a hospital room for observation. Only when she threatened to sue did they remove the restraints and provide her with a telephone. She immediately called Elena.

"She's out in the field, ma'am," said the receptionist in Crimes Against Persons.

"Well, I'm sure you can get her on a radio. This is an emergency. I'm Sarah Tolland, indicted for the murder of Angus McGlenlevie, and I'm in Thomason General. Have her call me immediately. Tell her—no, don't tell her anything. I want to talk to her myself."

Sarah lay in bed for another forty-five minutes, fuming, refusing sedatives, explaining that if her blood pressure was high, pure, unadulterated fury had caused the elevation.

"Sarah, what's wrong?" asked Elena when she finally called. "Were you in an accident?"

"Gus is alive."

"Now, Sarah—"

"I saw him in front of the library. And don't treat me like one of the criminally insane. His beard was about three inches longer, he was dressed more or less in rags—but that's nothing new—wearing a backpack, looking as if he hadn't bathed in several weeks, but it was Gus."

"Did he speak to you?" asked Elena cautiously.

"I don't know. I fainted when I saw him and evidently hit my head as a result of the fall. When I came to, I'd been put in an ambulance, and he was gone, so I don't know what happened to him after that, but I want you to come down here and get me out. Then we'll look for him together."

"Now, Sarah—"

"Elena, I'm accused of killing a man who's alive, and I shall file suit against the police department unless you get yourself down here within fifteen minutes."

"All right, all right, I'm coming," said Elena, and she arrived in ten minutes, just as a frantic Sarah managed to get rid of a nurse who insisted on taking her vital signs for the fourth time. They wouldn't give her an aspirin for her headache, and they wouldn't leave so she could get her clothes on. They seemed to think that shining lights in her eyes and taking her blood pressure every ten minutes constituted acceptable medical attention.

"We had an assault," Elena explained. "Some vagrant attacked a little girl in a park."

"Don't tell me about it," said Sarah, who climbed out of bed and peered into the hall to be sure no more nurses were about to invade her room. Then she dragged her clothes from the closet. Her head ached abominably, but she was determined to find Gus before he could disappear again.

"Don't you have to be released or something?" Elena asked doubtfully.

Usually a modest person, Sarah ripped off the hospital gown in front of Elena and began to climb into her underwear, then her light summer business suit. She stuffed her pantyhose into her handbag, slipped her bare feet into her heels, something she would never do under ordinary circumstances, and said, "Let's go."

Elena was three steps behind her and trying to catch up all the way down the hall. They picked up two nurses at the nursing station who sped after them crying, "You can't leave the hospital, ma'am."

"I'm accompanied by a police officer," said Sarah, gesturing toward Elena. "This is Detective Jarvis. She arrested me." Sarah didn't bother to add that the arrest had been five days ago. The nurses, round-eyed, stepped back. "We'll try his office and his apartment," said Sarah as they whisked into an elevator. "That irresponsible, unprincipled psychopath, he probably set this whole thing up. I don't know who the corpse was, but maybe Gus killed him."

"Well, if he did, why would he come back?"

"Why would *I* come back if I killed Gus?"

"Just calm down, Sarah." Elena patted her arm tentatively. "What did the doctors say about your injuries?"

"Everyone knows doctors are idiots."

Ordinarily Elena would have agreed.

"Do you have a car? Mine's still at the university."

"Yes, sure, but I had to leave Leo behind at the park. Now we're both without backup. I have to go—"

"Will you stop worrying about regulations? Just consider me your backup."

"For God's sake, Sarah, you're accused of murder, and you're a civilian. My considering you backup is even crazier than your thinking you saw Gus."

"Oh, shut up, Elena. Where's the car?"

By then they had moved from the cool hospital into the bright, hot sunshine. "It's over here in the emergency parking area," Elena mumbled. They climbed into an unmarked police car, headed toward the university, and stopped at the English Department, where Sarah demanded, "Has Gus been in?"

The secretary turned dead-white and rolled his secretarial chair backward until it collided with a file cabinet. "He's dead," said Lance Potemkin. "But you know that. You killed him."

"I did not. We'll try his apartment."

Elena trailed her out of the Humanities building, wondering how Sarah could walk so fast in those heels. The woman must be going three or four miles an hour. She'd have blisters on her feet before they could cut across campus. Elena caught up, grabbed Sarah's arm, and said, "We'll drive."

By a circuitous route among the palm trees, they reached the apartment building. "Take my space," said Sarah. "You won't get a ticket." However, Elena later discovered that she had been given a ticket—for parking in a reserved spot without the requisite sticker. That's what the ticket said. Violation number five, "Parking in a reserved space without the requisite sticker."

"He's on the fourth floor."

"I know that," said Elena. "I was the one who investigated the death."

They took the red elevator and sprinted toward Gus's door. Sarah pressed her finger firmly on his bell while she pounded on the door with the other hand.

"There's no one home," said Elena after a few minutes. She tried to move Sarah away, but Sarah wouldn't be budged.

"This is my life, my career, my freedom. We're damn well

going to stand here until he opens the door." Several minutes later he did.

"There," said Sarah. "Is that Gus McGlenlevie or isn't it?"

"Hey, babe," said Gus. "Sorry I couldn't go to the hospital with you. I realize I have a big effect on women, but you're the first one who fainted, at least when she wasn't in the throes of—"

"Oh, shut up," said Sarah.

Elena was staring at him nonplussed. "Where the hell have you been, McGlenlevie?"

Gus beamed. "I've been white-water rafting. Come in, come in. I've been getting in touch with my male persona. A man needs respite from the company of women."

"Oh yes? Who was putting pressure on you this time?" asked his ex-wife cynically.

"Well," he admitted, looking ingenuous, "Bimmie was pushing for a wedding date, but that's not the important thing. I've found the excitement, the primal energy, in male bonding— risking our lives, pitting ourselves against nature, men in the wilderness. That's what I'll call my next collection. *Men in the Wilderness.* You want to hear one of the poems I've written?"

"No!" they both said simultaneously.

Gus looked hurt.

"So when did you leave town?" asked Elena.

"Well—ah—May—I don't know. It was the Wednesday after my last final."

"He left before I did!" said Sarah, glaring at Elena.

"He did," Elena agreed. "Did you leave your keys with anyone, Mr. McGlenlevie?"

"Sure. I lent the apartment to Howard Margreaves. I'll never do that again. Look at the place. Its covered with dust, the bathtub's a God awful mess, and he's disappeared."

The two women exchanged glances. "The dust is fingerprint powder," said Elena, "and very likely he's the corpse we found in your tub. What did you say his name was?"

"Margreaves." Gus looked amazed. "I realized Howard was a little depressive, but I wouldn't have figured him for a suicide."

"And you'd be right. It's not likely that he crushed his own skull and then dissolved his own body. He'd need some help for that."

Gus's eyes lit up. "Maybe you should tell me what happened—in detail. Every sight, smell, touch. I feel my male muse kicking in."

"Oh, shut up," said Sarah. "Are you going to cancel my arrest?" she demanded of Elena. "I've never even heard of Howard whatever his name is." Her spirits soared. She'd have to call Colin with the good news—and the dean—and her lawyer. Maybe she'd celebrate—treat herself to a sinfully expensive new suit, give Karl Bonnard a terrible faculty rating so he wouldn't get a raise—no, that would be mean-spirited. He had, after all, told Elena that Sarah couldn't possibly have killed Gus, and he was right. No one had. Instead she'd celebrate by getting new stereo equipment for her car or giving a party—no, that was going too far. The last time she gave a party someone spilled red wine on her carpet. In fact, it had been Gus. "You psychopath," she said, scowling at him.

Elena was marveling because ladylike Sarah Tolland had said "shut up" three times in the last half hour—once to Elena, twice to Gus. For Sarah that was probably a record.

36
..

They were back in the interrogation room, Lieutenant Beltran behind the glass, chagrined that the woman they had arrested was now an unlikely suspect, Elena and Leo sitting on brown vinyl chairs, and the target of their questioning Gus McGlenlevie, who occupied the blue polka-dot sofa with his feet on the coffee table.

"Sarah probably did it," said Gus.

"Oh, right," Elena agreed. "She knocks on the door; this stranger opens it—or do you claim she knew this postdoctoral fellow in poetry?"

"She could have. Obviously Sarah had a thing for poets. She married me, didn't she?"

Elena thought, *Any woman can make a mistake.* But she didn't say it, since she wanted McGlenlevie's cooperation. "So the idea is, she knocks at your door, this stranger answers, she thinks, 'Oh, what the heck. Since Gus isn't here, I'll do this guy,' knocks him on the head, drags the body into the tub, and spends a couple of days in your bathroom soaking him in unslaked lime, all this while she's out of town."

McGlenlevie shrugged. "If you wanted to, you could figure out how she did it. And if you'd arrested her before, when she tried to blow my head off with that snail, this wouldn't have happened."

"Mr. McGlenlevie, let me put it to you this way," said Elena,

193

who was taking the lead in the interrogation. "Someone killed a man in your apartment, a man who was about your height. I assume he was quite a bit younger than you, but—"

"Not that much," said Gus. "I'm a man in my prime, a man in touch with his male muse."

"Right," Elena agreed before Leo could intervene with a sarcastic remark. "Anyway, what I want to get across to you is that there's a murderer out there, but Leo and I don't think it's your ex-wife, and if that murderer was after you, instead of your student, you could still be in danger."

Gus went white under his male-bonding tan. "I demand police protection."

"We'll get to that later. Right now we want to figure out who to look for. Who might have had it in for you."

"Why would anyone?" asked Gus. "I have friends everywhere."

"Many of them females," Elena suggested.

"I'm attractive to women." He gave her a seductive glance.

She tried to look at least tolerant. If you liked big beards and bright blue eyes, he was O.K. in the looks department, but she wouldn't have him if he came complete with a Mercedes and a designer wardrobe in her size. "Exactly," said Elena. "Which means that there are men out there who may have grudges against you."

"Oh, well, I—" Gus looked taken aback. "I've just spent two weeks in exclusively male company. We got along famously."

"You weren't boinking their ladies," said Leo.

"The act of love," said Gus stiffly, "is a poetic experience. A gift. *Boink* is hardly the—"

"I apologize for Detective Weizell. He's not a man with much poetic soul." Elena shot a warning glance at Leo. "And so although your lady friends may be quite happy with you, their gentlemen friends, present or past, could be jealous, even enraged. You see my point?"

"Love and greed," said Leo, "the two big motives for murder."

"About that police protection—"

"In a minute, Mr. McGlenlevie. We need some specific information about the women you've had relationships with during, say, the last year."

"The last *year*?"

His dismay at the prospect of remembering a year's worth of lovers made Elena wonder how many women would be on that list. How many hours would checking McGlenlevie's little black book entail? And would they be able to close the case before the person who killed Howard Margreaves corrected his mistake? Or was Margreaves the intended victim?

"I'm not one to kiss and tell," said Gus, who didn't look absolutely convinced of that precept.

"Let me help you along," said Elena. "There was the captain of the volleyball team, Lili Bonaventura."

"A charming girl," said Gus.

"With Mafia connections."

"What?"

"Her father's Fat Joe Bonaventura, a Mafia don in Miami."

"My lord, you think there's a Mafia contract out on me?"

"Well, that's a possibility. Old-fashioned father, violent colleagues."

His tan disappeared entirely.

"But we've got no evidence against the Bonaventuras," said Leo.

Elena, thinking of her vandalized living room, wondered if Fernie Duran had come up with anything about the Bonaventuras. She'd have to call him.

"It's just one possibility," Leo pointed out. "If we concentrate all our efforts there, someone else could get to you. So we need a list, see. Your best protection is for us to catch the killer."

"Why, for instance, did you leave town without telling anyone?" Elena asked.

"I told you. Bimmie."

"Betty Lou Kowolski, your fiancée?"

"Betty Lou! Can you believe I ever considered marrying a girl with a name like that? Bimmie decided it was time we set a date, and I, given my previous unfortunate experience in marriage to Sarah—well, I was having second thoughts about taking the plunge again."

"Do you think Bimmie would have tried to kill you?"

"She's strong enough. Wonderful muscles. In bed she's an Amazon."

Elena could see from the nostalgic gleam in his eyes that he was harking back to happier days with Bimmie.

"But Bimmie knew Howard. Why would she kill him?"

"The same argument could be used for Sarah," said Elena.

"You seem awfully defensive about Sarah," said Gus. "You're not bisexual, are you? Or lesbian? I remember how much more sympathetic you were to her than me. I'll bet you've fallen for Sarah." He was regarding Elena with malicious glee.

Elena, realizing that he was trying to get at her, replied, "You're saying you managed to turn Sarah, a heterosexual woman, into a lesbian?"

"People's sexual preferences are not at issue here," said Leo before the confrontation disintegrated into a brawl. He appeared to be on the verge of laughter.

"The answer is no, I don't think it was Bimmie," said Gus, evidently having thought better of needling Elena. "She wouldn't have killed the wrong person, and she wouldn't have had enough money to hire a hit man."

"Who else?"

"Well, I may have had fleeting relationships with some of the other volleyball players."

"Why was Margreaves wearing your volleyball ring?"

"He wasn't. He had his own," said Gus. "Howard was the assistant coach."

"Well, hell," muttered Elena. "No one told us that. We might have thought twice about identifying the corpse as you. Who else?"

McGlenlevie named several young poetesses.

"Isn't the university pissed about your getting it on with the students?" asked Leo.

Gus looked surprised. "It's not as if they're children. They're all women—young, but women. Except for Sarah, of course. Perhaps some of her charm for me," he mused, "was that she wasn't so young. She never giggled, for instance. I must visit her and apologize for—"

"I wouldn't," said Elena hastily. "Sarah's in a delicate emotional state. Being accused of your murder, when you were alive—"

"You mean you think she might kill me because—"

"No, of course not. I just think you might find her very— irritable. Besides, she's got a headache."

"Where have I heard that before?" muttered Gus.

"She's concussed, you—" Elena bit back an expletive and said, "Let's get back to a list of your women friends. And we'd like, along with them, a list of boyfriends, ex-boyfriends, husbands, ex-husbands."

"Oh, well, they're almost all single," said Gus. He named several other young women.

"And you have no idea about their previous emotional entanglements?" He didn't. Glancing at her notes, Elena pounced. "You said *almost* all single. Were you having relationships with any married women?"

"One," Gus admitted.

"And that was . . . ?"

"Mary Ellen Bonnard."

Elena swallowed. "What's her husband's name?"

"Ah—Karl. He's a member of Sarah's department."

Elena's mind went blank with shock. The silence stretched until Leo, glancing at her curiously, filled it. "Did Professor Bonnard know about the relationship?"

"Mary Ellen would never have told him."

"Did she ever talk to you about her relationship with her husband?" Elena prompted.

"God, yes," said Gus. "Endlessly. He was a perfectionist, criticized everything she did. His harassment—verbal, you understand—eventually drove her into the arms of one of those lunatic-fringe religious sects. Then the marriage deteriorated even further. Yet the poor woman, when I gave a talk to her book discussion group—they'd elected to read *Erotica In Reeboks,* my best-selling—"

"Yes, yes, we know about your book."

Gus's face lit up. "You've read my book? Wonderful, isn't it?"

Elena and Leo glanced at one another. Neither one of them had read the book.

"Well, we met over punch and cookies after my talk," Gus resumed. "She was a pleasant woman—lyrical breasts. Her breasts are a sonnet in themselves."

Leo and Elena scowled at him. He shifted uncomfortably in his seat. "At any rate, after the reception, she couldn't get her car started, so I offered her a ride, and one thing led to another."

"How long did the affair last?"

"Actually, we were still seeing one another when I left. Her husband was always out on Tuesdays. Some boring activity. Bowling. Who knows?"

Elena doubted that Karl Bonnard was a bowler, but the rest of it—about him driving his wife crazy with criticism—could that be true? Of course, it could; he'd said himself that Elena probably sympathized with his wife, which was just what she'd been doing, thinking no wonder the woman left him. By reading her thoughts, he'd disarmed her. And then he'd said something about the person you loved turning into an unpleasant stranger, and she, like a dummy, had thought, *Right on! That's what Frank did.* What Karl Bonnard had never said was that his wife had been having an affair with McGlenlevie.

What have I been doing? she asked herself. *Getting mixed up with two suspects in this case. Sarah, then Karl.* And she had another date with Karl tomorrow night. Well, she'd damn well keep it. She'd save questioning Bonnard for a time when he was off guard.

No, wait a minute. Would Bonnard have killed the wrong man? She searched her memory and remembered Bonnard saying, "I've never actually met McGlenlevie." So he might have.

Was he the jealous sort? Any man would be if he knew his wife was unfaithful. But Bonnard didn't know. At least, Gus didn't think so. Surely Elena would have sensed it if Bonnard were the killer. She'd been dating the man, for God's sake! She took a deep breath. She'd screwed up again, got mixed up a second time with a suspect, but not with a killer. She was pretty sure of that. And she'd turn the connection with Bonnard to her advantage. If he had killed Margreaves, which she doubted, she'd sure as hell find out tomorrow night.

"Well, if that's it on the girlfriends," Leo was saying, "maybe you can tell us something about Margreaves. Do you know anyone who would have wanted to kill him?"

"I wish I did," said Gus fervently. "Unfortunately, he seemed to be a dull fellow. Although he admired the example I set with women—what man wouldn't?—he never followed it."

"Why would he want to?" Elena demanded. "You act like you've never heard of safe sex."

"I like spontaneity," said Gus.

"Spontaneity is another word for AIDS," muttered Leo.

"Well, there's nothing like a bit of danger to—"

"You were telling us about Margreaves," Elena snapped. Frank had said something like that to her once, trying to talk her out of insisting that he be tested. Frank had loved danger; he was happiest living on the edge, undercover and hanging out with a bunch of low-life drug runners who'd kill him in a minute if they found out who he was. It turned him on. If he came home with bullet holes in his clothes, the first thing he wanted from her was sex. Elena sighed. She could cope with danger; it was part of her job, but she certainly didn't court it.

"I think Howard had a fiancée back in—New Jersey or somewhere," said McGlenlevie.

"Why didn't we find any of his stuff in your apartment?" Leo asked.

"Well, poor Howard. The university was very stingy about providing funds for him. He had a lease on some hovel in an unacceptable part of town, and he had very few possessions. I suppose he might have left them there. Howard was pathetically grateful when I asked if he'd like to occupy my apartment while I was out of town."

"What about his personal life?"

"Who knows? His poetry was admirable, fascinating Freudian imagery. His childhood must have been unusual. And of course, he was a good-looking fellow. As you say, he looked a bit like me." Both officers scowled at McGlenlevie, who hastened to add, "I must have a home address for him somewhere. He'd have had university benefits, so Personnel would have information on him."

"Would you know anything about his teeth, Mr. McGlenlevie?" asked Leo.

"His teeth?" Gus looked astonished. "He had some. Why would I—"

"How about the name of his dentist?"

"I don't know *any* dentists—much less his. Why do you care about his teeth?"

"That's what we've got left. Teeth and bones. Did he have a bone disease?"

Gus shrugged, obviously at a loss. Elena remembered Sarah insisting that Gus had perfect teeth. Jesus, they should have listened.

"We can identify remains from dental charts," said Leo impatiently. "But not with your help, I guess. Elena, anything else you want to ask?"

Elena realized that she'd said very little once she learned that McGlenlevie had been involved with Karl Bonnard's wife. What had Bonnard said about his wife? That she was out of town on a religious retreat. Elena had a really frightening thought that involved how much unslaked lime had been taken out of the E.E. storeroom—three boxes—and a recollection that the delivery man seen Sunday night had two on his dolly, which left one unaccounted for. Had Bonnard killed his wife and then used the last box of unslaked lime to—well, one box wouldn't do it, but he might have buried her in the back yard and then thrown the last box in on top of her to hurry decomposition. Or he might have used one box the night he killed Margreaves and then returned with two to hasten the dissolution of the body.

No, it was unlikely, very unlikely, that Karl had killed the poet at all. There was no more reason to suspect him than the Bonaventuras, except that someone had tinkered with the university computers to make Sarah look guilty. But of course, if you wanted to kill McGlenlevie and pin it on someone else, Sarah was the obvious candidate. Could the Bonaventuras have got into the computer? Well, why not? Maggie Daguerre said anyone could. No doubt the mob was as high tech as any other corporate group these days. On the other hand, Karl was right there at the university, in a department that dealt with computers. Except that he didn't know Gus—Oh hell!

"Mr. McGlenlevie, I guess that's it," said Leo. "But please don't leave town without—"

"Forget it," cried Gus. "Someone in Los Santos wants to kill me. I'm heading back to the wilderness."

"You're an important witness. You can't leave."

"I'm an important *poet*. Do you want to be responsible for the untimely demise of a possible Nobel prize winner?"

Leo and Elena exchanged glances. The budget year ended in August; the overtime money was gone, and they were operating on a special appropriation from the city council. Fat chance they'd get Beltran or Captain Stollinger to offer protection for Angus McGlenlevie, poet in peril. "Why don't you get a friend to move in with you? Murderers don't like witnesses."

Angus looked distressed. "Well, there's Sarah, but she might not agree."

"You're right about that," said Elena dryly.

"There's always Bimmie, I guess." He couldn't have sounded less enthusiastic.

Elena almost laughed aloud. "You can set the date for your wedding, and she'll move in."

"I could at least offer to talk about a date," he muttered.

"When she's at work," warned Leo, "stick around the university where there are lots of people."

"This is going to ruin my love life," said Gus mournfully. They had all risen, making ready to leave the interrogation room. "Unless I can invite women in—but that's it! Instead of knuckling under to Bimmie, all I have to do is invite a different girl each—"

Before Gus could finish, Beltran barreled into the room. "Hold it."

Gus looked alarmed at the sight of the stocky, grizzle-haired police lieutenant.

"What's the matter with you people?" he said to Leo and

Elena. "There was no forced entry at that apartment. We need to know who had keys."

Elena's heart sank. If Sarah had had a key to the apartment, it was marginally possible that she used it and killed Margreaves by mistake while his back was turned. "So who had keys?" she asked Gus with a belligerence that made him back up a step.

"Ah—I did. Margreaves, of course. And—Bimmie had a key. That's it."

"The hell it is. Lili Bonaventura had a key."

"Oh yes, Lili, right. Lili had a key."

"And Mary Ellen Bonnard?"

"Right. I forgot Mary Ellen."

"Any of those other coeds?" asked Leo.

"No, none of the others."

"Any previous lady friends who had them and forgot to give them back or who could have had copies made?"

Gus shook his head slowly but looked alarmed.

"Think about it. Once it gets into the paper that you're not dead, someone with a key could try again."

"I'll have the lock changed," said Gus.

"That won't tell us who got into your apartment and murdered Margreaves. What about Sarah Tolland?" asked Beltran.

"Sarah?"

"Well, you said she might have committed the murder—even though it was Margreaves who died. Did Sarah Tolland have a key?"

Still harping on Sarah, Elena thought. *He can't stand to be wrong.*

"No," said McGlenlevie.

"Oh, come on now, Mr. McGlenlevie. You were friendly enough to go to your ex-wife's house for dinner after the divorce."

"He invited himself," said Elena. "Isn't that right, Gus?"

"You didn't give Sarah Tolland a key?"

"No."

"Is there any way she could have got one?"

"Look, we lived at her place while we were married. I only

got my own apartment after the divorce. Sarah was so mad at me, she wouldn't have wanted a key." McGlenlevie scratched his beard. "I guess I owe her an apology. Oh, shit. After being arrested, she's not going to take it very graciously, but I see what you're getting at. She wouldn't have snuck up behind Margreaves unless she thought it was me, and if he answered the door, he'd have been facing her. Oh boy. Do I get police protection or not? Even if Sarah didn't try to kill me, she may want to now. I mean that's a stiff-necked woman. She was never willing to cut me even a little slack. Couple of little slips—girlwise—and . . ."

Elena couldn't believe he referred to his extramarital activities as a couple of little slips. According to Sarah, his girls were bombarding the apartment with calls. He was hopping in and out of beds all over campus, and he wanted Sarah to cut him a *little* slack?

"Have someone stay with you," advised Leo again, "and change your lock."

Beltran agreed, glaring at McGlenlevie. Elena put her hand over her mouth to hide a smile. Beltran was a family man. He didn't approve of promiscuity in either sex.

"But who will I ask? What if Bimmie's the one who tried to kill me?"

"You just told us she wouldn't do it."

"Mr. McGlenlevie," said Beltran, "if no one knows that you're back in town; in fact, if no one knows that you're alive, there won't be another attempt on your life."

"Right," said Angus. "I'll hide out in my apartment until you've caught the criminal."

"Sounds like the safe thing to me."

McGlenlevie's face lit up. "I can order out for Chinese and finish my book—*Rapture on the Rapids*."

"That's what you now want to call your male-bonding book?" asked Elena, deciding to see how the great woman chaser would take a counter-suggestion of homosexuality. "Watch what you write," she cautioned. "You know those critics. They see all kinds of things that aren't there. They might figure you're gay."

Gus looked alarmed. "You're right. My God, you're right."

Elena hoped she'd just given his male muse a swift kick in the balls.

As the door closed behind Gus, Leo began to laugh. "You devil," he murmured.

"What did I do?" she asked innocently, then sobering, turned to Beltran. "We're going to have to drop the charge against Sarah Tolland."

"Give it a few days," he said. "If we drop it, we have to reveal that McGlenlevie is back."

"Listen, she's got a real shark for a lawyer. We'll be hit with a suit we don't even want to think about if we leave her hanging in the wind a day longer than we have to." She knew she was pushing her luck with Beltran, pointing out that he had been wrong. "If we're going to keep the identity of the victim quiet, we need to let her know she's off the hook and ask for her cooperation."

"She might still be guilty," said Beltran.

"Hard to see how," said Elena.

"Two days won't make any difference. She doesn't have to know—"

"She's the one who saw Gus. She called me from the hospital." The two men seemed to have forgotten that.

"God," Leo muttered. "We're back to square one on this thing, and half the suspects have left town. Lili Bonaventura, for instance—she's long gone, and probably all those other girls he was getting it on with. But maybe not the Bonnard woman."

"She's at a religious retreat," said Elena, thinking that if Karl were the murderer, which she could hardly believe—well, hell! Maybe she owed Mrs. Bonnard a call and warning that an attempt might have been made on Gus McGlenlevie's life. Still, Bonnard had showed no signs of jealousy. And Gus didn't seem to think the man knew about the affair. Elena wondered if she could have been that stupid about Bonnard.

"I guess we start all over tomorrow," said Leo, "but, by God, I'm going home to bed. I'm tired. I'm tired of this case. I'm tired of that dumbass McGlenlevie. I'm just plain tired."

Elena wanted to get home too, but the thought of home reminded her that as soon as Sarah was publicly cleared, Lili

Bonaventura became a suspect again. And the Bonaventuras— She sighed, wondering which room they'd trash next. Assuming they were the ones who had broken in the last time. *I should have been a schoolteacher or a rock star,* she thought irritably. *Either one would have pleased Mother.*

37
..

Sarah Tolland was angry. All day she'd waited to receive
word that the charge against her had been dropped. She'd
called her lawyer three times, and he'd said, "The legal system
moves slowly, Sarah," or something equally frustrating. It
seemed to Sarah that, as her lawyer, he should have been giving
the legal system a nudge.

And even if the courts were slow, Elena could have called to
apologize. The police hadn't identified the body correctly,
much less the murderer. Surely they didn't think she'd kill
some stranger just because he was in Gus's apartment. She
considered calling the police to point out to them the illogic of
their position, but didn't; her lawyer wouldn't approve of such
an expedient.

Instead she called both newspapers and three TV news
departments to inform them that Gus was alive. That ought to
get some action out of the authorities, she had thought smugly
as she enjoyed a container of yogurt at her desk. Herbert
Hobart was, as far as she knew, the only university that had
yogurt machines in all the buildings—Greta Marx's innova-
tion. The doctor had confided to Sarah at one of the president's
cocktail and prayer fests that the consumption of yogurt would
combat vaginal yeast infections among the female student
population and thus save her, Dr. Marx, numerous time-
wasting consultations that distracted her from her more impor-

tant mission, the promulgation of safe sexual practices. Sarah hated to get cornered by Greta Marx. The woman always had something embarrassing to say, especially when she was drunk.

At six o'clock Sarah had rushed home to turn on the local news in the hope of hearing that the accusation against her had been withdrawn. Instead she heard that Howard Margreaves was now thought to be the acid bath victim instead of Angus McGlenlevie. Who *was* Howard Margreaves? And why had he been in Gus's apartment? Nothing was said about her. Evidently she still stood accused.

She snapped off the news and went into the kitchen to see what frozen delight she could dig out of her freezer. Sarah ate regularly, cooked seldom, and took no interest in food unless it was served to her in a good restaurant, where she could enjoy a meal without preparing it or cleaning up afterward.

Chicken and herb sauce. That ought to do. She took the little tray out of its box, locked it in the microwave, and set the controls. Just as the timer dinged, her doorbell rang. Impatiently she removed her TV dinner from the oven and returned to the living room to peer through the peephole, where she spotted, of all people, her ex-husband. "Go away." she ordered.

"Come on, Sarah," said Gus. "I'm here to apologize. O.K.? I'm taking my life in my hands even being outside my apartment, so open the door, will you, before someone kills me in your hallway?"

Sarah debated briefly, then unlocked the dead bolt and took the chain off. "I really don't want to see you, Gus. I'd be perfectly happy if I never had to see you again," she said, closing the door behind him and relocking it.

"Why are you doing that?" asked Gus.

"Doing what?"

"Locking me in here."

"You idiot. Do you still think I tried to kill you?"

"Well, there was the snail," said Gus defensively.

"Gus, if I wanted to kill you with a snail or any other way, believe me, I could figure out how to do it, and I wouldn't be satisfied with any substitute victim that I'd never seen before, much less heard of."

"Well, I guess I do believe you, Sarah, and I am sorry they arrested you. I know you wouldn't kill Howard."

"Who *was* Howard?"

"My postdoctoral fellow."

"*You* have a postdoctoral fellow? What does he do? Experimental poetry?"

"No, actually, Howard rather liked the traditional forms. He—"

"It was a joke, Gus."

"Making jokes is unlike you, Sarah. You're not going to become hysterical, are you?"

Sarah gave him a long cold look and said, "Before you leave my apartment, Gus, maybe you'd be so good as to explain why you left town without telling anyone where you were going. You didn't tell the apartment superintendent; you didn't tell Mr. Potemkin or your chairman; you—"

"Say, you needn't act so high and mighty. It could have been a professor in E.E. that tried to kill me."

"What?"

"Bonnard."

"Why would Bonnard want to kill you? I don't think you've ever met the man."

"Exactly," said Gus. "I never have. Otherwise, he'd have known who he was hitting on the head when he killed Howard."

"All right, but why would he want to kill you?" She stared at Gus. "My lord, you seduced Mary Ellen. Is that what you're saying?"

"Well, I'd hardly call it seduction," said Gus. "She needed kindness—a sensitive lover."

"And she picked *you*? I realized she must be having psychological problems when she joined that strange religious sect, but—"

"Actually, it's quite an interesting group," said Gus. "Overly strict in some matters."

"Like sex," Sarah suggested.

"Yes, but very interesting. They believe in psychic powers, faith healing. I've never—"

"Are you saying you seduced Mary Ellen as a sort of

research project?" Sarah interrupted. "Are you going to write a new poetry collection called *Sex Among the Fundamentalists*?"

"Probably not," said Gus. "I'm currently interested in male bonding, the male wilderness muse."

"Oh, spare me," said Sarah. "I can't think of a single man who would want to spend more than ten minutes with you."

"Well, you're wrong. I've just returned from a white-water rafting trip. All male. We spent ten days together, communing with nature, pitting ourselves against—"

"I don't want to hear about it, Gus. It doesn't interest me any more than *Erotica in Reeboks* did. However, I will suggest to you that if you're experimenting with homosexuality and you write a book about it, Harley Stanley is going to see that you're denied tenure. Oh, he wouldn't admit that it's because you're gay—"

"I'm not gay. How could you even think that?"

"Why wouldn't I think it? Maybe you've run out of girl students, so you plan to try boys."

"Well, Sarah, except for that obnoxious policewoman, nobody has ever suggested that I might be bisexual, much less homosexual. You of all people—"

"—know that you're promiscuous—blatantly, multitudinously promiscuous."

"I don't know why I bothered to come up here to apologize to you. Here I thought we had an amicable relationship."

"After being arrested and spending a night in jail—"

"I'd love to hear about the jail part."

"I'm sure you would. Now, go away, Gus. And don't come back."

"All right, but would you mind calling me in about three minutes to see that I got back safely."

"Yes, I would mind. There's the telephone. If you want someone to check on you, call your fiancée in the designer jogging suit."

"I do believe you're jealous, Sarah."

"And I do believe that you're a fool. Now do you want to use my telephone or not?"

"Oh, forget it." Gus stamped to the door. "How do I get out of here?"

"Take off the chain. Unlock the dead bolt. If you don't have the same safeguards on your door, you ought to. Especially if someone wants to kill you."

"You're right," said Gus, looking alarmed. "If Bonnard or the Mafia—"

"The Mafia?"

"It turns out that one of my friends is the daughter of a Mafia don."

Sarah started to laugh.

"It's not funny. There might be a contract out on me."

"You're right," she gasped, still laughing, "in which case, if someone comes around with a submachine gun, I'd just as soon they didn't spray my apartment with hundreds of bullets."

"Well, look, since you know about these dead bolts and things, could you call someone to—"

"No, I couldn't, Gus. We're divorced. You're on your own. Good-bye."

She brushed past him, turned the dead bolt key, unchained the door, and swung it open. "Good-bye."

"Check the hall first."

"Check the hall yourself. As I said, I don't want to be killed by someone who's already made one mistake."

Gus edged cautiously out of her living room and then sprinted for the elevator. Sarah slammed the door behind him and locked up. Angus McGlenlevie had more gall than any three obnoxious men she knew. She went into her kitchen to retrieve the rapidly cooling TV dinner. *Oh well,* she thought, *it's not going to taste much worse cold than it would have warm.* She poured herself a glass of white wine, put a rough-weave place mat and a napkin on her teak table, dumped the chicken onto a plate, carried it with silverware to the dining room, and sat down to eat while she considered the possibility that Karl Bonnard might have attempted to kill Gus in a fit of jealousy.

Suddenly she remembered what she had forgotten in the shock of discovering that her ex-husband was still alive. She had been arrested, not just because they thought she had a motive, but because there was evidence pointing to her—the initial appearance that she had left town after deleting her forwarding address from the computer, the unslaked lime rerouted from Buildings and Grounds and sent to her. Those things didn't just happen on their own. Someone had to tamper with the computer. Someone who understood computers. Someone who hated her. Not just Gus or Margreaves—but her!

Sarah laid down her fork because her hands were trembling. Bonnard! Who wanted to be chairman. Who at university functions treated his wife with a rather ugly disdain. Who, when Mary Ellen joined that sect, talked about it to everyone, as if his wife had entirely lost her mind. Yet even considering that strange passage in her life, Mary Ellen Bonnard had not seemed insane. If anything, her religious foray seemed to have tipped Karl toward neurotic behavior.

Furious, Sarah took a bite of her lukewarm chicken in herb sauce and a sip of wine—contrary to her mother's fixed principles, that anger was unbecoming in a lady, and eating while angry caused gastric disorders, not to mention lines in the face. In defiance, Sarah took another bite. And two large gulps of wine. Bonnard could have done it. Killed Gus—or tried to. Framed her. Rushed off to offer himself to the dean as the obvious person to take over her job. Of all the vicious, unprincipled, underhanded . . .

Sarah looked down at her plate in surprise. She had bolted the whole unappetizing puddle of herbed chicken and drunk all the wine. Just as her mother had warned, she felt the onset of an unladylike gastric upset. Another of her mother's precepts was that respectable people did not approve of or give in to violent impulses. Such doings were entirely the province of the lower classes. Sarah's mother was a terrible snob. But was she right? Now that Sarah had calmed down somewhat, her anger quenched by stomach acid, the idea that one of her faculty members could have killed his wife's lover and framed his chairman seemed bizarre. She'd never really liked Karl Bonnard much, and he had certainly proved himself to be no friend of hers, but that didn't make him a murderer. Just an opportunist.

Then she remembered that Bonnard had called the department that morning, having already missed one appointment, and informed Virginia that he'd have to be out of town for a few days. Had he heard that Gus, his intended victim, was still alive? If Sarah had seen her ex-husband on campus, others must have. Maybe Bonnard had left town in a panic. And where was Mary Ellen? Still at that religious retreat? Bonnard might be following her there with the idea of killing her so that she couldn't reveal her liaison with Gus and thus Bonnard's motive for murder. Sarah couldn't believe she was having such thoughts. If Gus hadn't mentioned the affair, she'd have thought that anyone accusing her colleague of murder was crazy.

As she rose to carry her plate, goblet, and silverware into the kitchen, another thought bobbed up. Maybe Gus had lied about the Bonnards. Maybe he'd killed Margreaves himself. And what were the police doing? Who did they think had killed the poet? Surely not her? Still? But if they suspected Gus, why were they letting him run around free? And if they suspected Bonnard, why weren't they protecting Gus—and Mary Ellen?

Sarah decided to call the Bonnard house to see if anyone answered. She got the answering machine, with a message that no one was available to take the call. She tried three times during the evening, the last at 11:30. Still no one answered, and she couldn't be sure what it meant.

The last time Sarah had seen Mary Ellen, she'd said that she planned to spend several weeks at a religious retreat in Cloudcroft, New Mexico. Perhaps she was still there, but Sarah had no idea how to reach her, and now that she thought of it, she didn't know what she'd say to Mary Ellen. In order to warn her against Karl, Sarah would have to reveal that she knew about the affair with Gus, if there had been an affair. Such a conversation would be horribly embarrassing.

Still, if the woman was in danger, she deserved a warning. Sarah shook her head. Tomorrow she'd ask Virginia if she had a telephone number for Mary Ellen in New Mexico. If anyone but Karl had that information, it would be Virginia. With that thought, and hoping her warning wouldn't come too late, she prepared for bed. Before she fell asleep Sarah marveled at how bizarre a situation it was, when she planned to warn the wife of a faculty member that her husband might be a murderer.

38
.．

Elena hadn't been out of headquarters all day. There'd been meetings with Escobedo and Beltran trying to scope out their next moves in the acid bath case, meetings with the D.A.'s office about what to do with the warrant against Sarah Tolland. How sure did they need to be that Sarah was innocent? Elena had wondered. Sarah hadn't even known the deceased. The screening attorney finally decided not to take the case to the grand jury, but to send it back for further investigation. There had been long sessions on the telephone trying to track down Gus McGlenlevie's sexual contacts and their sexual or family contacts. There was also a futile effort to investigate the Bonaventuras and any activity they might have initiated in Los Santos, like the vandalism of Elena's house; Fernie said rumors were beginning to circulate about a Miami connection in Los Santos. Then there had been breaks for ordered-in food and trips to the ladies' room and the water cooler, the only exercise she'd had all day. After one such trip she returned to find Beto Sanchez, who had been called in, occupying his cubicle across the aisle.

"Looks like you and Leo blew it," said Beto.

"Blew what?" She sat down on her own chair and reached for the telephone.

"Saw in the last edition of tonight's paper that your corpse wasn't Angus McGlenlevie after all."

Elena turned and stared at Beto.

213

"That bein' the case, don't it look like you arrested the wrong person? Why would she kill some guy she didn't know from Adam?"

Sarah or her lawyer had called the paper! If Beltran had agreed to drop the charges against Sarah, apologize and ask for her cooperation, this needn't have happened. Now McGlenlevie was a walking target for whoever had tried to kill him. Mrs. Bonnard too, if Karl was the killer. And Elena herself might be on the Bonaventuras' list. They'd figure if Sarah wasn't a suspect anymore, Lili was—Lili or some Bonaventura hit man.

"Well?" prompted Beto.

"Don't blame me," said Elena. "Beltran wanted her arrested in the first place, and he wouldn't let us cut her loose."

"Naughty, naughty," said Beto, grinning. "Beltran hates to be shown up."

"Then he shouldn't go out on a limb," muttered Elena. The lieutenant had been even unfriendlier since they discovered that Angus McGlenlevie wasn't the victim. "I told you that identification was worthless," he'd said. If he thought that, why had he been so hot to arrest Sarah?

"I hope you're not indulging in any dumb I-told-you-so's with the lieutenant," said Beto. He was scavenging through a pile of papers and came up with a scrap that looked as if he'd put a cigarette out on it. "I got a message for you from Frank. He called just a few minutes ago. I didn't even know you was in. Guess both of us are clockin' overtime."

"I'm not taking messages from Frank."

"This one's professional, babe. Frank says to tell you that the word on the street is a Bonaventura guy's in town."

Elena, who had been looking for a telephone number, turned back toward Beto. "Bonaventura?"

"Yep. Frank's snitch says the Bonaventura guy is looking to hire some local talent for a job."

A job on my house? Elena wondered. *A job on me?* Or were they moving in on the dope pipeline from Mexico? She'd had the security company update the alarm system on her house the morning after the break-in. Now all she had to do was keep her eyes open—on the job, at home, asleep, awake. Damn

Frank—he was probably making it up just to spook her. "Thanks, Beto, but Frank's information stinks—where I'm concerned anyway."

She flipped to the Yellow Pages in the telephone book. With McGlenlevie's resurrection on the front page, she was really worried about Mrs. Bonnard. Where was that religious retreat being held? She couldn't very well ask Karl, especially if he was out of town. And if he wasn't, how would she explain a sudden desire to talk to his wife? Someone had mentioned the name of the woman's church, some crazy long name. Elena ran a finger down the listings. There were three that sounded promising, and she decided to call the home number of each pastor.

On number two, she got lucky. The Reverend Owen Wister— Owen Wister? She almost laughed aloud. Was he the reincarnation of the author of *The Virginian*, a novel that she'd thought amazingly romantic if somewhat dated when she was eleven years old?

"Reverend Wister, this is Detective Elena Jarvis of the LSPD. Do you have a parishioner named Bonnard? I don't know her first name."

"Mary Ellen Bonnard?" There was a shocked pause. "I hope you're not trying to contact her with some—some terrible news—a death or—"

"Is Mrs. Bonnard on a religious retreat?"

"Yes, she is. I'm going up there myself tomorrow. As she's one of my flock, perhaps you'd like me to break the news to her."

That her husband may have tried to kill her lover? Elena thought wryly. "Sorry. I need to talk to her myself. May I have her telephone number?"

"Well, there's only one telephone at the camp."

"This is very important."

"Important enough to get her out of bed?"

"If necessary." It was already a quarter of ten, for Pete's sake.

"I see. Mrs. Bonnard isn't in any kind of trouble, is she?"

"I hope not." The Reverend Wister, obviously eaten up with curiosity, gave her the number, and Elena put through the call to Mary Ellen Bonnard. Fortunately the city had come through with more funding, so the ban on long distance calls had been lifted. Elena waited a good five minutes while Mrs. Bonnard was dragged out of bed. Then Elena introduced herself and launched into what was going to be a ticklish conversation.

"I have some bad news, Mrs. Bonnard. Well, half bad. There's been a murder here in Los Santos, a man named Howard Margreaves."

"Who?"

"He worked for Angus McGlenlevie."

"Ah . . . I'm afraid I don't—" Mrs. Bonnard was stammering.

"But we have reason to think that Margreaves was killed by someone who mistook him for McGlenlevie. The two men looked somewhat alike, and Margreaves was staying in McGlenlevie's apartment."

"But I—I don't—"

"Are you trying to say you don't know Angus McGlenlevie, Mrs. Bonnard?"

"I'm afraid I really don't—I mean I may have heard the name. I believe he was—"

"—the husband of your husband's department chairwoman," said Elena helpfully.

"Yes, yes, I do—know of him—but I believe they are divorced."

"I'm sure you know they are, Mrs. Bonnard. Mr. McGlenlevie says he met you at a talk he gave to your reading group and that you've been having an affair ever since."

"Oh, but Gus couldn't have—"

"Gus?"

Mrs. Bonnard began to cry.

"Mrs. Bonnard, do you think that your husband is capable of killing your lover?"

"My husband didn't know anything about—"

"Mr. McGlenlevie said the same thing, but neither of you can be sure, can you?"

"Is Gus all right?" asked Mrs. Bonnard, the query broken by stifled sobs.

"Yes ma'am, he is. He was out of town at the time of the

murder—getting in touch with his male muse," Elena added dryly.

"He's so talented."

"Mrs. Bonnard, I'm going to give you my home phone number and my office number." Weeping women didn't make useful witnesses until they recovered. "Please think about the questions I've asked and call me back collect. If you can shed any light on this murder, I'd appreciate the information."

"Like what information, Detective? I haven't been in Los Santos for over a month."

Elena sighed. "Have you, for instance, heard from your husband since you left town?"

"No."

"Isn't that rather surprising?"

"We weren't on very good terms. I'm thinking of getting a separation, even though my church doesn't believe in such things, and my pastor has advised me to—well—try again. But I really don't think that Karl—well, he was more unpleasant than usual the last two weeks before I went away on this retreat."

"You wouldn't describe your relations with your husband as amicable?" asked Elena, remembering that Karl Bonnard had initially expressed more dismay than anger with his wife.

"Heavens, no," said Mrs. Bonnard. "Amicable? I hope the Lord will forgive me for saying so, but I don't think there's a meaner man in the world than Karl Bonnard." She was crying again. "Would you mind if I hung up now?"

"Have you got my telephone numbers?"

"I do."

"Please call me. The situation could be dangerous to both you and Mr. McGlenlevie. If your husband was responsible for Margreaves' death and hears that McGlenlevie is still alive—and how could he help hearing, when the news was in the evening paper—?"

"Oh, my Lord," cried Mrs. Bonnard. "Oh, I've just blasphemed. Oh, this is terrible," and sobbing, she hung up.

Elena shook her head. What did these women see in Angus McGlenlevie? Even Sarah had once been taken with him.

Elena's fingers itched to tap out Sarah's phone number, but her next promotion might depend on not doing it.

She sighed, picked up her handbag, went home, turned on the patio lights, and out of sheer frustration, attacked the back of her house with whitewash, her service revolver shoved into the waistband of her jeans—just in case any Bonaventura employees showed up.

That damn Frank—getting me all upset, she thought. *And here I am whitewashing my house when mob thugs may be hiding in the bushes. I've become a home-repair freak.* Elena made another angry sweep with the roller. *And that's all Frank's fault too. If he were here right now, I'd throw some unslaked lime on him.*

What would it do? she wondered, fantasizing. *Take off a couple of layers of skin? Make holes here and there where it hit?*

The Bonaventuras too. If they show up, I'll dissolve them. She covered another square of adobe with the thick white liquid.

Hell of a note when you can't whitewash your house without worrying about the Mafia and your ex-husband and Sarah, who's probably madder than hell at the police department in general and me in particular.

Elena climbed down and shifted her ladder to the left. Mary Ellen Bonnard had said Karl didn't know about the affair. If he hadn't, he wasn't the murderer. So who was?

39
··

"You can't be serious," exclaimed Leo. "Frank's got the best information network in town."

"*If* some snitch really told him that," Elena retorted. "Frank probably made it up."

"Well, I guess he could have," Leo admitted, tipping his chair back and lacing his fingers behind his head. "Our best leads are the Bonaventuras, in town or out; former lovers of McGlenlevie; Bonnard; and someone who actually wanted to kill Margreaves."

Elena nodded. She had received word when they came in at eight that Margreaves had been positively identified by his dental work.

"So I'll see if I can track down Frank's info on the Bonaventuras in case they're really our perps."

"Check with Fernie," Elena suggested. "He's been hearing rumors."

"O.K., and I'll check out Bonnard. You stay here and get on the telephone. See what you can find out about the girlfriends. And say, someone needs to notify the Margreaves family, see what they know."

"And I'm elected? Thanks a lot!"

"Ask them if Margreaves had any enemies, if he had a weird childhood like McGlenlevie said. Maybe someone in his

219

family did him in. Course, you had a weird childhood, so maybe you did him in."

"I did not have a weird childhood."

"Yeah right. Didn't your old man belong to the Penitente Brotherhood?"

"Sure. Lots of men do."

"And they crucify people, right?"

Elena laughed. "Not lately. That's just a vicious rumor anyway. They help out their neighbors—that sort of thing."

"And your mother's a hippie, right?"

"Right, but Dad won't let her grow pot anymore or run around barefoot. He thinks it's undignified for a mother of five."

"I rest my case. You're the person to talk to the Margreaves."

Leo headed for the street and, as Gus McGlenlevie had suggested, Elena got the New Jersey number of the late Howard Margreaves from Personnel at Herbert Hobart University, still irritated that Leo thought her family was weird. None of them were fanatic tap dancers like some people she knew. Mrs. Howard Margreaves, Sr., of Murray Hill, New Jersey, answered the telephone.

"Mrs. Margreaves, I'm calling about your son Howard," said Elena, dreading the conversation to follow.

"Oh, I knew it," cried Mrs. Margreaves. "He's got another one of those terrible summer colds, hasn't he? I haven't had a letter from Howie in three weeks, and he has no telephone. You can't imagine the worries a mother suffers, Miss—what did you say your name was?"

"Jarvis," said Elena.

"Jarvis. I suppose you're from the university clinic. Well, I hope you're taking good care of Howie. His respiratory system is so delicate. It comes of living in New Jersey. Chemicals, you know. Of course, my husband says that's nonsense. Poppycock, that's what he calls it, but he just says that because he could breathe *anything* and it wouldn't affect him."

Mrs. Margreaves had a breathy little voice and an obvious inability to stop talking. Elena hated to cut her off with worse news than the woman anticipated.

"Scientists, you know," Mrs. Margreaves was saying. "Howard

Senior is a scientific administrator at Bell Labs—well, we don't call it Bell Labs anymore—A.T. & T. That was a crime, a governmental crime—don't you think?—breaking up the company the way they did."

"Mrs. Margreaves—"

"Howard Senior always said Howie should have become a scientist. He could have, you know. He had an S.A.T. of 1450. His father said, 'Why waste all those brains on a no-money endeavor like poetry where he'll be associating with people wearing sandals and long hair—and *beards*.'"

The emphasis Mrs. Margreaves put on beards made them sound like the mark of Cain, and maybe she was right, thought Elena. Gus had that big, messy beard, and he was a sort of sexual Cain. "Mrs. Margreaves, about—"

"Yes, yes, you're going to tell me that it's my fault because I smoked when Howie was little, but both Howie and I have been in therapy for that problem. Howie no longer blames me, and I—"

"Look, Mrs. Margreaves, I wasn't going to—"

"I stopped when Howie was seven years old, and if you think that was easy—"

"Mrs. Margreaves, your son doesn't have a summer cold."

"Bronchitis. He has bronchitis. Oh dear. Perhaps I'd better come down myself. No one knows how to treat Howie's bronchitis better than I."

"It's not bronchitis."

"Pneumonia? Oh, dear Lord—"

"Ma'am, Howie's dead." Elena would have liked to break the news more delicately, but she was afraid it might take another half hour before Mrs. Margreaves worked through her list of possible illnesses. "I'm afraid your son was murdered." The flow of chatter from Mrs. Margreaves stopped abruptly.

Elena gave the woman a minute to digest the news, then said, "I want to express my sympathy, Mrs. Margreaves, and also to ask if you can think of anyone who might have wanted to kill your son."

"Why would anyone want to kill Howie?" the mother said in a small, shocked voice. "He never did anyone any harm, just wrote poetry." She sounded bewildered. "The only person I can think of who ever got mad at Howie was Howard Senior," she added, as if that piece of information would nullify her son's death.

Mrs. Margreaves began to weep. Elena leaned her head onto her free hand while with the other she held the telephone away from her ear as she considered the possibility that Howie might have been killed by a disappointed and disapproving father. Lots of murderers turned out to be the victim's relatives, not that Elena anticipated any help from Mrs. Margreaves if questioned on the possibility that her husband had killed her son. This family *was* sort of weird. The fiancée, however, might be a source of information. "Ma'am," Elena began anew when the sobbing had abated, "do I understand that your son was engaged to be married?"

"Yes, yes. To Marguerite Dubois. A lovely girl, although Howard Senior didn't approve." She sighed, the sigh probably expressing years of mediation between father and son. "Howard Senior said, 'Why get engaged when you can't afford to get married?'" She was sniffling quietly. "Poor Howie, you see, was paid practically nothing at that university, living in a slum. How can they treat their poets that way?" Mrs. Margreaves wailed. "It was probably some slum dweller, some minority person, who killed him. Don't you think?"

"I doubt it," Elena replied, wondering if she should tell the mother that she was talking to a "minority person" and that Howie's death might have been a case of mistaken identity. Would that make her feel better or worse? Elena decided to say nothing until they knew more. "I wonder if you could give me Ms. Dubois' telephone number?"

"You're going to call her? That's so kind of you. I suppose you work for the university. I didn't mean to denigrate your institution. I'm sure it—"

"I'm with the Los Santos police, Mrs. Margreaves."

"The police?" Mrs. Margreaves now sounded totally bewildered, as if it had never occurred to her that the police would be interested in her son. "To think that my sweet Howie should end his life mixed up with the police," she said mournfully.

"Yes, ma'am. If you could give me Ms. Dubois' number." Elena had written onto her notepad, "Howard Margreaves, Sr.," and underlined it—the name of another suspect in a long, long list.

Ms. Dubois answered on the third ring, and when Elena said she was calling about Howard, Ms. Dubois said, "I knew it. He hasn't written in three weeks. You're a girlfriend, aren't you? He's found himself a new—"

"Ms. Dubois."

"Howard's so susceptible. Such a romantic. He's found himself a new—"

"Ms. Dubois, I'm sorry to tell you that your fiancé is dead."

"Dead? Pneumonia?" asked Ms. Dubois. "His mother warned me."

"He was murdered."

There was a short silence, then an uneasy, tinkling laugh. "This is a crank call, right? No one, I mean no one, would murder Howard. Howard is not the sort of man who gets murdered."

"Well, we think that possibly the murderer killed him by mistake, but still, Ms. Dubois, we wondered if you could make any suggestions as to someone who might have wanted to murder Howard."

"I told you, no one would want to murder Howard."

"What about his father?"

"That Philistine!" exclaimed Ms. Dubois. "The man thinks of nothing but his career. Murder would not advance his climb up the corporate ladder."

Elena thought about the state of Howard's remains. Howard's father was a scientist. Being a scientist, if he wanted to dissolve a body, couldn't he have thought of something more scientific and less time-consuming than unslaked lime? It rapidly became obvious that Ms. Dubois had little to offer in the way of clues, so Elena said good-bye and began to check airline reservations from the East Coast to Los Santos for the time frame during which Howard Margreaves was killed: May 6 when he moved into McGlenlevie's apartment to May 14 when Lili found and misidentified the body.

There were no passengers from Murray Hill leaving from Newark or any other airports in the area. Of course, the murderer could, probably would, have lied about his or her home address.

"Hang up," said Leo, his shirt collar open, his face streaked with sweat. Elena hadn't even seen him come in. "Gang action in Segundo Barrio. Three victims already."

Elena slapped down the telephone, scooped up her handbag, and sprinted after Leo, the murder of Howard Margreaves forgotten.

"Bonnard wasn't in his office, and I couldn't find out anything about the Bonaventuras," he called over his shoulder. "Maybe Frank *was* doing a number on you."

"Bastard," Elena muttered. As for Bonnard, she was supposed to have dinner with him tonight, and he was going to be pretty surprised at the direction the conversation took. Elena had never Mirandized a date, but there was always a first time.

40
##

Thursday, June 4, 7:15 A.M.

Barefooted, damp from the shower, clad only in a terry cloth
robe, and having awakened from a restless sleep not twenty
minutes ago, Elena dropped the receiver into its cradle. The
newsboy had skipped her house again, and she'd just had an
irate conversation with the newspaper's circulation department,
much good that would do. Maybe tomorrow she'd get up early,
catch him pedaling by her house without tossing her paper, and
scare the hell out of him. She looked up and called Karl
Bonnard's number. No answer there. Bonnard had stood her up
last night.

Rubbing her hair dry with a ragged towel, she turned her
thoughts to unslaked lime. Someone had rerouted that order,
making it look like Sarah's doing. Elena could understand
that. The murderer wanted to shift suspicion away from
himself—or herself. Maybe even had a grudge against Sarah.
Or just thought her a likely suspect. To know Gus, to know
Sarah, to have access to the university computers, the murderer
had to be connected with the university.

How many university people knew anything about unslaked
lime? Bonnard didn't seem a likely whitewasher. Scientists of
other sorts maybe? No, she'd decided that Howard Margreaves' father, if he'd killed his son, would have thought of
something better than unslaked lime; so would a university
scientist.

Did professors whitewash their houses? Not likely, she decided. So who—well, someone from Buildings and Grounds. *They* whitewashed things. They ordered and used unslaked lime. They might even know a thing or two about computers, and Gus could have infuriated someone from Buildings and Grounds as easily as he did everyone else. Maybe he'd got his hands on someone's wife or daughter—some Hispanic girl he'd forgotten about by the time Elena and Leo questioned him. But the girl's father, husband, brother, or boyfriend wouldn't have forgotten. So who? Probably not Hector Montes, the guy who had called her and brought Buildings and Grounds to her attention in the first place. Anyway, he was the only contact she had there. With luck, he started work early—before the heat got too bad.

She dragged out her telephone book again and in five minutes found out that Hector Montes had never met Gus McGlenlevie and didn't know of anyone in Buildings and Grounds who had. Mostly they took complaints from chairmen or other administrators, occasionally a problem at the faculty apartments, but then it was the wives calling usually. Most members of the faculty would never notice a guy from Buildings and Grounds unless he ran a power mower over their foot; that was Hector Montes' opinion.

Elena slumped against the headboard of her bed, where she had been sitting, clipping her toenails as she talked to Montes. Had the delivery of the lime been a fluke, some computer mistake, or some professor who wanted free lime and jerried the computer to get it? Was she back to the Bonaventuras? The only thing she'd gotten from pursuing that avenue was a trashed living room, and she wasn't even sure of that.

"Has anyone shown any interest in unslaked lime?" she asked in a last, feeble attempt to dredge up a lead.

"Why would anyone—" Montes paused. "Well, yeah. There was this one guy complained about the air conditionin' in his office. Came over himself, followed me right out to the storage area, carryin' this bottle of *agua mineral con gas*—mineral water. You know?"

"I know," said Elena.

"I got kinda sick of all his bitchin'. You got moisture in the air, the swamp coolers don't work so good. Nothin' I can do about it, so then he bumps into this container of lime, an' I tell him if he spills his fancy mineral water in that lime, it'll boil right up an' eat a hole in his leg. 'No kiddin',' he says, real interested, so I tell him about unslaked lime. He's the only one I can think of."

"Mr. Montes, you sweetheart!" cried Elena. "What's his name?"

"Wha'd you say yours was?" asked Mr. Montes, evidently turned on by being called a sweetheart.

"Jarvis," said Elena, grinning. "Jarvis-Portillo."

"Portillo? Say, that sounds good to me."

"Oh yeah? What about your wife and babies?"

"Some babies," he replied, disgruntled. "They're wantin' to go to college now—become bigger shots than me."

"Congratulations. Do you remember his name? The one who asked about unslaked lime—or what he looked like?"

"Anglo. Good lookin'. A real prick."

Bonnard, she thought. "Name?"

"Can't remember."

"If I got you a picture?"

"Yeah. Probably. You come by with a picture, an' I'll take you out for a Tecate."

"You devil," said Elena, laughing exuberantly. Bonnard. Ten to one it *was* Bonnard. This evidence wouldn't convict him, but it would take her a step along the way.

41
..

Thursday, June 4, 8:05 A.M.

"Big doings at your place last night, huh?" said the desk sergeant as she passed through the reception area at headquarters.

Elena stopped. "Nothing happened at my house, except I went to bed early, slept, and didn't get my paper again this morning."

"You mean you didn't even wake up?" Jaime McBain looked astonished, his round face split by a grin beneath a Pancho Villa mustache.

"Quit fooling around, Jaime. What happened?"

"Frank caught this guy in your back yard and beat him up." Elena frowned. "What was Frank doing in my yard?"

"Who knows? Maybe he come over to serenade you."

"Or steal my truck," Elena muttered. "And the guy he beat up?"

"Oh, you know Frank. He kicked the guy around some until he said he'd been hired by some new mob *jefe*, come to town to hassle you. Then Frank dragged him over here an' booked him."

Had Frank been watching her house since the Bonaventuras destroyed her living room? Elena shook her head. You'd almost have to like the guy—unless you were a woman who could take care of herself and who was opposed to being slugged by her nearest and dearest.

"I can't believe you never woke up or nuthin'."

"Never did," said Elena and headed upstairs.

42
..

Thursday, June 4, 9 A.M.

"Congratulations," said Virginia as Sarah entered the office the next morning.

"Why's that?"

Virginia looked at her in surprise. "The morning paper said that the charges against you have been dropped. Aren't you pleased—or at least relieved?"

Sarah felt a surge of anger. They hadn't bothered to call her. After leaving her accused of murder when they knew she hadn't done it, they hadn't even bothered to call her. Just figured she'd read the good news in the paper, which she hadn't. Unusual for Sarah, who always fell asleep as soon as her head hit the pillow and stayed asleep until it was time to rise, she'd lain awake for a long time, thinking about Karl Bonnard, and awakened several times during the night, uneasy with the bizarre possibility that a member of her faculty had committed murder and tried to frame her. As a result she'd overslept that morning and had to forgo breakfast and her morning paper.

"Your lawyer called. Probably wanted to know where to send the bill."

"The city of Los Santos would be an appropriate recipient," Sarah muttered, thinking of the twenty thousand dollars she'd paid the bonding company. And Formalee's bill—God knows what that would be. Maybe she'd sue the city. "Is Dr. Bonnard back yet?" Sarah didn't want to see him. She just wanted to know where he was—and that he hadn't killed his wife.

"As I told you yesterday, Dr. Tolland, he's left town," said Virginia angrily. "He wanted me to get someone to cover his class. I told him to do his own—"

"Where did he go?" Sarah interrupted.

"He didn't say."

"You didn't ask?"

"Of course I asked. He hung up on me."

"Oh, dear," said Sarah.

"Well, it's not my fault the man has no sense of responsibility," said Virginia, her voice cross and snippy.

"Of course, it isn't," Sarah agreed placatingly. "I wasn't worried about his class, anyway."

"Why not?" Virginia looked indignant, but Sarah ignored it because she didn't feel that she had time to smooth Virginia's ruffled feathers.

"I seem to remember Mary Ellen telling me that she was going to a religious retreat. Would you know anything about that, Virginia?"

"Cloudcroft, New Mexico, but *she's* back."

"She is?"

"Yes, she called this morning to ask if I knew where Dr. Bonnard had got to. How's that for odd? All I could say was, 'He's out of town and wouldn't say where he was going.' Imagine him thinking he could be chairman. He doesn't even get his grade sheets in on time or his class rolls or his—"

"Well, I'm going over to see her."

"Who? Mary Ellen? Dr. Tolland, you've got an appointment with Harley Stanley at ten o'clock."

"Maybe I'll get back by then. If not, call him."

"What am I supposed to tell him? You know what a stickler Vice-President Stanley is for—"

"I really don't care what you tell him, Virginia. It's not as if he's proved himself to be any friend of mine." Sarah turned and left the office, and Virginia, looking astounded because that sort of behavior wasn't at all like Sarah Tolland, turned back to her computer.

43
..

Leo dropped the newspaper in front of Elena. "You must be happy about your friend," he remarked.

HHU PROF EXONERATED

My God, thought Elena, *Beltran never said a word, and he must have known.* She skimmed the article, deciding before she'd finished that she needed to talk to Sarah. A phone call would be easier, but she felt she owed Sarah Tolland a face-to-face apology. After all, the woman was a friend, or had been. Elena picked up her shoulder bag and told Leo that she was going to the Westside to see someone about the Margreaves case. "Investigate a possible suspect," she said, thinking that she'd ask Sarah some questions about Karl Bonnard and pick up a picture of him from Personnel to show Hector Montes. Of course, Sarah would probably say, "Go chase yourself," and Personnel would—

"You mean without me?" Leo asked.

"You want to apologize to Sarah Tolland too?"

Leo laughed. "You're on your own, kid, but isn't this a personal-time trip?"

"No, I'm following a lead on Bonnard too."

Elena made one stop—at the campus police station—before she went to Sarah's office. The station had round corners,

windows framed in lavender tile, and a white tile plaque that
announced, "Herbert Hobart University Police Station" in
lavender. The desk officer checked records from the guard
stations and showed her the names of people who had entered
or left the campus in the time frame during which they thought
Howard Margreaves had been killed. Karl Bonnard had signed
out with the guard on a Sunday night. There was no record of
his entering, but the desk officer said he wouldn't have had to
sign in during daylight hours since he had a parking sticker.
Bingo! It was on Sunday night that a man in a delivery uniform
had been seen wheeling two boxes into the faculty apartment
house. Once she got Bonnard's picture, she'd show it to the
tenant who had seen the delivery man, as well as to Montes at
Building and Grounds.

Fifteen minutes later she was saying to Virginia, "I wonder
if you could give me a minute with Dr. Tolland? I realize I
don't have an appointment."

Virginia looked at Elena as if she were a piece of lint on a
dark suit. "I'm afraid I can't do that, Detective. Dr. Tolland just
went rushing off to see a faculty wife." Virginia slammed a
drawer shut, her face set in lines of disapproval. "I don't know
what's got into her. Dr. Tolland had an appointment with the
vice-president; she had no business haring off to see Mary
Ellen Bonnard."

"Mrs. Bonnard's at home?" Elena experienced a rush of
anxiety.

"Yes."

"Where's Dr. Bonnard?"

"I don't know."

"Damn." She thought a minute. "Give me the Bonnard
address."

"Look, we don't give out—"

"Right now," said Elena and rapped her knuckles sharply on
the desk.

Virginia, looking astonished and offended at such peremp-
tory treatment, wrote out the address.

"Call the Bonnard house," Elena ordered.

A worried frown began to form on Virginia's face, and she

tapped out the number without protest. "Answering machine," she said.

Elena nodded. She'd been calling there too and always got the answering machine. Karl had missed their date without a word of explanation. She'd sat there waiting for him, all dressed up, gun in her handbag, and he hadn't shown up, so she'd gone to bed—while Frank and some Bonaventura thug were fighting in her yard. "You're sure Mary Ellen Bonnard is at home?"

Now alarmed, Virginia nodded and even offered information. "She called this morning asking for Karl. That's her husband."

Elena knew who Karl was. A liar for sure, possibly a murderer. "And Sarah went over there?" At the confirming nod, she said, "Call Police Headquarters." Elena gave the number. "Ask for Detective Leo Weizell in Crimes Against Persons and tell him to meet Detective Jarvis at the address you gave me." Virginia agreed, pale by now as a result of Elena's brusque manner.

Elena turned and left, wondering where the missing suspect had gone; Bonnard was definitely a suspect. He had the means to commit the murder and the know-how, if he was the one who had asked Montes about unslaked lime, and he had the motive—his wife's infidelity. They might even be able to place him at the scene of the crime. Well, at least Mary Ellen Bonnard was alive. And so was Sarah. Yet Elena felt a sense of urgency, which she tried to quell by telling herself that the killer would probably turn out to be the Bonaventuras or Margreaves Senior. But in the meantime, she had a bad feeling.

Beltran would call it feminine intuition and tell her to ignore it if she wanted to be taken seriously as a policeman. He hadn't yet admitted other terms to his vocabulary, not policewoman, not policeperson, not—oh God, why would Sarah be going to see Mary Ellen Bonnard in the middle of the work day? And why had Mary Ellen come home? She was supposed to be up in Cloudcroft praying, asking forgiveness for her sins, whatever.

44
..

Thursday, June 4, 10:05 A.M.

Sarah studied the house anxiously as she swung her legs out of the BMW. No one seemed to be at home. There were no cars in the driveway. Of course, if she'd been expecting to find Karl, his car wouldn't be parked outside. He was the type who always garaged his, lest some errant hailstone dent its carefully polished surface or some wandering child leave a fingerprint. Karl's Buick sedan was as carefully maintained as his person. Mary Ellen too would have put her car away, not out of any concern for it but to placate Karl.

There had been such a charming, fly-away quality to Mary Ellen when Sarah first met her. Then after a year or so the fly-away quality took on overtones of desperation. She joined that religious sect, talked about it for a few months, then fell silent. It was as if Mary Ellen weren't really there at the faculty gatherings, the Wednesday afternoon prayer and cocktail parties, for instance. Mary Ellen attended, but she no longer drank, and although she might smile, she no longer bothered to say much, especially if Karl was in the same circle. Well, Sarah could understand that. Before Mary Ellen isolated herself behind a wall of religion, anything she said provoked an unkind response from her husband. Maybe that's why it had been hard for Sarah to like him.

Sarah knocked at the door, thinking again that the warning she had come to issue was going to be embarrassing to both of them. Then the door opened, and her thoughts were thrown into disarray because she faced Karl, not Mary Ellen.

"I thought you'd left town," she blurted out.

He looked as surprised as she. "I just got back."

"Where did you go?"

"Is this an official inquiry?" He opened the wrought-iron security door and took Sarah's arm to usher her in, giving her a merry smile, as if his question were a little joke—except that Karl Bonnard seldom made jokes and wasn't a merry person, any more than Sarah herself.

And he was touching her. She didn't think Karl Bonnard had ever touched her, unless perhaps they had shaken hands on first meeting. "It's not an official inquiry," she responded nervously, "although you've upset Virginia by failing to leave word where you could be reached."

"I never understood why that was necessary for me. Now, in *your* case—being chairwoman—"

His voice took on a nasty tone, and Sarah thought, *He really does resent my being chair.* "Well, I suppose in the event that some student wants to sue you, as that girl did Radna. What do you make of that?" Ordinarily Sarah didn't care what he made of anything. She had avoided him if she could and consulted him on departmental business only as a matter of professional courtesy. Now, however, she found herself making conversation because she felt uneasy in his presence. How could she forget that the murderer had left clues pointing in her direction and that Bonnard had a motive to kill Gus, perhaps even resentment enough to frame her? He'd certainly jumped at the chance to claim the chairmanship. "Is Mary Ellen at home?" she asked.

"Mary Ellen?" He looked as if he couldn't connect the name to a person. "You wanted to see Mary Ellen?" His glance sharpened, and Sarah realized that she had to account for this unusual morning visit.

"Yes, Virginia mentioned that Mary Ellen called, asking where you were. I thought I'd drop by before I started work to—ah—speak to her about the departmental picnic. I wanted to ask Mary Ellen if she'd handle it this year."

"Mary Ellen's out of town," said Karl.

"But I understood from Virginia that Mary Ellen had called from home."

"Did Virginia *say* my wife called from home?" Karl asked sharply, his tone almost threatening, reminding Sarah that she was dealing, possibly, with a murderer, and that Mary Ellen, who was supposed to be at home, evidently wasn't available. Had he killed his wife—just this morning, perhaps minutes after Virginia talked to her? "Virginia must have misunderstood," Sarah stammered.

"Mary Ellen's at her mother's. Or so the Reverend Mr. Ambruster told me at Cloudcroft when I went to see her."

"How long does she plan to stay at her mother's?"

"Mary Ellen and I are separated. Perhaps you didn't realize that, Sarah."

"No, I didn't." Sarah was not sure that Virginia had said where Mary Ellen called from. Maybe Virginia hadn't known.

"Yes. I went up to the retreat to talk to her about a divorce, but it seems she left and went to her mother's."

"Well, in that case, I don't suppose I can ask her to handle the departmental picnic."

"No, it wouldn't seem appropriate. And you do like to do the proper thing, don't you, Sarah?"

"I suppose I do. Well, I guess I'll be—"

"Which makes me wonder why you married Angus McGlenlevie."

Sarah could feel the hairs rise on the back of her neck.

"Another thing. You don't like lying, do you, Sarah? And I can see that you haven't believed a word I've said."

She admitted silently that she hated lies and that she found some of his statements questionable. "I don't understand, Karl. Why wouldn't I believe you?" She hoped the fear wasn't audible in her voice.

"Maybe I'm lying to you; maybe you're lying to me." His hand closed around her arm once more, just as it had when he drew her into the house. "Maybe you'd like to tell me why you think I'm lying about my separation from Mary Ellen."

"You misunderstand," she said. He had a surprisingly strong grip for a man who, she was sure, didn't lift weights or whatever people did to develop strong grips. He was walking her very forcefully from the entry hall into the living room.

"Sit down, Sarah." He pushed her into a puce-colored chair whose down cushions seemed bottomless. "In what way did I misunderstand?"

Sarah clutched the brocaded arms, and the protective covers shifted beneath her fingers, increasing her sense of unease.

"Well, you seem to think that I think—" She stopped because all the *thinks* sounded ridiculous.

"What, Sarah?" he prodded impatiently and leaned against the mantel of the fireplace, his hand only inches away from a heavy fire shovel in an ornate brass stand on the hearth.

Sarah stared, transfixed, as she remembered that the unfortunate Howard Margreaves had died from a blow to the head. "It's not that I think you're lying," she assured him. "I was just surprised to find Mary Ellen away. Because I misunderstood Virginia, you see."

"You seem nervous, Sarah."

"This is a peculiar conversation, Karl. Are you feeling all right? I suppose the separation has been difficult for you."

"Not at all," said Karl. "I consider myself well rid of her. Would you want to be married to a person who espoused creation scientism?"

Since he seemed to be waiting for an answer, he obviously didn't consider the question rhetorical. "I certainly find it a strange world view. However, our Constitution guarantees citizens freedom of religion."

"How tolerant you are, but then you're obviously not as particular about the views and habits of your mate as I am."

Sarah stared at him. This was the second time he'd referred to Gus.

"McGlenlevie is hardly the proper sort of person for a woman like you, Sarah."

"Yes. Well, Gus and I have been divorced, as you know, for some time."

"Unfortunate, isn't it, that the rest of us couldn't divorce him?"

"I beg your pardon?"

"Your husband—when you divorced him, he didn't leave the university."

"He's tenure-track, Karl, and Harley Stanley considers him one of the stars in our crown." She managed a wry smile.

"If he knew anything about McGlenlevie, he wouldn't tolerate him for a minute."

"Perhaps not," Sarah agreed.

"As you already know, having borne the brunt of Stanley's disapproval for your husband's indiscretions."

"I'm afraid I don't understand—"

"Why, your arrest for his murder. Stanley was quite ready to throw you to the wolves. Didn't you know that? It was the dean, not Stanley, who refused to put you on leave."

Was Bonnard unaware that Gus hadn't been killed?

"Unfortunately, after all you went through on his behalf, it turns out that McGlenlevie isn't dead."

So much for that idea, she thought.

"Surely you read about *that* in the paper. The case of the mistaken victim."

"Yes, of course. Actually, it turns out that the victim was some fellow living in Gus's apartment."

"But you assume, do you not, that the intended victim was McGlenlevie?"

"I've no idea." Sarah couldn't take her eyes away from Karl's hand—so near the heavy fire shovel. She didn't know what the safest course would be—to keep him talking perhaps, but then he might admit that he'd killed Gus—or rather Margreaves. If so, he'd have to kill her too.

"Well, I have to get back to the department. I have a ten o'clock appointment with Harley. In fact, Karl," she added in a moment of inspiration, "I wonder if you'd consider coming along. I could use some support in the matter of adding faculty. You know how popular computer science has become. We'll find ourselves teaching three, maybe four courses each if we don't add new faculty members." *I'm babbling,* she thought miserably.

"Given our endowment, I doubt that you need support in getting anything you want, Sarah. In fact, Harley may be falling all over himself to accommodate you, having proved to be such a fair-weather friend when you were arrested. Now he'll be forced to admit that you didn't deserve that kind of treatment."

"It's very good of you to say so, Karl," said Sarah, pushing herself partway out of the deep chair, determined to leave if she could.

"Sit down," he snapped and moved toward her. She sank back. "It's all your fault, you know." He returned to his position by the fireplace. "If you hadn't married him, none of this would have happened."

Was he about to admit that he had tried to kill Gus? Oh God, she didn't want to hear it. "Perhaps we belong to a doomed profession," she said, "people who make unfortunate mistakes in marriage." She essayed a smile, one more comradely than she'd ever have considered sending his way. "I'm divorced, and you're separated." Or was it a mistake to remind him of his wife, considering that he might have killed Mary Ellen too. Sarah fought to keep her terror from showing. "I suppose all we can do is get on with our lives."

"I must tell you, Sarah, that you're a poor dissembler. I'm sure Gus has already bragged about his affair with my wife."

Sarah could feel her own face stiffening with alarm. The admission she didn't want to hear was coming, the admission of murder. Karl was flushed, rage shining in his eyes, his mouth set in a fierce grimace.

"How could she consider offering what was mine—" he snarled. "Her body was mine! And she gave it to your disgusting husband."

"I—I—didn't realize," Sarah stammered. "Perhaps—she was—unhinged by her association with that sect."

"Yes, that sect. My God, that any woman would dare to humiliate me by associating with a group of crackpot fanatics."

Sarah nodded quickly. "It must have seemed very strange," she said, feigning sympathy, hoping to get him onto the subject of Mary Ellen's church. "I understand they believe in faith healing as well as—as creation science."

He nodded. "They probably rolled around on the floor, talked in tongues, her among them."

"Then you never actually attended one of their services?"

"Of course not."

"I wouldn't have wanted to myself," Sarah agreed, wondering if now was the time to jump up and make a dash for the front door. But no, he'd locked it and, she thought, taken the dead bolt key with him. She had to keep him talking while she thought of some other way to escape. "I'm afraid I'm not a religious person myself. I don't really understand the impulse to join even the most ordinary denomination. Were you ever religious?"

"Are you trying to distract me, Sarah?"

She manufactured a look of surprise.

"I ask because you've never manifested any interest in my beliefs before."

"Well, Karl, you're really a very private man. This is the most personal conversation we've ever had, but then this is the first time"—her mind whirled hectically, searching for words that would divert him—"we've had a traumatic event in common. I suppose that bad marriages will get people talking."

"Yes, your marriage wrecked my life. It caused me exceptional embarrassment."

"I hadn't heard a thing," Sarah mumbled.

"Your husband—"

"Ex-husband."

"—ex-husband hasn't boasted about his affair with—"

"Really, Karl. I don't see Gus if I can help it. I'm sure you can understand why. He did, after all, make that ludicrous accusation of murder when a snail exploded on his plate in my dining room."

"Too bad it didn't kill him."

"And now he's accused me again." She wondered unhappily if mentioning the murder had been a mistake. Since she had, she couldn't very well drop the subject, so she said, "As you pointed out, he's responsible indirectly for bringing me into embarrassing contact with the police and costing me a great deal of money. I don't suppose it was his fault that the other person was killed in his apartment, but frankly I never intend to say another word to Gus McGlenlevie as long as I live."

"Yes, as long as you live." He paused, as if he were considering how long that might be.

"And I do want to thank you for your offer when I was in jail. It was very kind of you." And an amazing piece of hypocrisy if her arrest was Bonnard's fault.

"Stop trying to change the subject, Sarah. I don't believe that McGlenlevie hasn't told you about his fling with Mary Ellen. Men like that can't keep their mouths shut about their sexual exploits."

"Believe me, Karl, I'd never have known if you hadn't—"

"It has undoubtedly occurred to you that I might be the person who mistakenly killed—what was his name?—Margreaves."

She wanted to deny that she'd had any such thought, but couldn't quite get it out.

"I don't believe that you've come here to see Mary Ellen about the departmental picnic. She told everyone at the last prayer meeting that she was going on a religious retreat. In fact, I heard her tell you, so stop lying to me, Sarah. It won't do you a bit of good." His hand had closed over the fire shovel. "You can't fool me any more than she could. I heard her talking to him on the telephone. That's how I found out, listening on the extension. The silly twit took a call from him when I was in the house. So I followed her." His eyes had narrowed, as if he were watching himself tracking Mary Ellen. "Every time she left the house without me, I followed her. All those church meetings. I was sitting outside. To be sure that's where she was going. But Tuesdays it wasn't church. Tuesdays she was meeting your husband."

The venom in his voice made Sarah shiver.

"Then I followed her every Tuesday for a month, and while I was sitting outside that apartment building, while your husband was screwing my wife, I made my plans. Brilliant plans. I made sure the police would never know exactly when he was killed. And all the evidence would point to you. You'd be arrested. And you were. I had a problem, and I found the most logical solution. The only mistake I made was killing the wrong man."

His fist closed so tightly over the fire shovel that Sarah could see the whitened knuckles from her chair.

"He deserved to die. The young fool. Imitating McGlenlevie—

the beard, the T-shirt that said 'A Poet Is a Metaphor for Good Sex.' How was I to know it wasn't McGlenlevie?

"I should have realized that McGlenlevie would get tired of Mary Ellen and want to escape from her. That was my mistake. I should have anticipated that he'd get out of town as soon as the semester was over. I didn't think about that part of it carefully enough. But my one mistake can be rectified. My second plan will be even more brilliant than my first."

He smiled at Sarah. "Do you know what I'm going to do first, Madam Chairwoman?"

Now thoroughly frightened, Sarah shook her head.

"I'm going to bash your head in, just the way I did that stupid boy's. That was very carefully planned so it would look like you'd done it. Did I tell you that?"

He's demented, Sarah thought. *He can't even remember what he's said.*

"If I'd just got the right person, I'd have Mary Ellen back, and you can be sure I'd make her very, very sorry that she ever soiled herself in Angus McGlenlevie's bed. You'd have gone to jail, and I'd have taken over as chairman, which is as it should be. Women have no business chairing departments. They have no organizational skills, no flair for leadership, no . . ."

Sarah felt trapped. She was at a physical disadvantage because she was smaller than he, because even if she tried to defend herself, she had no experience with physical violence, and because she was enfolded in this deep, low chair with no weapon to use against a man who already held the implement with which he intended to crush her skull. Although she kept her eyes on Karl Bonnard, waiting for the moment when he stopped ranting about women and sprang at her, she concentrated on her peripheral vision. There was nothing within reach to the left of her.

"But all those mischances can be remedied," said Karl.

To the right on a small end table stood a table lamp with a tall, slender brass base and an antique satin shade.

"This time," said Karl, "I have a plan that won't fail."

The lamp, thought Sarah, was probably heavy, heavy enough to fend him off if she could wield it with any authority.

"I'm going to use Mary Ellen," said Karl. "She's going to be the means of killing you all."

But the lamp might be too heavy, Sarah realized, noting with a sort of detached relief that Mary Ellen must be alive if she figured in Karl's plans. Sarah acknowledged to herself that seated as she was, she might not be able to sweep the lamp off the table one-handed, and how could she get out of the chair and grasp it with two hands before he hit her?

"Mary Ellen's going to call McGlenlevie and get him over here." Karl smiled with satisfaction.

"Why would she agree?" asked Sarah. The longer she kept him talking the better.

"Because she's terrified of me, but she'll believe me if I tell her that I want to keep her alive to make her pay for what she's done."

She might indeed, thought Sarah, wondering whether Karl had always harbored that strain of calculating violence.

"I just have to choose the most likely murderer in the murder-suicide scenario. It can't be McGlenlevie unless you know of some reason he might have killed his postdoctoral fellow. Can you suggest anything, Sarah?"

"I don't know." He was playing with her—enjoying her terror, but still—the longer she could keep him talking, keep him involved in his cruel game, the longer she'd stay alive. *Concentrate, Sarah,* she told herself. Brass lamps were all very well, but her intelligence had always been her best weapon. She ought to be able to outthink Karl Bonnard—at least for a while. A murder-suicide scenario, he'd said.

"What's the matter, Sarah? Don't tell me you've run out of ideas. All those brilliant scholarly articles, and now you can't come up with a thing, can you?"

He was wrong, she thought, applying her mind to the problem; she'd offer him enough options to keep him occupied until nightfall if she had to. He planned to kill all three—Gus, Mary Ellen, and herself—making two deaths look like murder and one suicide. She did a quick calculation of the number of plans that could entail. And then one had to factor in not only alternate plans, but alternate motivations. Suddenly she felt more confident. Math could be applied even to murder. "I suppose Gus might have been irritated with Margreaves if Margreaves took over one of the volleyball girls," she suggested. "Margreaves was assistant coach of that team. Maybe they were competing for the affections of the players."

"That sounds like McGlenlevie," Karl agreed.

Sarah had no idea whether it sounded like Margreaves, but Karl didn't know that. "Then he'd kill Mary Ellen and me because—" She stopped, thinking desperately. "Because—"

"You're being stupid, Sarah. McGlenlevie, would do it because he was tired of both of you! Because women are irritating, inferior creatures, and men get tired of them. But that's not a good enough story, Sarah. You'll have to do better if you want to stay alive long enough to see this through to its solution."

"I suppose Mary Ellen might have killed Margreaves by mistake. Maybe she didn't know Gus had left town. She hadn't heard from him. Terribly angry, she went to see him. Used her key. Hit Margreaves with something while his back was turned, thinking he was Gus."

"I'm not sure she has the guts. We can't have the police saying, 'Oh, that one's not guilty. She hasn't the guts to murder anyone.'"

"The woman-scorned motivation is very traditional, very convincing." Sarah was again trying to estimate how much that lamp might weigh and whether or not she could twist her body in the chair to grasp it with both hands.

"I suppose that's possible." Bonnard didn't look convinced. "That would explain why she kills him this time, but what about you? Why does she kill you?"

"She—he—he told her he was breaking off the relationship, that he wanted to remarry me. In a fit of jealous fury she—"

"I'd never have guessed you had such a melodramatic imagination, Sarah."

"Maybe you're right," she conceded. "And then there's no way to be sure the police understand the whole story. Since it's not true, there'll be no evidence."

"I'll be around. When all of you are dead, I'll be here like the last actor to speak in a Shakespearean tragedy. I'll be your Greek chorus."

"But how would you explain knowing?"

"Let's see. Maybe you told me that Gus was after you to remarry him. Two colleagues exchanging personal confidences."

No one would ever believe she had confided in Karl Bonnard, Sarah decided, but she said nothing. "Would it be prudent to admit that you knew about Mary Ellen's infidelity?"

"Not before today—I wouldn't have known before today. I'll tell the police that she called me—no, I called her—from Alamogordo. The concerned husband, trying to find his unbalanced wife. I went to her mother's house to look for her, you see, after I'd found that she left the retreat. That much is true. Then I'll tell the police that I called to see if she'd returned home, and her confession spilled out, her infidelity, her plans to kill you, the rival for his affections, and McGlenlevie, her fickle lover."

"Yes, but did you actually call here? The telephone companies have long-distance records, don't they? And then the police will want to be sure that she was in town when Margreaves was killed."

"That's the beauty of it," said Bonnard. "I made sure that they couldn't tell when he died. That was not only very smart of me but very satisfying. To watch the flesh disappearing from his bones, avariciously devoured. I wiped out almost every trace of him, and then I covered up how it was done—so they couldn't trace the method to me."

She supposed he meant the unslaked lime that he had charged to her computer account, but he hadn't covered up having used the lime. Of course, he was half crazy; she couldn't expect everything he said to make sense.

"I think I should make *you* the triple murderer, Sarah," Karl decided. "That would be the most satisfying."

He was smiling, swinging the heavy shovel. She could almost feel it connecting with her skull. "You'd have to presuppose that I mistook Margreaves for Gus, which isn't likely."

"Yes. Well, if you opened the door yourself and hit him on the back of the head before he turned around, it wouldn't be any different from the scenario you proposed with Mary Ellen as murderer."

"Except that she had a key; I didn't."

"You tried before to kill him and came close to being arrested; the police did arrest you this time. If it turns out to be you, after all, think of all the criticism they'll take for letting you go when McGlenlevie returned. All the law-and-order advocates will scream about the police and courts turning dangerous criminals loose. I like it."

"Aren't you afraid they'll pin all the murders on you? You'll be the last one alive."

"My dear, Sarah, I'm out of town. Nobody knows I'm here. I am, in fact, registered at a motel in Alamogordo, waiting for a call from Mary Ellen or her mother. I'll actually be back there tonight."

"Oh, I see. That is clever."

"Yes, I thought so. Now, back to you. Mary Ellen has a key to McGlenlevie's apartment. And I have a key. That's how I got in. With a copy of her key. So I'll just put my copy with your fingerprints on it in your purse. Simple."

"But wouldn't the police have found my key when they searched my apartment?"

"We'll just assume that you cleverly hid it somewhere and that it now turns up when they search your purse. You missed killing McGlenlevie on your first try—with the snail. And your second try. My, you're a very inefficient murderer, Sarah. You'll find Gus here with Mary Ellen. Say, in bed. And kill them. Jealousy. Just as you tried to kill him the first time over his new fiancée."

"But why would I come here—to your house?"

"The departmental picnic. Isn't that what you told Virginia?"

"What would I kill them *with*? I wouldn't bring a weapon to talk about the departmental picnic."

"You would if that was just an excuse, when you really knew they were having an affair and planned to—"

"The police don't know about the affair, Karl," she lied in the most reasonable tone she could muster. "That being the case, they won't be able to find any motive for my killing Mary Ellen."

"I'll tell them."

"Then you'll be a suspect too, because you'll have a motive as good as mine."

"Well, maybe you don't know they're having an affair. You come about the picnic and find his car here, find them in bed together. You kill them in a fit of jealous rage. What does it matter? You'll all be dead, and I'll have been in Alamogordo while you're killing off the others—and yourself. Have you forgotten that? I'm in Alamogordo. At a motel. Waiting for Mary Ellen's mother to tell me where Mary Ellen is, because, after all, if my wife told those idiots at the retreat that she was going to see her mother, then she must have done it. A fine religious person like Mary Ellen wouldn't lie. Right?"

Sarah noticed that his hair was disarranged and there was sweat on his forehead, although the temperature in the house was comfortable, and she could hear the steady hiss of cooled air through the vents.

"So I believe she'll come to Alamogordo. I'm waiting for her. She wouldn't rush back to Los Santos to be sure that her lover was safe, to be sure that her wicked husband hadn't killed him. Would I believe that? Never. Not of my virtuous, devout wife." His laughter rose between them. "It'll work, Sarah. You'll be dead, she'll be dead, he'll be dead—and I'll be alive. And laughing. And chairman!"

"There's another flaw in your plan," Sarah objected.

"What's that?"

"I can't bash in my own skull with that fire shovel. I doubt that I could kill them that way either."

Bonnard looked startled. "True," he admitted, calming down. "So glad you pointed that out to me, Sarah. I'm going to have to shoot you." Still swinging the shovel, he began to move sideways, toward a long table by the window.

Did he have a gun in that drawer? Because he was facing her instead of the table, he didn't see what she saw through the sheer curtains of the window behind him. A pickup truck. Elena's truck pulling up in front of his house. At least she hoped it was Elena's. All those trucks looked alike to Sarah, and she'd only seen the vehicle at night when they'd gone to the support-group meetings and met for dinner, but the color seemed familiar. Sarah didn't dare take her eyes off Karl for a closer look. "You can't kill me until after you've killed the other two."

"Of course, I can."

"Coroners can tell the time of death by body temperature and—and degree of *rigor mortis*. It may take you a while to get Gus over here. It may take even longer to convince Mary Ellen to call him."

"You're getting desperate, aren't you, Sarah? Really frightened, aren't you?"

"Of course, but what I'm saying is logical."

"Maybe."

Someone was coming up the walk. It looked like a woman. "I think you'd be wrong to chance it," she said. The doorbell rang. Karl's eyes darted toward the hall. "Especially when there's someone at the door," added Sarah.

"Just keep your mouth shut," he said, and his hand darted to the drawer. "We'll wait till they leave."

Dear God, Elena, don't leave, thought Sarah. "I think it's the police."

He glanced out the window, gun in one hand, fire shovel in the other. "It's a pickup truck."

"Elena Jarvis drives a pickup, and she'd recognize my car."

"Damn," he muttered. "So I invite her in. You'll have to kill her too, Sarah. You stay right where you are and keep your mouth shut. Cooperating with me is, after all, your only hope."

He'd have to pass close to her chair on his way to the door. How far past before she was blocked out of his peripheral vision? Sarah wondered. Every muscle in her body tensed, anticipating the spring for the lamp. She had to get him before he turned the gun on Elena.

"Stay right where you are," said Karl smoothly. "It's going to work out perfectly." He raised the gun. "I didn't like that Jarvis bitch anyway."

She watched him glide past her; then she rose, turning. It seemed to take forever to get the lamp, and it was heavy. She jerked its cord from the wall socket as she swung the other

way, letting it go just as he began to turn, just as she heard a
thud against the front door and the splintering sound of wood
tearing around the lock as the door burst open. The lamp was
already in flight. She watched, paralyzed, as the elaborately
ruched shade hit the side of his head. A shade would never stop
him.

He stumbled sideways as Elena appeared in the arch to the
living room, gun in hand. Karl regained his balance and raised
his own gun, but Sarah, released from her paralysis, rushed
forward three steps and, hiking her straight skirt, kicked out at
his hand. The gun flew loose and, desperate, he swung the
shovel at Elena. Sarah, a muscle cramp arching her back, saw
the flash of Elena's gun, saw the blood well and run down his
arm as he dropped the shovel. In the same second, she felt, with
a jolt of surprise, a searing pain in her own arm.

She looked down, saw blood, and realized she'd been shot.
Still she was alive, not dead, as she'd expected to be. Just dealt
a minor gunshot wound by the woman with whom she'd shared
disgusting burritos when Elena was choosing, excellent pâtés
and crêpes and soufflés when she was choosing, and after
dinner the trials of being a divorced woman when they attended
the support group together. She rubbed desperately at the
cramping back muscle. Damn! That hardly ever happened
except when she stretched in bed, trying to get comfortable
after a long day at the computer. She hadn't done any computer
work today and wasn't in bed, so why—

"Sarah, are you all right?" Elena's voice was sharp with
alarm.

She evidently wanted some assurance that Sarah wasn't
about to lose consciousness. However, Sarah did not consider
herself in danger. Just in pain. She bent forward to ease the
cramp. It was Karl who might be in danger, his well-tailored
coat sleeve dark and limp with blood. Actually, the whole thing
seemed rather anticlimactic. Sarah supposed she should be
grateful for anticlimax. Cramps. A dribble of red on her arm.
No one died in an anticlimax.

"Why the hell did you move into my line of fire?" Elena
demanded, her face pale and anxious as she moved toward
Sarah.

"Well, I believe it was because I've always wanted to kick a gun out of someone's hand," said Sarah wryly.

"And an impressive job you did."

As Sarah straightened, the two women smiled at each other for the first time since Sarah's arrest.

45
••

Relieved that Sarah had not been seriously injured, Elena moved carefully toward Bonnard. She could see that he was in shock, staring at his arm, from which blood dripped steadily. A movement behind him distracted her, and she glanced again toward Sarah, who, being a practical person, had whisked a scarf off the end table, the table from which she had plucked the monster lamp. She was binding the scarf around the wound where Elena had winged her. "Sorry I yelled at you," Elena muttered. "And shot you."

Sarah glanced up. "I don't believe there's any serious damage to my arm." She smiled weakly. "In fact, if you hadn't arrived, I'd probably be dead."

"Well, you weren't doing so badly on your own, considering that he had two weapons and you only had that lamp—and the football kick, of course," said Elena. "Ever punted for a team?"

"Ballet lessons," said Sarah.

"Right." How much different Sarah's childhood had been from her own. Chimayo, New Mexico, didn't offer ballet lessons, among other non-opportunities.

They both looked at Karl Bonnard, who had dropped into a straight-back chair by the arch. The violence seemed to have deserted him, leaking out along with the blood that soaked his coat sleeve.

"Get up, turn around, and put your hands behind your back,"

Elena told him. Where the hell was Leo? she wondered. Karl just sat there. "Did you hear me, or do I have to shoot you again?"

He got up, trying to look both confident and accusing, as if she were a friend who had suddenly turned unpleasant for no good reason. "I need medical attention."

"I don't suppose luck was with us and he confessed?" Elena asked Sarah, the gun in one hand as she punched out 911 on the telephone with the other.

"Yes, he did. He said something about logical solutions."

Elena shivered, remembering his statements about engineers and problem-solving. She'd been reassured at the time by the thought that Sarah wasn't crazy and therefore wouldn't consider murder a logical solution. It hadn't occurred to her then that *Karl* was the crazy one.

"She's lying," he said, face flushed with malice. "She's a lying bitch, and you can be sure that if you arrest me, you'll be facing a suit for—"

"Shut up and put your hands together behind your back." Now she was seeing a Karl Bonnard she could believe had killed someone. "C.A.P. Detective Elena Jarvis," she said tersely into the telephone. "I have a homicide suspect shot. Send an E.M.S. unit, backup, and a Shooting Review Team." Elena gave the address, hung up, and snapped the cuffs on Bonnard's good wrist and then on the wrist slippery with blood.

"Sarah planned to kill both me and Mary Ellen." His voice, which had started the sentence strong and accusatory, faltered when he mentioned his wife.

"Does that mean your wife's still alive?"

"She's been manifesting symptoms of insanity. I had to lock her in the bedroom. I was, of course, going to call a local psychiatric unit and would have done so except that Dr. Tolland arrived."

"Right. Sarah arrived, unarmed, planning to—"

"It was her gun," said Bonnard.

"I never owned a gun in my life," said Sarah indignantly.

"All right, you," Elena snapped at Bonnard, who had moved

several feet toward the door. She swung a straight-back chair out from the wall. "Sit on it backwards," she ordered.

"I don't—"

"Swing your leg across. Right now."

"You're arresting the wrong person, Elena. Surely you know me well enough to realize—"

"Do what I tell you," she snapped, furious that he still thought he could play her for a fool. "You look like you're about to keel over, Bonnard. That arm will really hurt when you hit the floor, and the bleeding will start up again."

He obeyed, almost falling in the attempt to lift his leg across the seat, then slumping against the chair back.

"What did he say about the murder, Sarah?"

Looking rather pale herself, Sarah sat down in an armchair by the window table.

"You're getting blood on my upholstery," Bonnard complained.

"You're getting blood on your carpet," she retorted. "He said he'd killed Margreaves by mistake. I don't think he'd ever seen Angus up close, so he was fooled by the beard and one of Gus's disgusting T-shirts."

"They never met at President Sunnydale's prayer meetings?" asked Elena, grinning.

"Gus refused to attend those. Some sort of protest against prayer in the schools. Probably he was meeting a girl while I was doing my chairmanly duty," said Sarah.

"That sounds like McGlenlevie," Elena agreed. "Look, I'm really sorry about your being arrested. There wasn't a whole lot I could do about it."

Sarah nodded and leaned her head against the high, curved back of the chair, her eyes closed.

"You all right?"

"I'm probably suffering from post-traumatic stress disorder." She smiled weakly. "Expecting a shovel to crush one's skull and being shot are new experiences for me."

"Post-traumatic stress symptoms come later," said Elena. "What did he tell you?"

"His plan was— Oh well, he explored several of them, but the plan of choice was to force Mary Ellen to lure Gus over here, then kill both of them and make it look as if I'd committed suicide after murdering them in a fit of jealousy. Then, when you arrived, he was going to shoot you too."

"She's lying," said Karl.

"Sure, she's lying, and that's her gun. Her fingerprints will be on it, won't they?"

Karl's eyes darted nervously from one woman to the other. "My prints would have obscured hers once I got the gun away from her."

"No, not really. We'll find partials on her too if what you're saying is true."

"I never touched the gun," said Sarah. "He says he's registered at a motel in Alamogordo. That was going to be his alibi; he wasn't in town."

Elena nodded, checking out the room, examining Karl Bonnard's possessions, darting quick glances at him every few seconds to be sure he hadn't moved from the chair. "My God!" she exclaimed as she peered at the huge aquarium that occupied the wall across from the door. "Those fish have teeth!"

"They're piranhas. He used to take great delight in warning Mary Ellen not to fall in when she fed them."

"What did he make her feed them? People?" Elena blinked, a grisly thought occurring to her. "They're flesh eaters, right?"

"Yes, they can strip a body clean."

"We never could figure out how he managed to get all the flesh off Margreaves' body with unslaked lime. One of your chemists said it would have taken a couple of days. Did you bring the fish along, Karl?" Elena asked, whirling on him.

"You have a lurid imagination," Bonnard retorted.

"He—he said something about Gus's flesh being devoured, but I thought he was speaking figuratively." Sarah was paler than ever.

"I wonder if we could autopsy the fish. You remember I asked you if Gus had a bone disease?"

"Yes, but I couldn't imagine why you'd think that."

"The coroner found scrapes on his bones—well, Margreaves' bones. No one ever thought they might be tooth marks. No, I take it back. That crazed doctor at the university asked if the body had been attacked by wild animals, but I never— Are you O.K.?" Sarah had turned a little green.

"More or less."

"It doesn't get any pleasanter, does it? I wonder if there's any of Margreaves left inside the fish."

"Those fish are expensive," said Bonnard. "If you think I'll give permission for you to kill them in order to explore some bizarre theory—"

"Oh, shut up," said Elena. "I don't need permission from you if I want to grind up every one of them."

"How did you get through the security door?" Karl demanded. "You're in my house illegally."

"It was open," said Elena smugly.

"You forgot to lock it, Karl," Sarah agreed. "You remembered the dead bolt and forgot the security door."

"Damn lucky too," muttered Elena. "I couldn't have kicked in an iron door."

"Well, kicking my door in was illegal."

"Not when I saw you through the window with a gun on Sarah." As she turned away from Karl, she saw Leo coming through the arch. "Hey, it's about time!" she said. "Look through the house for this guy's wife, will you?"

"Who is he?"

"Bonnard. He killed Margreaves and, according to Sarah, planned to kill her, McGlenlevie, his own wife—even me—in a quadruple murder-suicide, Sarah looking like the murderer and the suicide."

"Don't listen to them," said Bonnard. "Sarah—she did it all. Killed McGlenlevie, Mary Ellen . . ."

Leo's eyebrows shot up. "McGlenlevie isn't dead, is he? You sure you shot the right person, Elena?"

"Actually, Elena shot both of us," said Sarah. "With one bullet. Wouldn't that merit some sort of commendation?"

"What it will get me is a hell of a long stay here with the Shooting Review Team and an appearance before the grand jury," said Elena morosely.

"You mean you could be indicted for saving my life and your own?" asked Sarah.

"Not likely, but even if I shot myself in the toe by mistake, the S.R.T. would have to investigate, and the D.A. automatically presents it to the grand jury when a cop shoots anyone."

"There's something wrong with the system," said Sarah. "First me, then you. I really—"

Bonnard was looking smug. "Detective Jarvis shot me without provocation," he said to Leo. "Hysterical women should not be allowed in law enforcement."

"Bullshit," said Leo. "Elena never had hysterics in her life." He turned contemptuously away from Bonnard. "I'll see if I can find this maggot's wife." In a few minutes he was back, looking satisfied. "We've got him cold. He complained to Mrs. Bonnard about killing the wrong guy and said he was gonna get both Gus and her, anyway."

"Hearsay," Bonnard mumbled.

"You better get a lawyer, fella," Leo advised. "If you're planning your own defense, you're not doing too well."

"My wife and Sarah have conspired against me. Mary Ellen wants to divorce me, and Sarah wants me out of the department. She's afraid for her job."

"What a lie!" Sarah exclaimed. "The dean wouldn't even give you my job when I was accused of murder."

"Harley—Harley will—"

"The wife's getting dressed," said Leo.

"Leo, take a look at those fish over there," said Elena. "Maybe those two boxes he hauled up to the apartment on Sunday night weren't just unslaked lime. One could have been a container full of fish."

"I'll be damned." Leo bent over to peer at the piranhas. "Look at the teeth on those babies! With fish like that, he wouldn't need lime."

"But the lime was in the tub."

"Just to clean up, probably, and to throw us off. He's not gonna leave a fish there to finish the job. You don't find too many people with pet piranhas."

"She's the one who did it," said Karl.

"I don't have fish of any kind, Karl," said Sarah, "*or* unslaked lime, *or* guns."

"For God's sake, have you people forgotten that she's

already tried to kill her husband once?" cried Bonnard, beginning to sound desperate.

"Oh, yeah, right," said Leo. "With a snail. Well, man, no court's gonna think a snail is more dangerous than a piranha—or a guy with a club in his hand. What'd you use on Margreaves, anyway?"

"Sarah killed him," said Bonnard stubbornly.

Leo and Elena exchanged glances. "Don't worry, we've got him. I heard what Sarah had to say," said Elena.

"And I heard what Mrs. Bonnard had to say," Leo agreed. "Jealous husband. Best motive in the world."

"Sarah was the jealous one," said Karl.

"If necessary, I can testify that she didn't give a hoot about Gus McGlenlevie as long as he stayed away from her," said Elena. "So can all the women in the support group—some of them still in love with their ex-husbands, some of them jealous of new wives and girlfriends, and Sarah's only problem seemed to be worrying about how she came to marry him in the first place."

Mary Ellen Bonnard appeared in the doorway, a pretty woman with blond hair curled under in an old-fashioned pageboy, wearing a periwinkle-blue shirtwaist dress and high heels. Elena stared at her in astonishment. She looked like something out of—what?—the fifties. Elena wasn't sure.

Mary Ellen eyed her husband with loathing. "You sinner," she said. "God will punish you."

"God won't have to, Mrs. Bonnard," said Elena. "The courts will do it for Him."

The wailing of an ambulance siren swelled, then died in front of the house as Mary Ellen Bonnard nudged the crushed shade of the brass lamp with her toe. "That was my grand-mother's lamp, Karl," she said angrily. "I hope they hang you."

"How like you, Mary Ellen," he retorted contemptuously. "You don't even know what method of capital punishment is used in Texas."

46
∷

Thursday, June 11, 6 P.M.

"Would you explain to me, Elena," said Sarah Tolland as she opened the restaurant door, "why the Boston police called my brother yesterday. He arrived home from Brazil to a ringing telephone and a police sergeant asking if he had a relative named Sarah who was wanted for murder in Texas?"

"Two for dinner?" asked the *maître d'*, having sidled up to them with a toothy smile. "I am Armand, and your waiter tonight will be Pierre."

Elena looked him over skeptically, then turned to Sarah. "I asked those turkeys in Boston for help weeks ago, while you were still missing and unaccounted for. It must have taken them all this time to track you and your brother down."

Armand led them to a table, whisked out Sarah's chair, and left Elena to shift for herself.

"Maybe you ought to call them back—just so they don't arrest me the next time I visit my brother," said Sarah.

The *maître d'* gaped at her and asked in a weak voice whether the ladies would care for a drink.

"We'll have wine with dinner," Sarah informed him. "I can assure you that my brother was quite astonished to hear that I was wanted for murder."

Armand scurried away, looking over his shoulder apprehensively.

"I can imagine. What does this restaurant serve, anyway?" Elena eyed the spindly chairs, the pink tablecloths, and the travel posters featuring towering cathedrals and misty bridges with old-fashioned street lamps.

"The best French food in Los Santos," said Sarah, "and it's my treat, my way of saying thank you for saving my life."

"Come on, Sarah, you might have got him with the lamp." Elena remembered with relish the sight of ladylike Sarah Tolland swinging that huge brass lamp at Karl Bonnard's head. The pity was that she'd only hit him with the shade. And what a kick! Sarah had whipped up her skirt like a can-can dancer.

"I don't think I could have held that lamp thirty seconds longer," said Sarah. "It was terribly heavy."

"The wine list, madam," said their waiter, presumably Pierre.

"Maybe you ought to consider joining a health club and working out," Elena suggested.

"I do, madam," said Pierre.

"Not you. Her."

Sarah blinked in astonishment. "You mean with weights? I hardly think I'm the type."

"Well, you never know when you'll have to fend off a another murderer."

Round-eyed, the waiter disappeared in the same direction as Armand.

"I'd be very surprised to hear, Elena, that your average university professor is likely to encounter a murderer more than once in a lifetime," Sarah replied.

"Maybe you're right. Anyway, you'll be glad to know that the D.A. thinks his case against Bonnard is ironclad. The fish's stomach contents, unfortunately, weren't helpful. I guess the piranhas had already digested and passed Howard Margreaves."

"Elena, we're about to *eat*."

Pierre, who had returned with menus after a short, vehement argument with the *maître d'*, turned pale, handed them the menus, and ran.

"You know," said Elena, looking at hers, "Bonnard likes this kind of food too."

Sarah frowned at her. "How do you know what Karl likes,

and now that I think of it, why was he calling you Elena that morning?"

Elena flushed. "I went out with him a couple of times," she admitted.

"Elena Jarvis, you *dated* Karl Bonnard?"

"Well, he said he and his wife had broken up, and he's good-looking. How was I to know he'd murdered Margreaves? There wasn't a thing to connect him to the killing until Gus got back and admitted that he and Mary Ellen had been having an affair."

"I can't believe it. You dated Karl Bonnard! Where did he take you?"

"Santa Maria del Valle in Mexico, and the Camino Real here in Los Santos."

"Stranger and stranger. Ordinarily he doesn't like to spend money on anyone but himself. Did he let you order anything?"

"Of course, he did. I had a wonderful dinner in Mexico. It warms my heart to think of how much that evening must have cost him. And the dinner at the Camino Real was even more expensive—not to mention this delicious stuff called Bailey's Irish Cream afterwards under the Tiffany dome. That was to make up for subjecting me to Calvados with dessert. Calvados is a very nasty-tasting apple brandy."

"I know, Elena," said Sarah, grinning. "He must have been desperate to bamboozle you. Did he?"

"For a while," Elena admitted, thinking, *This ought to be the final blow to my friendship with Sarah.*

Sarah was shaking her head. "I think you may have even worse taste in men than I do. We both picked miserable husbands, but as far as I know, I've never dated a murderer, and in fact," she added, her face lighting up, "I'm hiring a very charming electrical engineering professor from the state of Washington."

"Ah ha! Tell me about this man. Have you been out with him?"

"Both here and in Chicago. If you hadn't arrested me, no telling what might have come of it."

"I wonder if he's the one who glared at me from behind a potted palm at the Camino Real."

"I really couldn't say, but I'd certainly have glared at you if I saw you there with Karl Bonnard while my future chair-woman was languishing in jail."

"Right. And I suppose he's the one who came to visit you in jail."

"He was."

"He must be in love. No *sane* person would visit the Los Santos County jail."

Sarah frowned. "I think I'm going to start a committee to do something about that facility. Both the clothes and the food are inhuman."

"Wait till after Bonnard leaves for Huntsville," Elena advised. "He probably hates jail clothes."

"And food," Sarah agreed. "That's an excellent thought. I was delighted to hear that he'd been denied bail."

"He's a danger to the public—particularly you and Mary Ellen. Did you read that interview with Mary Ellen? She said part of God's vengeance would be that in a community-property state half their assets are hers, and he's not using a cent of her half to pay his lawyer."

"Good for her," said Sarah. She closed her menu and looked around impatiently. "Where's that waiter? He seems to have disappeared."

"You frightened him away. He probably thinks you're a hit person."

"Hit person? Well, I guess that's more politically correct than, say, assassinette," murmured Sarah, "but I do resent being tainted by Bonnard's crime."

"Which reminds me, did you see the headlines in the paper last Friday? 'Acid Bath Case Solved.' I can't believe they're still calling it that. Lime bath, maybe."

"Or piranha bath," Sarah suggested. "That has a certain sensationalist appeal."

"You know, Sarah, for such a conservative woman, bizarre things seem to happen to you. First the snail, then the—"

"The bizarre things happen to Gus," said Sarah primly, "not me." Then she beckoned imperiously to the reluctant Armand, who was cowering behind a wine rack. "The first-course special tonight is snails in garlic butter," she informed Elena. "Shall we try them?"

Elena stared at her suspiciously. "I'd rather eat a hand grenade," she replied.